# THE NECESSARY ENGAGEMENT

ELIZABETH KELLY

EK PUBLISHING INC.

# CHAPTER 1

G rayson climbed the stairs and knocked on his grandmother's bedroom door. "GG, are you in here?"

When there was no reply, he frowned and returned downstairs to the kitchen of the large farmhouse. He drummed his fingers on the worn wood of the table that dominated the kitchen. Where could his grandmother be? He hadn't told her he was coming home today but hadn't thought it necessary. It was Saturday evening. GG should have been home starting dinner just like she always was. He felt a thin thread of fear ripple through him. Had something happened to her?

He cursed under his breath. He had told GG repeatedly that she needed to hire someone full time to help with the chores around the barn and the house. Although they had drastically reduced the number of cattle and horses in the last couple of years, there were still way too many for someone her age to care for.

It had been difficult enough to convince her to hire Derek on a part time basis. Ultimately, he'd had to threaten to

1

cancel his entire trip before she would relent and allow him to hire Derek to feed and water the animals four days a week.

Maybe she was in the barn? He stepped onto the front porch, which badly needed staining, and stared at the barn. He was heading toward it when a light in the small guest house caught his attention. Why would GG be in the guest house? He shrugged and headed towards the small, cozy cabin, ignoring the badly rusted Honda parked beside it.

He climbed the steps of the small porch and tried the front door. It was unlocked, and he slipped inside. The cabin was quiet and dark. The light he had seen from the main farmhouse was spilling out of the half-open bedroom door. He walked confidently down the hallway toward it. He had lived here for many years, choosing to spend his late teens and early twenties in this cabin and away from his domineering, alcoholic father. He couldn't live under the same roof as his old man, but he had been equally unable to abandon GG completely. The day after his father died of a bourbon-assisted heart attack, he'd moved back into the farmhouse with his grandmother, and there he had stayed until a year ago.

"Son of a bitch!" Pain radiated across his leg when he ran into a small side table just outside of the bedroom door. The table hit the wall with a loud bang, and the decorative vase on it teetered precariously on the edge before tumbling toward the floor. He caught it a few inches from the hardwood and carefully placed it on the table. He rubbed his shin where he had banged it on the table and glanced around, his brow furrowed. The side table used to be in the living room. He was sure of it.

Shaking his head, he entered the bedroom. "GG, are you -"

There was a flash of white to his left, and he turned to see a small, blonde woman wrapped in a white towel. She had a large glass jar of cotton balls raised over her head and murder in her eyes. He ducked back instinctively as she brought the jar toward his head. The force of her momentum sent her tumbling forward, and he caught her neatly, knocking the glass jar from her hand as he did so. They stared at each other for a long moment, and he just had time to notice how blue her eyes were before she punched him hard in the stomach.

He grunted in surprise but didn't release her. She turned and tried to skitter free of his grip, but he tightened his arms around her and pulled her back against his chest. She writhed and wriggled against him like a wild cat. She was panting harshly, one hand holding her towel closed and the other trying to scratch at his face.

"Enough!" he said and grabbed her wrists in his hands. He crossed her arms across her body and pinned her hands down at her sides.

"Stop moving," he growled into her ear.

She ignored him and stomped with her bare heel on the top of one boot-clad foot.

He barely felt it, but she winced with pain.

"Goddammit!" she shouted.

"I said stop!" he growled again and squeezed her slender body with his arms.

"I can't breathe," she complained.

"Stop moving, and I'll loosen my grip," he said.

She tensed and then relaxed against him. He cautiously loosened his arms around her but kept his hands wrapped around her wrists.

She took a few deep breaths and then twisted her head to glare up at him. "What do you want? If you're breaking in to steal money, you're out of luck. I don't have any."

"I'm not -"

"And if it's something else you want," she swallowed hard

and tensed against him, "I'll kill you before I let you touch me."

"I'm not a thief, and you're not my type," he said.

She relaxed slightly, her breathing harsh and loud in the silence.

"I want you to tell me what you're doing here," he demanded. "Who are you, and why are you living in my home?"

"Your home?" She craned her neck to stare up at him again. "This is my home, and you're breaking into it. I swear to God, the minute I get free, I'm going to kick your ass and then have you arrested for breaking and entering."

He stared down at her. The woman was barely over five feet and so slender that he would have been shocked if she weighed over a hundred pounds. The fact that she had tried to take him on and was now threatening him was more than amusing. The corners of his lips turned up, and she scowled at him.

"I'm tougher than I look, you asshole," she snapped. She struggled again, and he immediately tightened his arms around her.

"Let go of me!" she wheezed angrily.

He shook his head, staring down into her upturned face, watching her eyes darken with anger and something else. She wasn't his type. He preferred his women to be tall with dark hair, dark eyes, and plenty of curves. Soft, round bottoms and large, firm breasts that filled and overflowed in his hands. That's what he was attracted to and always had been.

The woman in his arms was small and blonde, and although the towel was still wrapped around her, it had loosened enough for him to see the slight swell of her small breasts. She was a B cup if she was lucky. She had obviously just come from the shower, and her shoulder-length blonde hair was damp and incredibly curly. She smelled like some type of exotic fruit, and her skin was so pale it was nearly translucent. Despite her threats, her tiny body was no match for his large one. Still, he admired her fierceness and determination.

"Stop struggling, and I'll let you go," he said.

Snorting like an angry horse, she glared at him again before relaxing.

"Tell me your name and why you're in my grandmother's home."

She stiffened against him. "Oh my God – you're Grayson."

He blinked at her in surprise. "How do you know my name?"

When she didn't answer, he released her, turning her swiftly and holding her wrists in one hand. He slipped his hand under the mass of curls at the nape of her neck, cupped the back, and squeezed lightly. "Where's GG? Have you hurt her?"

"I haven't hurt GG! I rent this place from her," she said.

"Where is my grandmother?" he repeated.

Despite his worry for his grandmother, he couldn't help but notice how full her lips were and how soft the skin on the back of her neck felt under his hand. He briefly wondered if the rest of her skin was as soft, and he studied her slender body. He paused at the hem of her towel and then stared at her pale legs.

She immediately squeezed her thighs together and glowered at him. "Stop looking at me like that."

"Don't flatter yourself," he said. "I told you – you're not my type."

She pulled at his hand, which still held her wrists captive. "Let go of me."

"First, tell me where GG is."

"She's at dinner with Alex," she said. "She always has

dinner with Alex on Saturday nights. She should be home any time now."

He continued to hold her captive for a moment, his head cocked to the side as he stared at her. She looked familiar to him, and he tried to place where he knew her. A faint memory started to surface in his brain as he stared at the mass of curly blonde hair. Before it could fully form, she pulled irritably against his hand again.

"Let me go, you big lug."

He grinned a little and released her. She stepped away from him, rubbing her wrists before readjusting her towel.

"What's your name?"

"Sydney. I've rented this place from GG for the last ten months," she said.

"I'm sorry. She never told me she had rented the place out. I thought you were a -"

The rough sound of an engine interrupted him, and she pointed toward the door. "That will be GG."

He nodded but continued to stare at her. She sighed. "Do you mind? I need to get ready for work. I'm going to be late, thanks to you."

"Right, sorry again." He gave her an apologetic smile and left the room.

\* \* \*

"You're late, girl." Belinda grinned at her.

"I know, I know. My car was acting up again." Sydney hurried into the staff room and quickly opened her locker. She hung her jacket and purse on the hook and yanked her apron from the top shelf. She tied it around her waist and turned to Belinda.

"How do I look?"

Her dark hair sleek and shining, and her make-up impeccable as usual, Belinda looked her up and down. "Not bad. Just a few minor adjustments needed."

She reached out and tugged up the waistband of Sydney's skirt, folding it under until her formerly knee-length skirt fell to the middle of her thighs. She undid the top two buttons of Sydney's shirt and stared critically at her small breasts.

"You bought the push-up bra." Belinda grinned at her.

"Yeah," Sydney said. It was a purchase she could barely afford, and she'd had to give up two meals to buy it, but if Belinda were right, it would eventually pay for itself.

"It looks great!" Belinda reached out and, ignoring Sydney's gasp, grabbed her small breasts. "They look much bigger and perkier."

"Belinda, knock it off!" Sydney laughed and shoved Belinda's hands away.

"Trust me, honey. The more skin you show and the more you flirt, the more money you make. Especially later at night when the beer's been flowing for a while." Belinda reached into her locker and pulled out a small lip gloss tube. "Just one more touch. Hold still."

She smoothed the gloss onto Sydney's lips, and Sydney looked in the small magnetic mirror inside Belinda's locker door. "It's much too red."

Belinda rolled her eyes. "No, it isn't, Sydney. Trust me, honey. Your mouth is your best looking feature – you need to play it up."

She slammed her locker door shut and took Sydney's hand. "C'mon, we'd better get out to the bar and start serving drinks before Wayne fires us both."

\* \* \*

"You look great, GG." Grayson drank iced tea as his grandmother warmed up soup on the stove.

"Thanks, honey. You're very tanned. Did you have fun travelling?" His grandmother continued to stir the pot of soup, stopping to taste it before frowning and adding more spice.

He shrugged. "It was a good experience. I'm glad to be home, though. I've missed you."

GG smiled at him. "I've missed you too, Grayson."

She ladled some soup into a bowl and set it down before him. "I'm sorry it's only reheated soup. You didn't mention you'd be home today when you called last week. If I'd known, I would have cooked something special."

"Soup is fine. I've missed your soup." Grayson smiled at her as she sat in the chair beside him. "How have things been at the farm?"

"Oh, fine, fine." She picked at the worn wood of the table. "Derek has been a great help around this place. And I rented out the guest house to a young woman named Sydney. She's a little slip of a thing, but she's been real good to me and helping me with stuff around the house."

She pointed to the warm yellow walls of the kitchen. "She repainted the kitchen, my bedroom, your bedroom, and both bathrooms this past summer in exchange for a month of free rent."

Grayson glanced at the walls before tipping up his bowl and drinking the rest of his soup. His grandmother stared at him, and he grinned. "Sorry, GG. I lost some of my manners while I was travelling."

He stood and spooned more soup into his bowl before sitting at the kitchen table again. "I met Sydney earlier. I didn't realize you had rented out the guest house, so I went over when I saw the light. I thought it might have been you in there. How did you meet her?"

"Barbara Stanwick - you remember Barb from church, I imagine - introduced me to her. Sydney works two days a week at her bookstore, and Barb knew I was considering renting out the guesthouse. Sydney couldn't afford the rent at her place and was looking for something cheaper. Barb introduced us, we got along like a house on fire, and Sydney's been renting the place ever since."

Grayson reached out and took his grandmother's hand. "GG, why are you renting out the guesthouse? Has something happened while I was gone? You shouldn't need the money."

GG shook her head. "No, sweet boy, nothing happened. It's just – sometimes a person gets lonely. It was nice to have another person living out here with me."

Grayson winced a little. He had worried about his grandmother being lonely and even discussed it with her when he was thinking of leaving for the year, but she'd assured him she would be fine.

"I'm sorry, GG." He looked down at his bowl of soup, feeling shame burning in his belly. "I shouldn't have left you."

She shook her head. "Hush, child. You had to leave, and both of us knew it. You'd spent twenty-six years in this town – it was time you got out and saw the world."

She took his hand. "Frankly, I'm surprised you even came back."

He squeezed her hand. "I would never leave you like that, GG."

She stared at him with her brow furrowed. "Grayson Stephen O'Reilly – tell me you did not return solely because you were worried about me."

"No. I missed you and was worried about you, but it wasn't just that. I missed the farm, the town, hell, I even missed Dawson's."

He stared earnestly at her. He wasn't saying that to make

her feel better. After twenty-seven years of living in the same town, he thought he couldn't escape it fast enough. A year of traveling the world had shown him that despite the bad memories of his bastard of a father – the town and the farm he had lived his entire life in - was the place he was meant to be.

"I mean what I say, GG," he said.

GG smiled at him. "There's no place like home."

# CHAPTER 2

Sydney muttered a soft prayer and stepped hard on the gas pedal. The Honda groaned and moaned its way up the steep hill just before the farm, and she released her breath in a harsh rush when it crested the hill and began its descent.

It was just after two in the morning, and she was exhausted and freezing. It was late fall, and the weather was growing steadily colder. The Honda's heater had broken weeks ago, but there was no way she had the money to fix it. She would just have to dress warmly.

She turned into the driveway and shut off the Honda with relief. She climbed out of the car and ran through the frosty air to the guesthouse. She kept the heat low to save money, but the house was blessedly warm compared to the icebox that was the Honda.

She turned the light on in the kitchen and opened the fridge. It was empty besides a small bag of salad, some apples, and a piece of cooked chicken. She was starving. Wayne gave them a discount on the food in the bar, but she didn't get paid until Thursday. Although she had made more tonight in tips than she had since she started at Dawson's a month ago, she had to pay her electricity bill on Monday. That would leave her just enough to cover her gas money and buy a little something for Emma tomorrow.

She sighed and reached for the bag of salad and piece of chicken. She made herself only cut up half the chicken into the bowl of salad, even though her stomach growled and her mouth watered. She sat at the table and took small bites of her salad, forcing herself to eat slowly and savour each bite.

Her mind kept mulling over this afternoon when Grayson had broken into her house. Well, broken into wasn't exactly true. She rarely locked the guesthouse. They were in the middle of the country, and the crime rate was so low that the deputy sheriff spent most of his time at the local gym. It was one of the reasons that Jacob had lobbied so hard to stay here when she'd suggested they move away.

"Think about it, babe," he'd said, "it's a great place to raise children."

It was a Sunday afternoon, and they'd spent most of it in bed. He'd placed his hand on her expanding belly and smiled at her. "We've lived here our entire lives. This town is special, and you know it. Do you really want to leave?"

She'd shaken her head no. Despite the bad memories and the occasional rude comment about her mother, deep down, she hadn't wanted to leave. There were good memories here, too. Saturday night dinners with her father at Ivan's. Standing downtown during the annual Christmas light-up, bundled up against the cold with a thermos of hot chocolate in one hand, and watching with delight as thousands of twinkling Christmas lights came to life on the main street.

She'd wanted those same memories for the child growing in her belly, and she was naive enough to believe that she and Jacob would make it work.

She sighed and ate the last of her salad before rinsing the bowl and setting it in the sink. She didn't bother with the light in the bedroom as she undressed. The bedroom was the coldest room in the house, and she shivered wildly as she yanked on her flannel pajamas before crawling between the cold sheets.

She pulled the quilt and the sheets up to her nose and curled into a small ball in the middle of the bed. She was tired, but her mind refused to shut down. For once, it wasn't thinking about Emma and how much she missed her, but rather what it felt like to be pressed against Grayson O'Reilly. She frowned and sat up, punching the middle of her pillow before burying her head back into it.

It had taken her a while to recognize him, and it wasn't surprising that he didn't remember her. He'd been in his last year when she started high school, and he wouldn't have looked twice at her. He was athletic, bouncing from sport to sport with an easy grace. Despite his quiet and guarded personality - or perhaps because of it - girls had fallen over themselves trying to get his attention.

He had dated a tall, dark haired beauty named Donna for most of high school. They seemed serious enough to Sydney. But after graduation, Donna moved away to university while Grayson stayed and worked on his family's farm.

Sydney had only one encounter with Grayson, but it was enough to cement a full-blown schoolgirl crush on him. A month after she started high school, Erin Drenning and Mary Bines, along with their oafish boyfriends, had played a cruel prank.

She'd thought she could escape them once they were in high school. Believed it would be easier to blend in with the larger crowds and avoid the torment that Erin and Mary had been inflicting on her for most of her school years. It had started the first day of grade one when she arrived at school wearing a thrift store shirt and jeans and sporting a terrible haircut, courtesy of her mother. Tired of trying to tame her daughter's naturally curly hair, Sydney's mother had taken the scissors and cut it so short that Sydney was mistaken for a boy for the months it took for her hair to grow out.

Sydney could still remember how furious her father was with her mother. He'd been a soft-spoken man who rarely raised his voice in anger and never spanked her, but his face went white when he saw Sydney and sent her immediately to her room. He and her mother fought bitterly while she curled up in bed and put the pillow over her head.

She shook her head, angry with herself for allowing the bad memories to creep in on her. She tried hard not to dwell on the past, but sometimes it was nearly impossible. She closed her eyes and took a few deep breaths to clear her mind.

Immediately, the memory of being pinned against Grayson's body flooded through her head. She groaned and opened her eyes. She hadn't gotten laid in years, and it was affecting her. Grayson was attractive with his dark hair, broad shoulders, and tanned skin, but she needed a man in her life like an extra hole in her head.

Still, she couldn't help but shiver a little when she remembered how he'd held her so closely, his hands around her wrists and his hard chest pressed against her. He was much larger than her, and his deep, gravelly voice gave her goosebumps.

Even before she figured out who he was, she was still a little turned on at the way he had so effortlessly held her captive. She could feel her cheeks reddening, and, with a muttered curse, she flipped to her other side and yanked the blankets completely over her head. Even if he hadn't made it clear that she wasn't his type, she couldn't risk Jacob using her sleeping with someone as ammunition. It was stupid to torture herself with thoughts of what it would be like to have him in her bed. She would think about tomorrow instead, about her precious time with Emma, and ignore the tremors in her stomach at the memory of Grayson's hard hands and deep voice.

* * *

GRAYSON SIGHED AND STARED AT THE CEILING OF HIS bedroom. It was good to be back in his own bed, but the jet lag had played havoc with his system, and despite the late hour, he still couldn't sleep. It didn't help that every time he closed his eyes, a vision of Sydney, her slender body barely covered in a towel and her full lips trembling with anger as she fought against him, flooded his head.

He grimly ignored the growing hardness below his waist. Sydney was not his type. He'd never even slept with a blonde before, and it was stupid of him to keep reliving how it had made him feel when she struggled against his body. He could admit that he had found it more than a little erotic to know that she was helpless against him, that if he wanted to, he could have pinned her hands behind her back and kissed her.

Not that he would have. He would never force a woman to do anything she didn't want to, but the idea of having a woman at his mercy, of kissing her and touching her until she was moaning with need, was something he'd fantasized about.

He stared at the alarm clock next to the bed. It was nearly three in the morning, and he still wasn't tired. He concentrated hard, trying to remember how he knew Sydney. After almost five minutes, he grunted with satisfaction – of course, that day in the locker room. He closed his eyes and let the memory wash over him.

*Like always, Grayson waited for his teammates to finish and leave before he got into the shower. It was easier to avoid the questioning altogether than to come up with an excuse. He'd let the water ease the aches from the basketball practice and the soreness in his back before shutting off the water, toweling dry, and slipping into his shorts.*

*He was almost at his locker before he even noticed her. Dangling from the wall, hung neatly from the metal towel hooks by the pink backpack strapped around her, she stared miserably at him, her face bright red and her full lips trembling.*

*He stared silently at the tiny, skinny girl with the giant halo of frizzy blonde hair. She returned his look defiantly, her blue eyes large with anger and embarrassment and her hands hanging limply at her side.*

*He was so surprised to see her there that he might have stared at her forever if he hadn't noticed how the backpack's straps dug into her shoulders and arms. She wore a sleeveless shirt, and the thin straps revealed the red marks spreading on her pale flesh.*

*Cursing under his breath, he walked toward her and tried to pull the straps down from her arms to free her. She hissed with pain, and he muttered an apology. Whoever had hung her there had wrapped the shoulder straps around the hooks and then cinched them so tightly that there was no way he could slide her out of the backpack.*

*He ran his hand through his damp hair. "I'll have to lift you to try to unhook the backpack. Ready?"*

*She nodded, and he wrapped one arm around her thin waist and lifted her as much as the backpack would allow. It provided a bit of give in the straps, and he tugged at one strap, first trying to loosen it from the metal hook and then, when that didn't work, trying to pull it down her arm using brute force.*

*She grunted with pain, and he gently lowered her again. She made another small moan of pain as the straps resumed digging into her arms, and he raked his hand through his hair again.*

*"New plan. I'm going to lift you again. Are you strong enough to hold your body weight up if you wrap your legs around my waist?"*

*She nodded, and he lifted her again. She wrapped her thin thighs around his waist, and he gave his own groan of pain when she hooked her feet together in the small of his back and brushed against the bruises.*

*"I'm sorry." Her voice was soft and low. "Am I too heavy?"*

*He grinned. "Hardly. Ready?"*

*She nodded, and he released her waist. She squeezed her legs around his waist, and he used his lower body to help support her weight against the wall as he grabbed the buckle of one strap with both hands. With a grunt of effort, he yanked repeatedly on the piece of plastic until it loosened.*

*She sighed with relief when the strap lengthened, and he helped her ease her arm free of the strap. She put it around his shoulders as he slipped her other arm free and stepped back, putting his arm around her waist.*

*Her blue eyes stared into his hazel ones, and he cleared his throat nervously. Her face flushed when she realized she still clung to him like a monkey, and she let her legs fall away from his waist. He gently dropped her onto her feet, and she rubbed one arm and the other.*

*"Thank you," she said.*

*"Yeah, no problem. Who put you up there anyway?"*

*"A bunch of childish idiots," she muttered.*

*He ducked around her to pull her backpack from the hooks, and she gave a soft gasp of dismay. Too late, he remembered he wasn't wearing a shirt, and he almost shoved her backpack at her before crossing the room and pulling his shirt out of his gym bag. He shrugged into it, covering the bruises on his back, and turned to face her.*

*"What happened to your back?" she asked.*

*He opened his mouth to lie like always but couldn't get the words out. He didn't know why, but he had the oddest feeling that this tiny, flat-chested girl would keep what he told her to herself.*

For the first time, he told the truth about his bruises. "My old man. He... he drinks a lot."

She nodded, giving him a clear look of sympathy, but didn't say anything.

He picked up his gym bag. "You'd better go before Mr. Baker catches you in here."

"Yeah," she said. Holding her backpack, she walked to the locker room door. "Thank you again."

"Hey," he called.

She paused in the doorway and looked over her shoulder.

"What's your name?"

"Sydney."

"I'm Grayson."

She smiled. "I know."

# CHAPTER 3

"Grayson! Dinner's ready," GG called up the stairs. She returned to the kitchen and smiled at Sydney. "I told him to take a nap for a few hours. The time change is messing with him something terrible."

"I bet," Sydney said. "Should I put the butter on the table?"

"Yes, please. Can you grab the cloth napkins from the sideboard in the hallway? Let's fancy up the dinner tonight," GG said as she carved the roast into thick slices.

Sydney headed down the hall, looking over her shoulder as she said, "Which drawer are the napkins in, GG?"

She yelped in surprise when she bounced off of something warm and hard. She tripped over her feet, but before she could fall, hands grabbed her upper arms and held her upright. She inhaled sharply at the sight of Grayson's half-naked body.

*Holy shit, he's beautiful!*

The last time she had seen him without his shirt, they'd been teenagers, and while he was as tall then as he was now, he'd been much skinnier. He'd filled out considerably over the years, his shoulders now broad and his upper arms thick with muscle. His chest was perfect – all tanned skin and lean muscle with a light dusting of dark hair.

She bit her bottom lip at the sight of his six pack. She followed the thin trail of hair below his navel to where it disappeared inside his jeans, and she had to clench her hands into tight fists to stop herself from reaching out and tracing it with her finger. She dragged her gaze to his face when she realized he was speaking.

"I'm sorry, what?" she said.

"I asked what you were doing here." He frowned as he pulled his t-shirt over his head. He looked her up and down, taking in her baggy jeans and faded t-shirt.

She bristled in defense. "GG invited me."

"Why would she invite you for dinner?" he asked.

Before she could answer, GG stuck her head out the kitchen doorway. "Sydney, did you find the – oh, Grayson, good. Be a love and grab the napkins from the second drawer, please. Sydney, come help me with the rest of the food."

Hoping the look on her face didn't scream *I want to fuck your grandson*, Sydney followed GG to the kitchen.

GG STUCK HIS HEAD INTO THE KITCHEN. GG WAS ALONE AND tidying up, and he breathed a sigh of relief. Sydney must have left while he was taking the garbage out. Dinner was excruciatingly uncomfortable. He had been annoyed with GG for so obviously trying to set him up with Sydney, and he'd spent most of the dinner eating silently and giving one-word responses while Sydney filled the silence with nervous chatter.

"I know what you're up to, GG," he said as he stepped into the kitchen.

"What are you talking about, child?" she asked.

He rolled his eyes. "Don't play innocent with me."

She piled a plate with potatoes, vegetables, and leftover roast. "Grayson, I have no idea what you mean."

"Really? I've been back one day, and you invited Sydney for dinner tonight. You have to stop trying to set me up with every woman you meet, GG. Sydney seems nice enough, but -"

"But what? Sydney is a lovely girl." GG pointed a potato-covered wooden spoon at him. "Frankly, you'd be lucky to have her. I hate to tell you this, child, but you're not getting any younger. If you weren't so fussy, you'd be married with kids by now."

"I am not fussy, GG," he said through gritted teeth. "And I'm sure Sydney is lovely, but she's not my type."

"Not your type," GG scoffed. "Why, because she has a brain in her head, and her boobs aren't the size of melons?"

"GG!" Grayson stared at her in shock.

"Well, admit it, Grayson."

"Look, I get the feeling that you like Sydney a lot, and I'm glad you're friends, but stop trying to set me up with her, okay?"

GG frowned at him. "Grayson, lower your voice, she -"

He kept going, speaking over his grandmother. "She's too skinny, too pale, too blonde, and she talks too much. I've seen how she looks at me, and I'd appreciate it if you didn't encourage her."

GG's gaze flickered to the right. He looked behind him and groaned. Sydney stood behind him, her hands cupping her elbows and her face red.

"Well, I think this is my cue to leave. GG, thank you for a lovely dinner."

She started toward him, and feeling ashamed, he stepped back so she could sweep past. She kissed GG on the cheek.

His grandma hugged her and then handed her the plate of food.

"Here, honey. Take this home with you."

"Thank you, GG." She gave his grandmother a warm smile. "That's so nice of you."

She stopped in front of Grayson and gave him a smile that didn't reach her eyes. "Grayson, it was nice to see you again."

His face blazing red, he nodded and avoided her gaze as she left the kitchen. He heard the click of the front door closing and forced himself to look at his grandmother. She gave him a look of disappointment, and he could feel his cheeks burning even brighter.

"GG, I'm sorry."

"Dear boy, I'm not the one you need to apologize to." She poured herself a cup of tea and sat down at the table. After a moment, he sat down across from her, feeling like he did when, as a little kid, he'd broken her favourite candy dish.

"I wasn't trying to set you up with Sydney. She joins me every Sunday night for dinner," GG said.

"I'll apologize to her, GG. I promise."

"You'd better," she warned. "I won't make you a single meal until you do."

\* \* \*

"Why, Grayson O'Reilly! You are a sight for sore eyes!" Barb, her brown eyes sparkling, pulled him into a hug. "I saw your grandmother at church Sunday morning, and she said you were back in town. I was surprised you didn't join her at the service."

He smiled at her. "I was still suffering from jet lag."

She patted his arm. "Eleanor sure is glad you're home. She wouldn't admit it, but she missed you terribly."

"I missed her too."

"Well, we're all glad you're home. What can I help you with today?"

He glanced around the store. "I'm looking for Sydney. GG said she worked here Tuesdays and Wednesdays."

"She sure does. She's such a sweet little thing. I wish I could afford to give her more hours. Lord knows she could use the money." She smiled at the short woman with grey hair in a tidy bun who'd just entered the store. "Hello, Edith! Be right with you!"

Barb pointed to the back of the store. "Sydney's at the back shelving books."

With a nod of thanks, Grayson headed to the back. He found Sydney standing on a stool, stretched to her tiptoes as she reached for the top shelf. He studied her ass for a few seconds before saying, "Need some help?"

She jumped and then shrieked as she tumbled off the stool. The book she held fell from her hand, bounced off the top of his head, and landed on the floor. He winced but caught Sydney before she could join the book on the floor.

She stared at him before pushing against his chest. "Put me down."

She weighed about as much as a feather, and he frowned at the feel of her ribs under his hand. "Christ, Sydney. How much do you weigh?"

"That's none of your business."

"You need to eat more."

She smacked him lightly on his chest. "Could you put me down?"

"I can lift you with one arm." Keeping one arm firmly around her waist, he dropped his other arm. She gasped and grabbed onto his broad shoulders as she dangled helplessly against his muscular body.

He grinned at her. "See? I told you so."

She didn't reply. Instead, her pretty blue eyes roamed over his face. She studied his nose – slightly crooked thanks to a broken nose during a high school football game – before her gaze fell to his lips and lingered. He was suddenly intensely aware of how her tiny breasts were pressed flat against his chest and how her pussy lined up perfectly against his dick.

Her hands squeezed his shoulders, and she tilted her head and parted her lips, making him drop his gaze to her mouth. It was amazing, he decided. Lush and soft looking and her bottom lip practically screamed to be sucked on. She was still staring at his mouth, and there was a look in her eyes that he recognized well.

He didn't like blondes. And he certainly wasn't attracted to a tiny, skinny, pale blonde that his body weight would crush the minute he tried to take her to his bed. Of course, her mouth *was* begging to be kissed, and he could admit he was curious if her lips were as soft as they looked.

*Besides, she could ride you in bed. Problem solved.*

Before he could give in to his urge to kiss her, Sydney's face turned bright red, and she pushed at his shoulders. "Put me down, please."

He dropped her gently to the ground, and she took a few steps back. She smoothed her t-shirt down with the Barb's Bookshelf logo stitched across the front and glared at him. "Do you understand the concept of personal space?"

"I didn't want you to get hurt falling off that stool," he said.

"Thank you," she said begrudgingly.

She bent to pick up the book from the floor. Her shirt rode up, and Grayson eyed the tattoo on the lower right side of her back with interest. She straightened, and he took the book from her hand and easily placed it on the top shelf.

"I hate being so short," she said.

He grinned at her. "Being tall does have its advantages. May I ask what your tattoo means?"

She flushed a little, her hand reaching behind her to touch the spot where her tattoo was. "It's the Chinese symbol for soup."

He stared at her. "You're kidding."

"Nope, I'm not."

"Why do you have the symbol for soup on your back?"

She shrugged. "I like soup."

He paused, waiting to see if she was joking, but she just stared at him, her teeth worrying at her full bottom lip before she sighed. "Is there a book I can help you find?"

"Actually, I came here to apologize to you for Sunday night."

"Why? You were only being honest. I am too skinny and too pale, and I did talk too much that night. I tend to babble when I'm nervous."

"It was rude of me to say what I did. I'm sorry," Grayson said.

"Don't trouble yourself about it. Trust me. I have thick skin, and I'm not taking your complete lack of interest in my too-skinny, too-blonde body personally."

The disdain in her voice made him wince. This wasn't going the way he thought it would. Not that she had to be upset that he wasn't interested in her, but he'd grown used to women falling all over him. After how she'd looked at him in the hallway and just now, he assumed she would be the same. It was a little disconcerting to find out that he was completely wrong.

She gave him a stiff smile. "But so that you know, I didn't ask your grandmother to set us up. I have dinner with her every Sunday night."

"I know, GG mentioned that. Will you accept my apology for being so rude?"

"Will you feel better if I do?" she asked.

He nodded. "Yeah, I would."

"Not to mention, GG will start cooking for you again, right?"

He flushed, and she gave him a cheeky grin. "Then I accept it. We can't have a big strapping boy like you starving to death now, can we?"

Before he could respond, her pocket rang, and she pulled an old, battered cell phone from it. A smile lit up her face, her full lips parting to reveal even white teeth. "If you'll excuse me – I need to take this."

She turned and walked away, answering the phone as she did. "Hi, honey! I'm so glad you called me. Are you having a good day? You did? That sounds like so much fun!"

She disappeared into the back room, and Grayson sighed and headed toward the front of the store.

* * *

"BELINDA, YOU ASKED ME TO MEET YOU BEFORE WORK SO WE could go here?" Sydney stared at the sign over the store's front door. The sign boldly announced the new opening of Dirty Little Secrets in red cursive lettering.

"Really?" She arched one eyebrow at Belinda, who giggled and grabbed her hand.

"C'mon, Sid, let's check it out." Belinda pushed open the door, and a small bell jingled as they entered the warm, dimly lit store. A young woman with her hair gelled into spikes and numerous piercings on her face smiled at them from behind the counter.

"Hello, ladies. Are you looking for anything in particular today?"

Sydney shook her head as Belinda said cheerfully. "Just browsing today, thanks."

26

The young woman retreated behind the counter. "Just let me know if you have any questions."

As they wandered through the store, Sydney glanced at Belinda. "Why exactly did you drag me in here?"

Belinda grinned at her. "I need to spice up my sex life with Bill. A year of marriage, and we think it's time for some new toys." She wiggled her eyebrows at Sydney.

Sydney laughed and gave her a gentle push. "Go on then. Take a look around and see what you can find. I'm going this way."

"What? You're not going to help me pick something out?" Belinda picked up a bottle of red gel and stared at it critically. "I wonder if this tastes like strawberries. Bill loves strawberries."

"Yeah, I don't need to know anything more about your sex life, thanks." Sydney grinned before walking away.

"You're too buttoned-up, Sid. You gotta learn to have fun," Belinda called after her.

Sydney walked through the store, staring with wonder at the multitude of products. She wasn't naive when it came to sex, but she had never been in a store like this, and she was a little shocked at what they had on display. It was a small store but well-laid out, with plenty of stock hanging from the walls and on shelves, and she took her time walking through the aisles.

She stopped abruptly in front of a display case near the back wall. Laid out on blue velvet was a thin leather collar. Beside it, draped over a small display stand, were two red silk scarves with a large black feather lying on the stand base.

Sydney's heart sped up in her chest, and she could feel her cheeks reddening. She couldn't stop staring at the collar, couldn't stop wondering what it would feel like to slip that smooth leather around her neck, tighten the buckle until it was snug and -

She closed her eyes, clenching her hands into tight fists. It didn't help. Immediately, an image of herself wearing the collar and nothing else while Grayson wrapped her wrists in those bright red scarves flooded her mind. Her bed was an old four-poster bed and perfect for being tied to. She shivered a little at the thought of being tied to her bed with those red silk scarves. Of a naked Grayson hovering over her and doing all sorts of delicious things to her while she was helpless and –

"It's beautiful, isn't it?"

She jumped, her hand flying to her chest, and opened her eyes. The store clerk stood beside her, giving her a friendly smile.

"It's one of our best sellers. We sell it separately and in a kit with the feather and the scarves. Of course, the kit gives you the best value for your money. Would you like to take a closer look?"

"Oh no! That's fine, I'm just -"

It was too late. The store clerk was using a small key to open the display case, and she pulled out the collar and dropped it into Sydney's hands before she could stop her.

Her hands trembling, Sydney ran her fingers along the smooth leather. It was incredibly soft and supple, and the buckle was small and lightweight.

"Here, feel these as well. They're silk." The clerk draped one of the scarves over Sydney's arm. "Isn't it lovely?"

Sydney nodded mutely as she stroked the scarf.

"Of course, there are other choices." The store clerk pointed to the wall in front of them, and Sydney glanced up, her mouth dropping open a little.

Leather collars, scarves, handcuffs, ropes, and other restraining devices covered the wall. Sydney stared at them as the clerk reached up and snagged one of the collars. It had small silver studs embedded in it and was thicker than the one Sydney held. The clerk held it up to Sydney's neck and frowned a little.

"I think you'd be better off with the thinner collar. You're pretty tiny, and some of these collars can get kind of heavy. I doubt your partner would find it sexy if you couldn't keep your head straight."

When Sydney stayed silent, the clerk went on, her pierced face becoming increasingly animated as she spoke.

"We've got a great selection of handcuffs as well. These," she pulled a pair from the wall, "are your basic handcuffs. There is a button here that you can press to unlock yourself if you want. They're also pretty weak, all things considered. Now, if you're interested in ones where you're completely restrained, these are great."

She pulled a heavier pair free of its hook from the wall and held them in front of Sydney. "These are heavy duty. There's no way you can free yourself from these babies. They require a key to release them."

She paused. "Do you have a preference for handcuffs?"

Sydney shook her head, and the clerk gave her a close stare. "Have you been restrained before?"

"Um, I well... no." Sydney's face burned with embarrassment, but the clerk seemed unfazed.

"If it's your first time, I suggest you start with the scarves. When you're first starting in bondage, most people prefer the feel of the scarves to handcuffs."

She placed the handcuffs back on the wall and then stared at Sydney's body critically. "You have a smoking body. A little small on top, but if you gained, say, fifteen pounds, I bet it would go straight to your chest and butt. You'd be kick-ass curvy then."

Sydney stared open-mouthed at her. She had never been so embarrassed but couldn't figure out how to politely escape the store clerk. She tried to return the scarf and collar to the woman, but the clerk had turned away and was rummaging through a lingerie rack just to her left.

She pulled a black corset from the row of clothing, shook her head, and put it back. She sorted through a few more pieces before giving a small grunt of satisfaction and pulling out a red corset.

"This would look great with the red scarves and black collar." She grinned at Sydney and held the corset up in front of her. "It laces up in the back, but you can also use the fasteners in the front to put it on or take it off."

Sydney stared at the tiny bit of fabric the store clerk held up to her body. It was made from a bright red shiny material and covered in black lace. The back had a long, black ribbon laced through it, tied into a bow at the bottom, and on the front, there were six silver eye and hook fasteners spaced evenly down the bodice.

"You can wear it with the straps," the clerk pointed to the shoulder straps, "or you can wear it strapless. This is a size small. There's a dressing room in the back if you want to try it on."

Sydney's mind whirling, she reached for the corset when Belinda suddenly popped up beside them.

"Ooh, that's gorgeous." She eyed the collar and the scarf in Sydney's hand and poked her in the side. "My God, Sid. I had no idea you were so kinky. Collar and scarves...nice."

Sydney practically shoved the items into the clerk's hands. "Knock it off, Belinda."

Belinda grinned as Sydney smiled apologetically at the clerk. "I'm sorry. I didn't come in to buy anything today. It's a little out of my price range right now."

"No problem." The clerk returned the items to the display case before turning to Belinda. "Did you find what you were looking for?"

Belinda nodded. "I sure did. C'mon, Sid. Let's buy these and get to work before we're late."

She led Sydney towards the front of the store, linking her arm around Sydney's and squeezing it. "You know, with your new push-up bra and a can-do attitude when it comes to flirting, I bet you could make enough in tips in one night to buy that stuff."

"Hush, Belinda," Sydney said. "I'm not interested in it. I was just being polite."

Belinda laughed. "Sure you were, girl. Sure you were."

# CHAPTER 4

Grayson drove down Main Street and turned left at Denver Avenue. It was Saturday night, and he had driven into town about an hour ago, feeling restless and bored. GG was out with her friend Alex, and Sydney's piece-of-crap car wasn't parked in front of the guesthouse.

He had been driving aimlessly and realized with a start that he was driving by Dawson's. He slowed down, staring at the parking lot, feeling sick in the pit of his stomach. Too many times, he had been forced out of his bed at two in the morning by a phone call from Wayne, asking him to come and pick up his father. He had dreaded Saturday nights for years, knowing that he would have to drag his drunk, usually crying, father home from the bar and practically carry him into the house.

Despite his fondness for Wayne, the owner of Dawson's, he hadn't been back since the day his father died. He stepped on the gas, anxious to get away from the memories of his father, when he caught sight of the familiar rusty Honda parked in the lot. He hesitated only briefly before pulling into the parking lot.

Despite the darkness, he was positive it was Sydney's car, and he threw his truck into park and shut it off. Sydney didn't seem like much of a bar type to him, and he had to admit he was curious about why she was there. Was she on a date? He'd assumed she was single. In the two weeks since he'd returned home, he'd seen a couple of women stop by to visit Sydney, but no men. He ignored the little voice in his head that immediately asked why he was paying so much attention to Sydney's houseguests and got out of the truck.

He ducked his head into the cold wind and walked quickly to the bar's front door, nodding to the bouncer Frank.

"Grayson! Hey, man, long time no see! I heard you were back in town." The large man with the ink-coloured afro held out his hand, and Grayson shook it firmly.

"It's nice to see you, Frank. How's Maria?"

Frank's face lit up. "She's good, man, really good. About to give birth to our second."

"Congratulations."

"Thanks." He opened the door. "Wayne will be happy to see you."

"Is he still working the bar?" Grayson asked.

"Nah. He hired a guy for that. He does some shifts, but he's been spending most of his time doing administration stuff. He used to bitch like hell about having to work the bar so much, and then he expanded the place six months ago. Now all he does is grumble about all the paperwork he has to do."

Grayson laughed. "That sounds like Wayne."

Frank grinned. "Yeah. Later, Grayson."

"Take it easy, Frank. Say hi to Maria for me."

Grayson walked into the bar, his eyes widening a little. The last time he'd been in the bar, nearly five years ago, it had been small and intimate, with only seven or eight tables and a small bar against the wall. It had almost doubled, with fourteen tables and a new and larger bar. The back wall had been knocked out, and what used to be a storage room was now a dance floor with a small stage. A band of five men, all wearing cowboy hats, sang and played instruments while three or four couples swayed to the music.

Grayson made his way deeper into the bar. He didn't recognize the bartender, but Mark, the bar's other bouncer, leaned against the wall beside the bar. His muscular tattooed arms were folded over his chest, and he held a glass of whiskey in one meaty hand as he surveyed the room.

His gaze landed on Grayson, and he grinned, holding out one large fist. Grayson fist-bumped him and then winced as Mark punched him hard on the arm.

"Goddammit, Grayson – where the fuck you been, boy?"

Grayson shrugged. "Traveling."

"Yeah, I heard a rumour about that. You back for good?"

Grayson nodded. "I'm thinking of expanding the farm again. Maybe get back into the cattle business."

Mark shook his head before tilting the glass to his mouth. He swallowed the amber liquid in one gulp and pointed his finger at Grayson. "Christ, if I had your money, I'd be doing nothing but lying on a beach all day surrounded by beautiful women in bikinis."

Grayson laughed and leaned against the bar next to Mark. "Yeah, I tried that for a few weeks. It got real boring, real fast."

Mark arched his eyebrow at him, "If you were bored surrounded by a bunch of bikini-clad women, then you weren't doing it right."

Grayson laughed again as Mark waved to someone behind him. "You want a drink?"

"Sure. How's school going?"

Mark shrugged. "Pretty good. Two more years, and I got

my degree. Course, if I hadn't spent my early twenties fucking up my life, I'd have been done a hell of a lot sooner."

"Yeah, I guess, but -"

Grayson stopped as a warm hand pressed intimately on the small of his back, and a voice spoke in a low purr. "What can I get you to drink, cowboy?"

He turned. "I'll have a -"

He stopped, staring in shock at the familiar blonde woman. "Sydney?"

Sydney pulled her hand from his back like she'd been burned. "Oh. Hi, Grayson."

Grayson could hardly believe it was her. The Sydney he had grown used to seeing, the one who wore baggy jeans and t-shirts and very little make-up, was gone. In her place was a tiny, blonde bombshell in a tight, low-cut tank top and an indecently short jean skirt. His eyes dropped to her breasts for a moment. They were still as small as ever, but whatever she was wearing under that tank top had pushed and cupped them in such a way that she had a sexy amount of cleavage peeking above the neckline. Her hair was piled on top of her head, with a few ringlets curling around her face, and her eyes were lined with dark shadow, making them seem even more blue than normal. But it was her mouth that had him captivated.

He had checked her mouth out already, of course. It was hard not to notice the lush fullness of her upper and lower lip, but they had always been bare with only a hint of something shiny. Tonight, they were painted a deep red, and they were so soft looking he was suddenly aching to kiss them.

His pulse thudded in his ears, and vaguely, he realized Mark was saying something to him, but he couldn't stop looking at Sydney's mouth. Her lips parted slightly, her small pink tongue slipping out to lick nervously at her bottom lip, and he inhaled sharply.

* * *

GRAYSON WAS STARING AT HER MOUTH, AND SYDNEY THOUGHT that after two months of working at Dawson's, she was used to men staring at her mouth. Since Belinda had convinced her to use the red gloss on her lips, nearly every man in the bar stared at them. She'd spent a few mornings looking at her mouth, the taunts of her school classmates echoing in her head. They had called her trout lips and duck mouth, and she'd grown to hate her mouth and had dreamed of having the same thin lips as the other girls in her class.

As she grew older, more and more men had begun to notice and comment on them, but she'd never really gotten the appeal. Jacob hadn't taken much notice of them one way or the other, and it had been a bit of a relief for her. But now, watching the way Grayson's eyes darkened and his nostrils flared as he stared at her mouth, for the first time in her life, she could feel an answering pull of desire deep in her belly.

She wet her lips nervously. A muscle in Grayson's jaw ticked lightly as he bent down. He was going to kiss her right in front of everyone, and rather than pull away, she opened her mouth even further, silently inviting him.

Instead of kissing her, he placed his mouth to her ear and placed his drink order. His warm breath on her skin made goose bumps scuttle to life on her arms and chest. She swallowed hard, cursing herself for being such an idiot, and nodded dumbly before turning and walking toward the bar. She took a deep breath, her cheeks burning and her hands shaking slightly.

*You are not his type,* she reminded herself. *Stop acting like a love-struck schoolgirl, for Christ's sake.*

* * *

Grayson watched Sydney walk away, his eyes dropping to her ass. The skirt hugged it like a second skin, and it was too easy to imagine sliding his hands under her skirt and cupping and kneading her warm, firm flesh. Mark gave him a friendly elbow to the side.

"For such a tiny little thing, she's got a pretty great ass. She's worked here for two months, and I've been trying like hell to get between those skinny little legs of hers the entire time, but she won't even go for coffee with me."

He shook his head. "She's too skinny, but who cares with a mouth like that? What I wouldn't give to have those red lips wrapped around my -"

He stopped, the grin falling from his face, when Grayson turned and glared at him. "Say one more word about her, and you'll regret it, Mark."

Mark put up his hands. "Whoa, man, sorry. I didn't realize you and her had a thing going on."

Grayson didn't bother to correct him as he watched Sydney pick her way carefully through the crowd. She had his beer on a tray, and he pulled his wallet out as she stopped before him.

She handed him the beer and gave him an awkward smile. "That'll be five dollars."

He handed her a twenty, and as she picked through her apron pocket for his change, he shook his head. "Keep the change."

She frowned at him and held out the ten and the five. "That's too much."

He refused to take the bills from her. "I said keep it."

She waited a moment longer and then stuck the bills into the smaller side pocket of the apron. "Thank you."

He nodded, and she walked away once more. His hand tightened around the beer bottle when a short man with a huge beer belly pulled on her arm. She turned toward him, and Grayson could feel his stomach clenching when she rested her hand lightly on his arm and gave him a slow and inviting smile. The man, weaving slightly, leaned forward and whispered into her ear, his hand stroking her bare arm. She nodded and squeezed his arm briefly before heading toward the bar.

Mark clapped him on the back. "Chill out, Gray. Your girl ain't doing anything behind your back. Trust me. You know how it is in here. All the girls try to make the customers feel special. It helps with the tips. Hell, half the men come here just in the hopes that Belinda over there will talk to them."

He pointed to a tall and leggy brunette with large breasts and straight, sleek hair. Her outfit was as tight, if not tighter, than Sydney's, and she stood at a table of men with a tray filled with shooters. She gave a husky laugh, pinching one of the men's cheeks playfully before pouring the shot glass filled with an exotic-looking green liquid down his throat. The rest of the men cheered, and as she handed the rest of the drinks out and turned to go, one of them gave her a light slap on the ass.

She turned and shook her finger at him, giving him a mock glare, before winking and walking away. She walked like a model, long strides with an exaggerated sway of her generous hips, and as she walked towards the bar, nearly every man's head turned to watch her.

Belinda was exactly his type, and until a couple of days ago, Grayson would have been right there with the rest of the men, flirting shamelessly and tipping her large amounts. Using his looks and natural charm to convince her to go home with him.

He shook his head. He had developed an obsession with skinny, blonde Sydney in the last couple of weeks and didn't have the faintest idea why. He scowled at the floor. It drove him crazy to lose control, and right now, he felt completely and utterly off-balance.

There was no reason why he should be attracted to her or why it should bother him to watch her flirting with the men in the bar. He barely knew her - hell, he couldn't even remember her last name. He had no right to feel any sort of proprietorship toward her, but here he was, his stomach churning with jealousy as he watched her work.

It was a small town. You bumped into the same people repeatedly, and yet, other than the moment in the locker room, he had zero memory of ever seeing her before or after that. Maybe she'd moved away for a while. It would explain why he didn't remember seeing her around town. He would ask GG about it.

Mark spoke into his ear. "Grab a seat at the bar. I'll get Wayne from the office. I know he'll want to see you."

Grayson nodded and made his way to the bar. He sat down on one of the smooth leather stools and took a drink of beer. He scanned the room, searching for Sydney and grunting with satisfaction when he spotted her near the dance floor.

* * *

SYDNEY SIGHED AND LEANED AGAINST THE WALL FOR A moment. She rubbed the small of her back as Belinda joined her.

"Only an hour to go, Sid. Hang in there," she said.

"I don't know you do it," Sydney said grumpily. "You've been wearing five-inch heels for nearly seven hours straight, and you're not even limping. I'm wearing tennis shoes, and my feet and back are killing me."

Belinda laughed. "Honey, I've been doing this for much longer than you. Trust me, you'll get used to it."

Sydney sighed. She didn't want to get used to it. The thought of waitressing at Dawson's for years filled her with a hopeless sort of despair.

"Tell me who that tall drink of water is who's been watching you all night," Belinda said.

"I don't know what you're talking about," Sydney said.

Belinda rolled her eyes. "Liar."

"He hasn't been watching me," Sydney said.

"He's watching you right now." Belinda turned and waved at Grayson, who nodded and took another drink of his beer.

"Belinda," Sydney said, "knock it off."

"What?" Belinda shrugged. "He's cute, and he obviously likes you. Go talk to him and find out his name."

"I already know his name. He's GG's grandson."

Belinda's eyes widened with shock, and she looked behind her for another glance at Grayson. "Holy shit. That's Grayson O'Reilly? Jesus, I think I've only seen him once or twice since high school. I was a grade ahead of him. He's certainly filled out nicely, hasn't he?"

Sydney shrugged. "I hadn't noticed."

"Well, you're the only woman in here who hasn't. He's been drinking the same beer since he got here, but Lisa's gone over to him at least seven times to see if he needs a refill. She told me she had to practically shove her way through a crowd of women at one point."

Sydney laughed and poked Belinda in the side as the bartender, Greg, frowned in their direction. "C'mon, we need to get back to work. Greg's giving us the evil eye."

* * *

SYDNEY HANDED THE GLASS OF WHISKEY TO ART, ONE OF THE regulars, and smiled when he handed her a dollar tip.

"Thanks, Art." She winked at him, and the older man blushed a little.

She started across the room, willing herself not to check the bar to see if Grayson still sat there. It was extremely difficult. She didn't need to look at him to remember the way his dark gray t-shirt clung to his broad shoulders and wide chest or how good his ass looked in his jeans. Even the dark brown cowboy boots on his feet were turning her on.

She scowled and picked up some glasses from the empty table closest to her. When Grayson moved to his seat at the bar, he moved out of her section and into Lisa's. Part of her was glad she didn't have to talk to him again, but a bigger part was jealous that Lisa had a reason to keep talking to him.

She picked up an empty beer bottle, carefully balanced it on the overflowing tray, and inched her way through the people milling about. Despite the late hour, the bar was still close to full, and she suspected it would take a while to clear them all out. She sighed as a large man, his bald head gleaming in the lights overhead, stepped in front of her.

"Hey, Ron, watch out," she called, tapping him on the back. She took a step back when he turned around and glared at her. "Ron? What's wrong?"

"Sorry, Sid." Ron took a deep breath. His anger had made his British accent thicken. "That goddamn wanker Darren is pissing me off."

"Why don't you go outside and get some fresh air?" Sydney said.

"Yeah, that's a good idea."

Before he could step around her, a short, fat man sidled up to him. "Hey, Ron? You running away like a little bitch?"

"Shut up, Darren," Sydney said sharply.

Darren glanced at her, his gaze falling on her mouth. "Mind your business, Sydney."

"You need to leave. Go now – walk home and sleep this off," Sydney said.

"Not until this asshole apologizes for calling me a wanker."

"I call it like I see it, you ignorant sod," Ron growled.

Sydney looked behind her, searching for Mark. He was at the far end of the bar, and she waved at him. He started walking over, and Sydney sighed with relief.

Ron and Darren were standing nose-to-nose now, and alarm bells went off in Sydney's head at how red Ron's face was. Ron was a good man, quiet and not prone to anger, but when he did lose his temper, things usually took a quick turn for the worse.

Hoping to ease the tension, Sydney balanced the heavy tray on one hand and placed her other on Ron's large arm. "Ron? Honey, why don't you come to the bar with me, and I'll get you another drink? What do you say, big boy?" She made her voice soft and cajoling, and when he glanced at her, she smiled invitingly at him.

He stared at her mouth and then nodded. "Yeah, I'd like that, Sid." He dropped one heavy arm around her shoulders, and she slipped her arm around his thick waist.

She was leading him away when Darren spoke behind them. "That's right, Ron, ya little bitch. Let a woman fucking tell you what to do."

With a roar of anger, Ron swung around, sweeping Sydney with him. She ducked under his arm and staggered backward, trying desperately to hang onto the tray of glasses and beer bottles as Ron cocked his arm back to hit Darren. Ron's elbow slammed into her shoulder, spinning her around and knocking her to the floor. She hit the dirty, sticky floor with a hard thud, wincing as she landed on the tray, and the bottles and glasses dug into her abdomen. There was the sound of breaking glass, and the front of her tank top was soaking wet.

There were shouts of anger as Ron and Darren began to fight above her. People rushed to crowd around them, and Sydney tried to gain her feet. It was impossible. The people were starting to crush her against the floor, and feeling panicky, she wrapped her arms around her head and tried once more to stagger to her feet. As Mark, shouting obscenities, pushed through the crowd towards the fighting men, Sydney screamed his name.

"Mark! Down here! Mark!"

He didn't hear her, and she cursed as a drunk woman stepped on her hip. The woman's high heel dug painfully into her flesh, and just when Sydney was sure she was about to be trampled to death, a familiar face leaned over her.

His face grim, Grayson reached down and hauled her to her feet. He put his arms around her and held her close, protecting her against the people still crowding around them. She rested her head on his chest and rubbed at her abdomen. It was stinging painfully and wet with beer and liquor, and she winced a little as Frank barrelled past them and helped Mark break the men apart.

"Back! Everyone get the hell back!" A familiar voice shouted. Wayne, his ruddy face covered in sweat and his dark eyes glowing with anger, walked through the crowd. He clapped his hands loudly before whistling piercingly.

"Jesus Christ! Are you all a bunch of animals?" he yelled. "Everyone get the fuck out! Now! Bar's closed, ya bunch of drunken bastards!"

When no one moved, he drew himself up to his full height of 5'4" and glared at the crowd. "Have ya gone deaf as well? Get out! Come back tomorrow when you've sobered up!"

The crowd slowly dispersed as people headed for the

exits. Sydney peeked around Grayson to see Ron and Darren, both of their faces bloody and starting to swell, sitting at separate tables. Frank stood beside Ron, and Mark had one meaty hand on Darren's shoulder.

"Sydney, are you okay?" Belinda asked worriedly.

"I'm fine." She tried to pull away from the circle of Grayson's arms, but he frowned and kept her against his side, one arm firmly around her shoulders.

His face a mask of shame, Ron said, "Sid, I'm so sorry. I didn't mean to knock you down like that."

"It's fine, Ron. I know it was an accident." Sydney rubbed at her abdomen again. It was really stinging now, and she was feeling a little sick to her stomach.

Wayne frowned at the two men. "What the fuck? Do you both want to be banned from here? Is that what you want? You know I don't allow any fighting in my goddamn bar."

"He called me a wanker!" Darren protested. "I'm supposed to just -"

"I don't fucking care!" Wayne yelled. "Christ, you are a wanker, and everyone knows it."

Ron snickered, and Wayne turned on him. "Something funny, you stupid bald oaf? You could have seriously hurt Sydney."

"I'm fine, Wayne," Sydney said. "I just got the wind knocked -"

She stopped at Belinda's gasp of shock, staring at the tall brunette. "Belinda, what's wrong?"

"You're bleeding." Belinda pointed to her abdomen, and Sydney looked down, groaning at the bright blossom of blood soaking through her tank top.

"Shit." Grayson lifted her tank top, sucking in his breath at the cut on her stomach just below her rib cage. It was bleeding freely, and she could see bits of broken glass embedded in her skin. She reached with one shaking hand to touch her stomach, and Grayson pulled her hand away.

"No, don't touch it. You need to go to the hospital."

"I'll be fine. I just need to rinse it clean and put a bandage on it. The cut's not that deep," she said.

"Are you crazy, Sid?" Belinda gave her a look of horror. "Grayson's right. You need to go to the hospital. You'll need stitches for sure."

"I'm fine. I'll rinse it in the bathroom right now." She pulled free of Grayson's embrace and walked quickly to the ladies' room.

She stood in front of the sink, untying her apron and placing it on the counter before easing up her shirt. She turned on the faucet as the door banged open, and Grayson strode through it, followed closely by Belinda.

"Hey!" Sydney frowned. "This is the ladies' room."

"I don't care," he growled. "You need to go to the hospital right now. You can let me drive you there or wait for an ambulance – your choice."

"I am not going to the hospital," Sydney said.

"Yes, you are." He folded his arms over his chest and stared at her.

She looked to Belinda for help, but she gave Sydney a grave look. "He's right, Sid. You need stitches."

"I don't have insurance," Sydney said, "and I can't afford a hospital bill right now. I'll clean it out well, and it'll be fine."

"Don't worry about the cost," Grayson said. "I'll pay for it, and you can pay me back."

"No, I don't want -"

"Sorry, Sid, this isn't a choice. You have to go to the hospital." He took her upper arm and led her out of the bathroom and across the bar. Belinda hurried ahead, grabbing a clean towel from under the bar before returning to them. She pushed the towel into Sydney's hand.

"Here, apply pressure to it until you get to the hospital."

Sydney pressed the towel to her abdomen.

Holding an icepack to his swelling cheek, Ron reached for her as they passed him. "God, Sydney. I'm so sorry."

Grayson knocked his hand away. "Don't ever touch her again. I'll rip your arm from its socket if I even catch you looking at her. Do you hear me?" he snarled. His face was red with anger, and Ron shrank back.

"Ron, it's okay. I'll talk to you later," Sydney called over her shoulder as Grayson led her from the bar and toward his truck. She shivered in the cold air and was thankful when they reached Grayson's truck. He opened the passenger door, cupped her elbows, and lifted her easily into the truck's cab.

He shut the door and slipped into the driver's side, reaching across her to snag her seatbelt and carefully buckle it around her. Without speaking, he started the truck, turned the heat on high, and drove out of the parking lot.

# CHAPTER 5

Sydney stared up at the dingy ceiling of the emergency room. To her left, hidden behind a curtain, a woman coughed steadily, and she could hear the low murmuring of a man to her right.

She sighed and fidgeted a little on the bed she laid on. For a Saturday night, the emergency room was surprisingly quiet. She'd had to wait less than half an hour in the waiting room before a nurse ushered her into the emergency ward. Grayson had been at the front desk, filling out paperwork, and she'd given him a quick wave.

"Don't worry. We'll bring him back as soon as he's finished filling out the paperwork." The nurse patted her arm. She'd shown Sydney to a bed, pulled the curtains, and helped her remove her clothes and slip into a hospital gown.

She examined the bloody gash on Sydney's stomach closely. The wound had started to clot, but there were still small shards of glass sticking into her skin, and the nurse lowered the bed before helping Sydney climb carefully into it.

She'd instructed Sydney to stay flat on her back before

tucking the sheets below her belly button and Sydney's gown just below her breasts.

"No getting off the bed, all right?" She'd smiled at Sydney. "The doctor won't be long, and I'll check if your boyfriend is done with the forms."

"Oh, he's not my boyfriend." Sydney had tried to clarify, but the nurse had already left, pulling the curtain shut behind her.

Now, the curtain pulled back, and the nurse reappeared.

"Found him," she said cheerfully, and Sydney had to fight the urge to pull up the sheet when Grayson appeared behind the nurse.

"Here, hon. You can sit here." The nurse pulled a chair over and placed it next to the bed. Grayson nodded his thanks and sat on the chair as the nurse laid instruments on a small silver tray.

"How do you feel?" he asked.

"Fine. My stomach is sore, and my hip hurts from where that woman stepped on me, but other than that, I'm okay."

He glanced at her stomach, and Sydney's cheeks heated when he leaned over her for a closer look. His warm breath on the bare skin of her stomach made her flesh break out in goosebumps, and he stared up at her. "Are you cold?"

"A little," she lied.

Before he could respond, the curtain opened, and the doctor ducked into the small space.

"So, I hear you got in the middle of a bar fight," he said. "Probably not the wisest – Sydney? Sydney Wright?"

Sydney smiled at him. "Chad! How are you?"

"I'm great." He grinned boyishly at her and sat on a stool on her right side. "I haven't seen you since high school."

He looked her up and down, his gaze lingering on her mouth. "You're looking really good. How did you get in the middle of a bar fight?"

Sydney laughed and then winced a little. "I work at Dawson's now."

"Dawson's? I thought you were going to college to get your teaching degree?" Chad said.

Sydney glanced at Grayson. "Well, I was, but then my dad, you know..."

Chad squeezed her arm. "Right. I'm sorry, I forgot about that." He paused. "I heard you and Jacob Yewn were an item."

"We were," Sydney said. "Not anymore."

She changed the subject before he could ask more questions. "You seem to be doing well. How long have you been a doctor?"

"I'm not quite a doctor yet, still interning. Three more years to go," Chad said as he studied her stomach.

Grayson swore under his breath. "Maybe we should get a real doctor to sew her up."

"Grayson," Sydney cut him a look, "don't be rude."

Chad glanced at Grayson before turning back to Sydney. "So, I'll numb the area first. I'll need to put it in a few spots since it's not just the cut but glass shards in your stomach, too."

He pulled on gloves and held up the needle. "The bad news is this will hurt like a bitch. The good news is you won't even feel me picking out the glass or sewing you up once it's done."

Sydney sighed. "So, I do need stitches? I hoped since the wound was clotting that maybe I wouldn't need them."

Chad shook his head and turned on the light hanging over the bed. He brought it down until it was just above Sydney's stomach and examined her skin carefully. "Sorry, Sydney. You'll need stitches. Not that many, though – ten maybe?"

He brought the needle close to her skin. "Here's the tough part. Take deep breaths and try not to move, okay?"

Sydney nodded and reached for the bed rail. Before she could wrap her fingers around it, Grayson had slipped his large hand over hers and held it loosely. She gave him a look of surprise as Chad slid the needle into her stomach. She winced and squeezed Grayson's hand. There was a burning sensation under her skin, and she tried to keep still as Grayson made a soothing noise under his breath. He rubbed her arm with his other hand, squeezing and stroking softly.

"Look at me, Sydney."

She stared at him, tears stinging her eyes, and he smiled encouragingly. "He's almost done."

"There." Chad set the needle down. "Now we'll just give it a few minutes to take hold, and then I'll start picking out the glass."

He pulled the light down a little further and flipped a small switch on the side of it. The light burned brighter, and he grunted with satisfaction before slipping a pair of magnifying glasses on.

Her stomach growled, and Sydney blushed when Grayson studied her stomach.

"When did you eat last?" Grayson asked gruffly. He stared at her flat stomach, how her hip bones jutted out and how the skin stretched tightly over her ribcage.

"Before work," she said. He didn't need to know it was an apple and half a package of crackers.

"You need to eat more," he said.

"He's right," Chad said. "I know you're small-boned, Sid, but this is too thin. He ran his gloved finger across one of her ribs. "You need to gain at least ten more pounds, maybe even fifteen."

"Right," Sydney said. She was embarrassed by her lack of money and even more ashamed that she could barely afford to feed herself.

Trying to pull their attention from her too thin body, she said, "I hurt my hip as well. Can you take a look at it?"

"Sure." Chad pulled the sheet down slightly and whistled under his breath. "Now that's impressive."

Grayson leaned over her and swore softly. Just below her left hipbone was a perfectly round red spot with an edge of white around it. The swelling and bruising had already started, and Sydney flinched and squeezed Grayson's hand again when Chad probed softly at it.

"That must hurt," Chad said. "What the heck is that round mark from?"

"A high heel," Sydney said. "Some chick stepped on me while I was lying on the floor."

Chad patted her arm. "Well, you'll have one hell of a bruise, but I don't think anything is broken."

"Maybe we should get x-rays done just to be on the safe side," Grayson said.

"No," Sydney said. Even though she fully intended to repay him, she was humiliated enough that Grayson was paying for the hospital bill. She already had enough hospital bills to pay – she was damned if she would add to it.

Grayson scowled when Chad said, "I don't think x-rays are necessary. If it isn't healing after a week and is still sore when you touch it, come back, and we'll do x-rays."

\* \* \*

"ALL FINISHED." CHAD PULLED OFF HIS GLOVES AND DISPOSED of them in the wastebasket beside the bed. Sydney stared at her stomach. Chad had picked out all the glass, cleaned the cut and the surrounding skin, and then sewn the gash shut with neat black stitches.

"Thanks, Chad, it looks much better." She pulled her

gown down and the sheet up, wincing a little, as Chad pulled another needle out.

"One last shot for pain," he said. "No driving after this."

"Then don't give it to me," Sydney said. "My car is still at the bar, and I have an appointment tomorrow that I can't miss."

"Give her the shot. I'll give you a ride home and bring you back into town tomorrow morning to get your car," Grayson said.

"I can't ask you to do that. You've already done way too -"

"Give her the shot." Grayson squeezed her arm gently, and Chad eased the needle into her other arm.

"This'll make you feel much better. You'll be loopy and might get a little drowsy from it, which is fine. You should go straight to bed anyway."

Sydney's stomach growled loudly again, and Chad looked at Grayson. "Correction – get some food into her and then put her to bed."

Grayson nodded as Chad pulled a prescription pad from his pocket and scribbled a few sentences. "This is a prescription for an antibiotic – just to be on the safe side. You can pick it up tomorrow at the pharmacy."

Sydney nodded, knowing she couldn't afford it but not wanting to admit that in front of Grayson. She took the paper, and Grayson deftly plucked it from her fingers.

"I'll get them tomorrow for you. You should probably try to rest as much as possible," he said.

"Okay, I think we're done here." Chad stood. "The stitches can come out in ten days – you can pop by here, and I'll take them out for you free of charge if you'd like. No stretching or bending for the first five days, and no lifting anything heavier than ten pounds."

"But I can go back to work, right?" Sydney said.

Chad hesitated. "You should probably take the week off."

"I'll take it easy," Sydney promised. There was no way she was missing a week of work. She'd ask Wayne if she could have a smaller section at the bar for a few days. He'd be fine with it.

Chad glanced at Grayson. "Remember – food and then straight to bed."

Grayson nodded as Chad squeezed Sydney's hand. "Good to see you again, Sid. Maybe I'll drop by Dawson's one night and say hello." His gaze fell on her mouth again, and Sydney could see the irritation in Grayson's face before he placed his hand on her arm in a weirdly possessive manner.

"I'd like that," Sydney said to Chad.

"Do you need me to send the nurse in to help you get dressed?"

"I'll help her." Grayson held out his hand, and Chad shook it. "Thanks, I'll take her home now."

Chad nodded and left as Grayson turned back to Sydney. He pulled the sheets back to the end of the bed and then slipped one hand around the back of her neck and the other around her waist. He gently pulled her forward until she sat up.

"Okay?" he asked.

She nodded, and he took her legs and swung them to the floor. Her clothes were piled neatly on the chair against the wall, and he picked up her tank top.

She wrinkled her nose at it. "I do not want to wear that. It's covered in blood and beer. Just throw it away, and I'll wear the hospital gown home."

He threw it in the waste basket and grabbed the next item of clothing. It was her bra, her pink lacy one, and he gave her a questioning look as she blushed. "I can go without it."

He shoved it into the pocket of his jacket and grabbed her skirt. A tiny pink piece of fabric fell out, and he caught it quickly before it hit the floor. He stared at it curiously for a moment, and Sydney yanked the fabric out of his hand just as understanding dawned on his face.

"I don't need help putting on my underwear," she said.

She started to lean over, then flinched and sat back up abruptly.

"Give them to me," he said roughly. "It's not that big of a deal."

He pulled her underwear from her hands, bent down, and slipped her panties over her feet and up her legs to just under the hospital gown. He put his hands in her armpits and lifted her from the bed, setting her down gently. She wobbled a bit, and he steadied her for a moment.

"Okay?"

"Yes."

He reached for her underwear, and she blushed again and grabbed at his hands. "I can pull them up."

He steadied her as she carefully pulled her panties up under the gown. Still steadying her with one hand, he reached for her jean skirt and bent down.

She rested her hands on his shoulders as she lifted one foot and then the other so he could slide the skirt up her legs. Without waiting for her permission, he pulled the skirt up over her ass and hips.

"Turn around," he instructed. She obeyed, and he zipped up the back of her skirt before helping her into her socks and shoes and placing his jacket on her. It was almost comically too big for her. The sleeves fell past her hands, and the jacket hem went past her knees. He zipped it up to her throat.

"Ready?"

"Yes, but you're going to freeze out there." She looked doubtfully at his bare arms in his short-sleeved t-shirt.

"I'll be fine." He took her hand and led her slowly toward the exit.

# CHAPTER 6

"I 'll take you home, cook you something to eat, and then help you to bed," Grayson said as he pulled out of the hospital parking lot.

"No, you don't have to do that," she protested.

She had three apples, half a package of crackers and a tiny bit of pasta in her kitchen. She had planned to boil the pasta and slice an apple into it, but she had a feeling that Grayson wouldn't consider that enough food.

"I don't mind."

"The thing is – I don't have a lot of groceries in the house right now," she said. "I was planning on doing some grocery shopping tomorrow."

"We'll grab something quick to eat before going home then." He glanced at the clock on the dashboard. It read 2:12 in steady green numbers, and he pursed his lips. "Any idea what might be open?"

She smiled a little. "I know the perfect place. Head downtown and turn right on Bowden Street. It's right across from the library."

She gave him a tentative smile. "I'll buy you dinner. It's the least I can do to -"

She stopped talking and slapped her forehead in frustration. "I left my apron with my tip money at the bar and my purse in my locker."

He grinned. "It's fine. I'll buy tonight, and you can buy next time."

* * *

"ARE YOU SURE THIS PLACE IS OPEN?" GRAYSON ASKED AS HE reached for the door.

"I'm sure," Sydney said.

The door opened, and Grayson ushered her into the warmth, staring around curiously. It was an old-fashioned diner with six booths in front of the window, a long counter with a display case of baked goods at one end, and a jukebox at the other. There were red leather stools with faded and ripped seats bolted to the floor in front of the counter, and the floor was scuffed and worn.

"I don't think I've ever been in this place before," he said.

She smiled. "It's a little off the beaten path."

The swinging door behind the counter opened, and a tall, heavy-set man with a thick beard walked through it. His broad, homely face broke out into a large smile.

"Miss Sydney!" His voice was heavy with a thick European accent, and Grayson watched as he lifted a hinged section of the counter and hurried towards them. "How are you?"

"I'm good." Sydney smiled at him and returned his gentle hug.

He turned toward Grayson, and Sydney said, "Ivan, this is my friend Grayson. Grayson, this is Ivan."

"Any friend of Sydney's, as the saying goes," Ivan said as he shook Grayson's hand.

He swept his arm out. "Sit wherever you want, my friends. I'll grab you some menus."

Grayson cupped Sydney's elbow and steered her toward one of the booths. She unzipped his jacket and took it off, laying it on the booth seat before carefully sliding in. Grayson sat across from her as Ivan dropped menus in front of them.

"Something to drink?"

"Just a water for me, please, Ivan," Sydney said as she opened her menu.

"I'll have the same." Grayson stared at the menu, trying to decide what to eat. With a soft sigh, Sydney closed her menu and gave him another tentative smile.

"The pasta is really good here."

"I was thinking of trying the meatloaf," he said.

"It's delicious, too."

He closed his menu as Ivan approached with two glasses of water.

"Do you know what you're having?" Ivan asked.

Grayson listened, his eyes widening a little as Sydney ordered. "I'll have the potato soup to start, please. And I'll have the spaghetti and meatballs. Oh, and can I also have a piece of garlic toast?"

Ivan nodded and turned to Grayson. He ordered the meatloaf with a salad, and Ivan grinned at him. "The meatloaf is my specialty. I'll give you a little extra, my friend."

He left them, and Sydney blushed slightly under Grayson's steady gaze. "What?"

"How do you know about this place?"

"My dad worked at the factory just outside of town. It closed down last year, but he worked there for years."

"I remember it."

"He worked shift work, so sometimes he didn't get home until midnight. About once a month, he would come home from work, wake me up, wrap me up in a blanket and carry me out to the car. We'd come here, just the two of us – me in my pajamas and him in his work clothes – and have dinner."

"That sounds nice."

"It was." She smiled wistfully.

"Do you and your dad still eat here?"

"No. He died three years ago."

"I'm sorry."

"Thank you. I miss him a lot." She shifted a bit in the booth.

"Does your stomach hurt?" he asked.

"Nope. Nothing hurts. In fact, I feel really, really," she paused, "good. Hungry, but good - and warm."

She grabbed the hospital gown and fanned it back and forth before sticking her head down it and blowing. He laughed, and she grinned in delight.

"I think you might be a bit high right now," he said.

She shook her head. "I am not."

Grayson liked this new, warm and relaxed side of Sydney, and he was anxious to learn more about her. "Why did you leave college?"

"It's a boring story." She picked at one nail before taking a sip of water.

"I'd like to hear it."

Before she could reply, Ivan set a steaming bowl of soup in front of her, and Sydney bent her head and inhaled deeply. Her stomach growled loudly in response, and she picked up her spoon and ate.

Grayson stopped with his forkful of salad halfway to his mouth and watched in amazement as Sydney ate her soup with the enthusiasm of a three-hundred-pound lumberjack.

She finished her soup in less than three minutes and, after wiping her mouth with her napkin, sat back with a sigh.

She noticed him looking at her and coloured slightly. "Sorry, that was rude."

"Not at all. You were telling me about college." He prompted as he finished eating his salad.

"Right. My college years – make that year," she giggled.

Ivan appeared beside them and placed the biggest plate of spaghetti Grayson had ever seen in front of Sydney. She clapped her hands with delight and grinned up at Ivan.

"It smells delicious, Ivan!" she crowed.

He winked at her. "I gave you an extra meatball, Miss Sydney. You're too thin now."

He placed a steaming plate of meatloaf and mashed potatoes smothered in gravy before Grayson.

"Eat, my friend, eat," he urged.

Grayson took a bite of the meatloaf. It was delicious – perfectly spiced and practically melting in his mouth - and he gave Ivan the thumbs up. "It's the best meatloaf I've ever had."

Ivan clapped him on the back. "Excellent. Enjoy, my friends."

He returned to the counter and sat on a stool, pulling out his phone and scrolling across the screen.

Grayson glanced at Sydney. She was almost shoveling the spaghetti into her mouth, her face flushed with happiness, and she looked up at him.

"So good, right?" she mumbled around a mouthful of pasta.

He nodded in agreement, secretly delighted at watching her eat the way she was. It had crossed his mind that she might have anorexia, and he was relieved to see how much she was eating. He didn't know much about anorexia, but he didn't think that people who suffered from it took that much enjoyment in their food.

She swallowed and then tore off a piece of garlic toast, popping it into her mouth and chewing it with great relish. She sucked the garlic butter from one finger, and Grayson felt a twinge of desire shudder through him as he watched those full lips close around her finger.

"So, when I was in grade ten, my mother committed suicide."

He winced. "I'm sorry to hear that."

She shrugged. "She had schizophrenia that she refused to get treatment for, and a drinking problem, and she abused both my father and me. I was as sad as you probably were when your father died."

She stared solemnly at him. "I know you don't remember me because we didn't travel in the same social circles at all, but there was this day in high school where -"

"The locker room. I remember."

She gave him a look of surprise. "That's right. I still remember how badly your back was bruised."

He shrugged. "It was a long time ago. Go on with your story."

"Anyway, as horrible as this is, life got a lot better once my mother was gone. We didn't have much money, but my dad saved and scrimped enough money to send me to college. I love kids and have wanted to be a teacher for as long as I can remember. A couple of months into my first year, I met Jacob Yewn. Did you know him?"

"Yeah, a little. We weren't friends, but I knew who he was."

"We fell in love. His parents disapproved, of course. It was the classic story of a rich boy falling for the girl from the wrong side of the tracks. Such a cliché, am I right?"

She put another forkful of spaghetti into her mouth and

chewed slowly. "His parents thought I was just after his money. They did what they could to keep us apart, but we were in love, you know? Or at least I was. I think Jacob was just in love with the idea of being in love. Or maybe he liked being the big, strong hero who swooped in and saved the girl from her miserable, poor life. I don't really know."

She stared at her plate of spaghetti. "Six months after we started dating, I got pregnant. His parents freaked out, but Jacob was excited. He loved kids as much as I did and had all these plans for us. He wanted to get married immediately, which threw his parents into a panic, but I refused. I didn't want his parents to think I was just some gold-digger, so I said no, but I promised that once we finished college and I was working, I would marry him then. We spent the pregnancy planning our future together. I would take a year off to raise the baby and then return to college for my teaching degree. Jacob was going into real estate, and we used to talk about the kind of life we'd give our child."

She had eaten over half of her spaghetti and paused and eyed Grayson's garlic toast. "Are you going to eat that?"

He shook his head and handed it to her. She bit into it and then took another bite of spaghetti. "Emma was born three days after her due date. She was perfect. Absolutely perfect. My dad was so proud of her. God, how he loved her. And even Jacob's parents were starting to come around. A baby has a way of doing that, you know? They bring people together."

He nodded and took another bite of mashed potatoes.

"The first six months of Emma's life were so good. Jacob and I were happy. Emma was an easy baby, and I was starting to think that we could make it work. But then Jacob started to change. I think he realized how different we were and that he didn't love me the way I loved him. We started fighting a lot, and at one point, I took Emma and moved in with my dad for a few days. I went back to him, though. Jacob swore he loved me and needed time to figure out what he wanted. I wasn't sure what would happen between us, and then..."

She swallowed hard and stared down at her now-empty plate. "And then my dad had a massive stroke."

"I'm sorry," Grayson said.

She cleared her throat. "He was recovering well at first. His left side was paralyzed, and he'd lost the ability to speak, but he was getting stronger every day, and he recognized us. I used to bring Emma to the hospital daily, and his eyes would light up. She would pat his face and snuggle on the hospital bed with him, and I would read stories to the both of them."

She took a large drink of water, her face pale. "Three weeks after his initial stroke, Dad had another one. He slipped into a coma, lingered for a few days, and then died."

He reached out and squeezed her hand. "I'm so sorry, Sydney."

She glanced up at him, tears caught in her lower lashes. "Thank you. Emma was just over a year old, and I was supposed to go back to college, but I used the money that Dad had saved to pay for his funeral."

She stared moodily at her plate. "My father didn't have health insurance, so the hospital bill was... large. Jacob and I limped along for another year or so. He continued going to college, and I worked the night shift at a convenience store to pay for my dad's hospital bills."

Grayson frowned. "Jacob didn't help you pay for it?" He didn't know much about the Yewn family, but he did know that they were one of the wealthier families in town.

"He never offered, and I wouldn't have let him anyway. By then, we barely spoke, and I didn't want to owe him any more than he thought I already did."

Ivan took their empty plates and returned with a pot of tea and two mugs. He set them silently on the table and left.

Grayson poured them tea, and Sydney sipped the fragrant liquid. "Eventually, Jacob told me he wanted out. I said fine. I would take Emma and move into a small apartment. He lost it. He and his parents had planned that Jacob would have full custody of Emma, and I could have her on the weekends. I told him that would never happen, and he sneered at me and told me to stop being so naive. He came from a good family, a *wealthy* family, and I was a nobody. My parents were dead, I had a massive hospital bill to pay, and I couldn't provide for Emma the way he could. He told me he'd take me to court over it and drag it out for years."

She stopped and stared into her tea.

"What happened then?" Grayson prompted.

She laughed bitterly. "I panicked. I was young and afraid of losing my daughter, so I packed up my car and took off with Emma. I had very little money and no idea what I would do or where I would go, but I was petrified that I would lose Emma, you know? I didn't get very far. Jacob called the police, told them I had kidnapped our daughter, and they arrested me about a day and a half from town."

"Jesus," Grayson said.

Jacob hired an expensive lawyer, and he and his lawyer convinced the judge that I was a danger to Emma. They brought up my mother's mental problems, my lack of money, my large debt, and my dead-end job. It was so easy for them, you know? I made it easy for them by taking off with Emma."

She sighed. "They gave custody of Emma to Jacob, and I was allowed weekly supervised visits with her."

"Asshole," Grayson muttered. Sydney's eyes were dark with pain, and he watched as she wiped the tears from her cheeks. He felt like an asshole himself for forcing her to share the story with him. "I'm sorry, Sydney. I shouldn't have been so nosy."

She shrugged. "It's fine. Most people in the town already know the story. Jacob doesn't have any problems talking about what a horrible mother I am. I'm surprised you don't know any of it."

"Working a cattle farm doesn't give you much time to listen to town gossip."

"I suppose not. It's not all bad. I graduated to unsupervised visits with my baby girl last year. I'm returning to court in a few weeks to get unsupervised overnight visits."

She finished her tea and gave him a small smile. "The only thing that comforts me is that as much of an asshole Jacob is to me, he is a wonderful dad. Emma loves him madly, and he would do anything for her. Anyway, that's why I never finished college. Told you it was a boring story."

"How old is Emma now?"

"She just turned four. I can't believe my baby will be starting school next year." She suddenly yawned and sat back in the booth, rubbing her stomach softly.

"Are you in pain?" Grayson asked.

"Nope. Just really full." She lifted her hospital gown and stared at her bare belly. She had a small pot belly from all the food, and she laughed and rubbed it. "I'm like a tiny, blonde Buddha."

He grinned as she yawned again. "Okay, Buddha. Time to get you into bed."

"Yeah, I'd like that." Her face turned red. "I mean – to sleep."

He laughed. "I know."

He helped her out of the booth, zipping her into his jacket again, and Ivan gave her another hug as Grayson paid the bill.

"I will see you and little Emma tomorrow afternoon, yes?"

She nodded. "Yes."

"Good. I will make a special cake just for her."

"She'll like that." Sydney smiled and kissed his weathered cheek. "Goodnight, Ivan."

Grayson and Sydney walked quickly to his truck, and he cupped her elbows and lifted her easily into it. She was already starting to shiver, and he cranked the heat as he drove away from the diner.

"Does Ivan always stay open twenty-four hours?" he asked.

She shook her head wearily. "No - just Friday and Saturday night. He used to do it for the factory workers who worked the midnight shift, and now I think he does it out of habit."

They drove silently for a while, and when Grayson glanced over, he wasn't surprised to see that Sydney had nodded off, her head resting against the passenger window.

He quickly drove home and parked next to the guest-house. He reached over and shook her gently. "Sydney, we're home."

She snorted and raised her head, blinking owlishly at him. "Home?"

"Yes. Sit up for a minute, okay?"

She nodded sleepily, and he slipped out of the truck and ran to the passenger side. He opened the door and unbuckled her seat belt. "C'mon, honey. Let's get you into bed."

She giggled as he picked her up, and she buried her face into his neck. "Yes – into bed. But only for sleeping. Nothing else because I'm too skinny and too blonde, and I talk too much."

She sighed. "I talked too much again tonight, didn't I?"

He shook his head as he carried her to the front door. "No, not at all."

"Do you have your keys?" he asked.

"Nope, but the door's unlocked."

He frowned. "You need to keep your door locked, Sydney."

"Yes, sir." She gave him a sleepy salute before giggling and burying her face into his neck.

He opened the door and carried her to the bedroom. He deposited her on the side of the bed and knelt, taking off her shoes and socks as she yawned again.

"God, Sid. It's freezing in here. You need to turn up the heat."

She snuggled up to him again, wrapping her small arms around his shoulders and her legs around his waist before pushing her face into his throat once more.

"You could stay and keep me warm," she murmured against his throat. The feel of her full lips against his skin was bad enough, but when she licked him, her tongue sliding across his flesh, his cock hardened, and his balls tightened almost painfully.

"I bet you're good at making women hot," she giggled. She licked him again, and he pushed her back, his breath exploding from his mouth in a long, drawn-out hiss.

"I think you should probably just get some sleep. What do you say?" he said.

"Okay," she said.

"Stand up, Sid," He tugged her to her feet. He took his jacket off of her and then turned her around and unzipped her skirt under the hospital gown. He pulled it down over her butt and hips and let it fall to the floor. She stepped out of it, and he hesitated for a moment.

"Do you want to leave the hospital gown on?"

"God, no."

He untied the gown, and she pulled it off and dropped it to the floor, keeping her back to him. He stared at her, his eyes dropping to her ass, and he groaned inwardly at the

sight of

firm

She

the bed.

quickly,

coloured ni

He heard

sighing with rel

He leaned ov

from her face. "Goo

"Good night, Gray

eye. "I have to be in tow

"That's fine. I'll drive

thirty, okay?"

"Okay." She closed her ey

kissing her forehead softly.

locking and closing the front do

# CHAPTER 7

"Thanks again for taking me to the hospital last night and for the ride into town today," Sydney said.

Grayson nodded. "You're welcome."

"If you let me know how much the hospital bill is, I'll pay you back as soon as possible."

He shrugged indifferently. "Yeah, I'll let you know. How's your stomach this morning?"

"It's good. A little sore, but my hip hurts more. I've got one hell of a bruise on it." She brushed some lint from her pants.

They were almost to the bar, and Sydney sighed with relief. Grayson had been quiet the entire ride, and she had a feeling that he was probably regretting asking for her life story last night. The pain meds had loosened her tongue, and she groaned inwardly as she recalled how much she had blabbed to him last night. He probably thought she was a first-class loser or, worse, as messed up as her mother had been.

*It's too late to worry about it now,* she told herself. *Besides, what do you care what Grayson thinks about you? He's made it clear he's not interested.*

He pulled into the parking lot and put the truck into park. The wind blew fiercely, and he frowned at her. "Did you not bring a jacket?"

She smoothed her thick sweater down self-consciously. Her old and ripped winter jacket did nothing to block the wind. She pulled on her mittens. "I don't get cold easily."

She opened the door and slid out of the truck, turning to give him a small smile. "Thank you again, Grayson. I'm grateful for your help."

"No problem."

She hesitated, shut the truck door, and walked quickly into the bar.

* * *

"Mama!" Emma barrelled toward her and slammed into her legs and hips. Sydney winced before dropping to her knees and hugging the little girl hard.

"Hi, baby girl! I'm so happy to see you!"

"I'm happy to see you too, Mama." Emma's cheeks and nose were red with the cold, and Sydney kissed them gently.

"C'mon, baby girl. Let's go to the library and pick out some books."

"And then we'll see Ivan?" Emma said hopefully.

"We will. I think he's making something special for you today."

"Yay!"

She glanced up as a man with dark hair and a short, muscular body approached them. "Daddy, Ivan made me something special today!"

"That's nice, Emma." He stroked her soft blonde hair. "Just

make sure you don't eat so much that you ruin your appetite for dinner."

"I won't," Emma said. She took Sydney's hand as Jacob stared stiffly at her.

"You're late."

"Just five minutes. It took a while for my car to start."

Jacob stared at the rusty Honda with distaste. "I don't want you putting Emma in that thing. It's a rolling death trap."

"I know, Jacob. I'm just taking her across the street to the library, and then we're going to Ivan's."

Sydney glanced at the tall, ivory-skinned blonde standing next to Jacob. She wore a long fur coat, shivering delicately in the cold air as she took Jacob's hand, and he gave her a loving look.

"Hello, Monica. How are you today?" Sydney asked.

"I'm good, thanks, Sydney. How are you?"

"Good." She turned back to Jacob. "I'll see you in two hours."

"An hour and fifty-five minutes," Jacob corrected her.

Sydney gritted her teeth and forced herself to smile. "Right. An hour and fifty-five minutes."

"Bye, Daddy! Bye, Monica!" Emma waved cheerfully at them, and Jacob blew her a kiss as Sydney led her across the street and into the library.

* * *

"Emma!" Ivan picked up the little girl and swung her in a circle before kissing her soft cheek. "How's my sweet girl today?"

Emma giggled. "I'm good, Ivan. Mama said you made something special for me today."

"That I have, little one. You look more and more like your mama every day. Did you know that?"

"Monica says I'm the spitting image of her," Emma said.

Ivan winked at her. "Go sit in the booth with your mama, and I'll bring your special treat to you, okay?"

"Okay." Emma slid into the booth beside Sydney, and Sydney helped her remove her jacket and hat.

"Sydney, can I get you something to eat?"

Sydney shook her head. "No thanks, Ivan. Just a glass of water for me, please."

He frowned but didn't say anything as he walked away. Sydney opened her purse and quickly counted her tip money. Her monthly payment on the hospital bill was due on Monday, and she bit her lip with frustration when she realized it only left her forty dollars until Thursday night. The Honda was low on gas, and she had finished off the pasta and apples this morning.

She thought quickly. GG would give her leftovers tonight after dinner, as she always did, and Sydney could stretch the leftovers into three small dinners. She would pick up another bag of apples, they were cheap right now, and that would cover her for food. She would use the rest of the forty bucks for gas money and on Emma today.

"Mama, who's that man?" Emma asked.

"Hmm?" Sydney said as she shoved her tip money back into her purse.

"That man? He's staring at us."

Sydney looked up, her pulse quickening when she saw Grayson sitting at the booth farthest from theirs. She waved weakly at him, and he nodded before eating his lunch.

"That's Mama's friend Grayson." She smiled at the little girl and kissed the top of her head. "Pick out a book, and I'll read it to you, baby girl."

Ivan approached their table and placed a glass of milk and

a large piece of chocolate cake in front of Emma. "Here you go, Miss Emma. A very special piece of cake for a very special girl."

Emma's eyes sparkled. "Thank you, Ivan. It looks so good. Doesn't it, Mama?"

"It sure does." Sydney smiled again at her. "Eat it slowly and put your napkin on your lap, okay?"

She took the glass of water from Ivan. "Ivan, when did Grayson get here?"

"A while ago. He said the meatloaf was so good, he had to come back for a second taste."

She studied Grayson, but he didn't look up, and after a moment, she smiled at Ivan. "Thank you again for being so kind and making Emma something special."

"Read to me while I eat, Mama," Emma demanded as Ivan left. With another look at Grayson, Sydney opened one of the books they had chosen from the library and began to read.

* * *

"WELL, IF IT ISN'T LITTLE SYDNEY WRIGHT. HOW ARE YOU?" A familiar voice spoke, and Sydney looked up from where she was curled up in the booth with Emma, looking through a picture book. She forced a polite smile on her face.

"Hello, Erin. Hello, Mary."

The two women were dressed in designer clothing, their fingers and ears dripped with expensive jewels, and their make-up was flawless. Erin and Mary had moved away, marrying rich men and divorcing them. They had returned to town within a year of each other, both sporting new noses and new boobs and flaunting their newly acquired wealth.

The two of them had been best friends since high school, and although it'd been many years since they'd hung her from her backpack in the locker room, Sydney still felt a burn of anger in her stomach when she saw them. She had no idea why they were in the diner. She'd always assumed they existed solely on vegetables, bourbon, and sarcasm.

"Having your weekly visit with little Emma, are you?" Erin asked.

Sydney nodded but didn't reply.

"It's so great that you don't have to be supervised now," Mary said. "Who knows, maybe eventually you'll be able to have her for more than a few hours at a time."

Sydney forced a smile. "I don't mean to be rude, but I'm kind of busy right now and I -"

"Oh my God. Is that Grayson O'Reilly?" Erin nudged Mary, who squinted across the diner.

"Ooh, I didn't realize he was back in town." Mary gave Erin a wicked grin. "Let's go and say hello."

Jealousy burned in her belly as the two women walked away without saying goodbye. She had no doubt that one of them would succeed in seducing and bedding Grayson. If his high school sweetheart was any indication, they were Grayson's type. They were tall, dark-haired with large breasts – *fake breasts*, a voice whispered viciously in her head - and they were elegant and graceful and practically oozed sexuality. They were the exact opposite of her in every single way.

She sighed and forced herself to stop thinking about Grayson. This was her only time with Emma, and she wouldn't waste it thinking about her high-school nemesis bedding her sexy neighbour.

* * *

GRAYSON SIGHED IRRITABLY AND TURNED THE WIPERS ON TO high. A storm had started while he'd been stuck in the diner with Mary and Erin, and the rain fell so hard he could barely see five feet down the road.

It wasn't just the weather he was irritated with. He had hoped to stop by Sydney's booth to say hello to her and meet Emma, but then Erin and Mary had descended upon him. By the time he managed to extract himself from the conversation, Sydney and Emma were gone.

He paid for his food and escaped the diner and the two women, nodding distractedly at their requests to call them. He didn't see Sydney's car, so he climbed into his truck and headed home.

He rounded a bend in the road and squinted out the windshield. "What the hell?"

He checked the rear-view mirror and then pressed on the brakes. He rolled his window down, staring into the small Honda on the side of the road. It was Sydney's car, but she wasn't in it.

Anxiety trickling into his belly, Grayson continued to drive toward the farm. He had only gone a mile or two when he spotted her. She walked on the side of the road, her head down against the wind and one hand resting against her side. He pulled up beside her and put the truck in park, hopping out as she stopped and peered at him.

"What are you doing walking in the rain?" He had to shout to be heard over the rain and the wind.

"My car broke down." Her lips were blue, and she was shivering wildly.

"Christ. Get in the goddamn truck." He took her by the arm and led her to the passenger side. He lifted her into the cab as she protested weakly.

"I'm soaking wet. I'll ruin the upholstery."

"I don't care." He slammed the door shut and stalked around to the driver's side. He climbed in and threw his cowboy hat into the backseat, running his hand irritably through his hair before turning the heat on full and starting down the road again.

"Why didn't you call me?" he asked.

"I don't have your number." She held her shaking hands in front of the heat vent.

"Do you know how dangerous it is to be walking on the side of the road like that? The road is wet, it's dark, and people drive too fast for the conditions. You could have been run over," he said.

"Sorry." She frowned at him. "I just wanted to get home."

"Your car is a piece of shit. You need to get a new one."

"Yeah, I'll get right on that," she shot back.

"I can't be rescuing you all the time. I do have other things I need to be doing."

"I didn't ask you to stop," she snapped. "You know what? Pull over. I don't need your help. I can walk the rest of the way."

She unclicked her seatbelt. Grayson snorted with annoyance and reached across the seat, grabbing one wrist in his hand and pulling her across the seat until she sat next to him. He put his arm around her upper body and pinned her against his side.

"Let go of me!" She smacked at him, and he grabbed both her wrists in one hand as the truck weaved on the road.

"Stop struggling. You'll rip your stitches out, for God's sake," he said.

Panting, her face red and her hair dripping water onto his arm, she stopped struggling and sat limply against him. After a minute or two, she tugged against his hand, and he tightened it around her wrists again.

"You can let go," she said dully. "I won't get out of the truck."

He didn't answer, and he didn't release her wrists either. She sighed and stared out the windshield as he drove over the hill, and the farm appeared. He turned into the driveway and shut off the truck, staring with annoyance at her. "You have to think, Sydney. You can't just -"

She surprised him by bursting into loud sobs. He stared at her in disbelief for a few seconds before pulling her against his chest. He pressed her head against his chest and rubbed her wet back through her sweater.

"I'm sorry. I shouldn't have been such a dick."

She didn't answer, just sobbed harder, and he pushed her wet hair away from her cheek before rubbing her back again. He didn't have much experience with crying women, but he knew there was sometimes a point where you just had to let them cry it out.

He continued to rub her back as she wrapped her arms around his waist and cried into his shirt. He murmured soft words of comfort, and after about five minutes, her crying subsided to a few watery sobs.

"I'm sorry, Sydney," he said again.

"It's not you." Her voice was muffled against his shirt.

"Do you want to talk about it?"

She straightened and stared miserably at him. "You know how I told you I was going back to court in a few weeks to get a couple of days with Emma by myself?"

He nodded and wiped a stray tear from her cheek with his thumb. She didn't seem to notice his touch. "After I brought Emma back to Jacob today, he told me that his lawyer had gotten the court date moved up. He pretended he was doing it for me, but he knows it makes it more difficult. I can't afford a lawyer, and I'm representing myself. I've been getting some books from the library, books on family law, and trying to read up on how best to present a solid argument for why I should get Emma, but they're so goddamn confusing that I need all the time I can get, you know?"

He nodded again. "When is the new court date?"

"Tuesday! This Tuesday at eleven. So now I have only two days to prepare a good argument for why I deserve to have Emma, and I have to lose my shift at the bookstore. That asshole Jacob did it on purpose."

She was starting to cry again, and he wiped the tears away.

"It'll be fine," he soothed. "We'll think of something."

She laughed bitterly and shook her head. "I don't even know why I try to fight him. I'll never win. He has too much money and power, and I'm dumb to think I have a chance. Even you think I'm dumb."

He shook his head. "I don't think you're dumb, Sydney."

She stared at him before her eyes dropped to his mouth. She took a deep breath and then suddenly pressed her mouth against his. She pushed her tongue eagerly against his lips, and he opened them as a shudder of desire went through him. She swept her tongue into his mouth, rubbing it against his tongue invitingly.

She abruptly pulled away from him. "I'm so sorry, Grayson. I shouldn't have done that."

He stared silently at her, still feeling the softness of her lips against his mouth and tasting her on his tongue, and she blushed furiously and slid across the seat.

"I'm sorry," she repeated and fled the truck.

# CHAPTER 8

Grayson knocked on the door of the guesthouse and waited patiently. When there was no answer, he tried the door, scowling when it opened easily. He entered the house and called Sydney's name, although he suspected she wasn't home.

She had joined them last night for dinner, but she had been very quiet and barely looked at him. She was obviously upset and had told GG briefly about the new court date, but when GG expressed sympathy, she took a deep breath and smiled at her.

"I'll just have to do my best. I'm a good mom, and I'll stay calm and make a good case for myself. I can do it."

Her obvious worry hadn't affected her appetite. She'd eaten two heaping platefuls and taken another plate of left-overs home at GG's urging.

He wandered into the kitchen and leaned against the counter, wondering where she was. Her car had broken down, and she hadn't borrowed GG's car. Feeling oddly unsettled by her absence, he paced the small room for a few minutes. He stopped before the fridge and pulled it open, staring absently into it.

He frowned. The fridge was empty except for the leftovers from GG last night. Sydney had split the food onto three plates, creating three laughably small meals.

What the hell? He closed the fridge and began opening cupboard doors. They were all bare. In the long pantry cupboard, he found half a package of crackers and an empty jar of peanut butter. At the rumbling sound of car engines, he headed outside. She had said she was low on groceries on Saturday night – maybe she was shopping.

He slipped out the door and onto the front porch. He watched Derek hop out of his truck and walk over to Sydney, who shut off her car and climbed out carefully. His eyes narrowed when Derek gave Sydney a lingering hug.

"Thank you so much, Derek. I owe you again. This is the third time you've gotten that rust bucket running." She squeezed his waist and stood on her tiptoes to plant a kiss on his cheek.

Nostrils flaring with irritation, Grayson descended the porch stairs and walked toward them as Derek blushed a little.

"No problem, Sid. Listen, maybe sometime you'd like to catch a mov -"

"Grayson?" Sydney blinked at him in surprise. "Where did you come from?"

"Hello, Derek." Grayson nodded to Derek.

"Hey, Grayson. How's it going?"

"Fine, thanks. Helping Sydney, were you?"

"Yeah, I got a bit of a touch with shit cars, and I think hers is the shittiest of them all."

"Cork it, you." Sydney gave him a threatening look, and Derek laughed.

There was an awkward silence. Grayson knew that Derek

was waiting for him to leave, but he just gave the younger man a casual grin and folded his arms over his chest.

After a moment, Derek cleared his throat. "Anyway, I'd better go. I promised GG I would brush Samson and Moonlight before I left." He reached out and squeezed Sydney's arm. "I'll talk to you later, okay, Sid?"

"Sure." She gave him another warm smile, making Derek blush again, and he nodded to Grayson before disappearing into the barn.

"Why didn't you ask me for help this morning? I could have gotten your car towed to a repair shop," he asked as she returned to her car and pulled out a plastic shopping bag.

She slammed the door shut and shrugged. "I had to run into town first, and Derek was going there for GG anyway, so I just hitched a ride with him. He wasn't kidding when he said he was good with cars, so I accepted when he offered to look at it on the way home."

She went to walk past him, and he took her arm and pulled her to a stop. "He has a crush on you."

She snorted. "Yeah, right. He's what - twenty? I'm a little too old for him."

"Yes, because at twenty-four, you're an old maid," he said.

She didn't reply, and he squeezed her arm again. "Next time, ask me."

"You made it clear last night that you didn't have time to keep rescuing me."

He sighed. "I didn't mean that. I was tired last night."

She shrugged. "It's all good. You've been very helpful the last few days, and I appreciate it, but you're right that I've been taking advantage of your generosity."

"You haven't." He glanced down at the shopping bag in her hand. "You went for groceries?"

She nodded, and he tugged it open. There was a single bag of apples in the bag.

"Just apples?" He raised his eyebrow at her.

"Yeah, I had more groceries than I thought."

He stared at her, and she pulled free of his grip. "Thank you again for your help this weekend, Grayson."

She walked into the guesthouse without looking back.

\* \* \*

SYDNEY STOOD AS THE JUDGE ENTERED THE COURTROOM. Jacob and his lawyer stood at the table next to her, and she could feel her stomach churning with a combination of nerves and hunger.

"Please be seated." The judge was a tall, gray-haired man with a loud, deep voice, and Sydney started a bit. She sat down, folding her hands neatly on the table as the judge looked over his glasses at them.

"What are we here for today?"

Jacob's lawyer stood, smoothing down his tie. "Your Honour, we're here to discuss Emma Louise Yewn's custody."

The judge looked through the folder of papers in front of him before turning to Sydney. "Ms. Wright?"

Sydney stood, squeezing the table's edge to keep her hands from shaking. "Yes, Your Honour."

"Where is your counsel?"

"Actually," Sydney's voice came out in a whispered squeak, and she cleared her throat and tried again. "Your Honour, I'm representing -"

The courtroom door banged open, and a short, balding man wearing a pin-striped suit and carrying a leather brief-case hurried into the room. "Sorry, I'm late, Your Honour."

He stepped between the swinging door that separated the viewing section from the rest of the courtroom and stood next to Sydney.

"Mr. Thompson, I assume you're representing Ms. Wright?" The judge raised one eyebrow.

"Yes, Your Honour."

"Bullshit," Jacob spat out.

The judge glared at him. "Ask your client to watch his language in my courtroom, Mr. Gentry."

Jacob's lawyer squeezed his arm, and Jacob leaned forward and whispered into his ear.

His lawyer nodded and stood up. "Your Honour, my client informed me that on Sunday, Ms. Wright said she would represent herself at today's proceedings. I'm questioning the -"

"Ms. Wright just hired me this morning, Your Honour," the man in the pinstripe suit interrupted smoothly.

Sydney stared blankly at the man as he smiled at her and turned back to the judge.

"I'd like to request that we postpone today's hearing so that I may go over the case details with my client. I've had limited time with my client to discuss the case, and I'll require more time to represent her effectively." He glanced at Jacob's lawyer and smiled broadly. "I'm sure you understand, Tobias."

Jacob's lawyer opened his mouth, but before he could speak, the judge shut the file folder and nodded. "That's fine. How much time do you need?"

"As much time as you'll give me, Your Honour."

The judge nodded again. "We'll reconvene Friday at two."

He grabbed his gavel, banged it briskly, and motioned to the bailiff. "Next case, please."

The man in the pinstripe suit took Sydney's arm and tugged her to her feet. She turned and followed him numbly out of the courtroom. As they stepped out into the cool air, she saw Grayson leaning against his truck parked on the street in front of the courthouse. She blinked in surprise as he started toward them.

"Hey!" There was a shout behind her, and she turned to see Jacob storming angrily towards her. "What kind of game are you playing, Sydney?"

"Jacob, I don't -"

He grabbed her arm. "Do you honestly think hiring a lawyer will convince the judge that you're a fit mother?"

When she didn't respond, he shook her hard. "I will never allow you to -"

Sydney flinched when Grayson shoved Jacob away from her. Jacob stumbled and nearly fell before catching his balance. He glared at Grayson, who put his arm around Sydney and pulled her back against his body before resting his hand possessively on her hip.

"Keep your hands off of her."

"Grayson O'Reilly? What the hell are you doing here?" Jacob looked at Grayson's arm wrapped around Sydney and laughed bitterly. "You always did have a taste for the rich life, didn't you, Sydney."

"Shut your mouth," Grayson advised.

"Or what?" Jacob asked. "Christ, Sydney. You can't fight your own battles? You need to have Grayson O'Reilly fight them for you?"

Jacob's hands tightened into fists, and Sydney watched in alarm as his face deepened to a dark red. "What? You spread your legs for him, and he buys you a lawyer, is that it?"

When neither Grayson nor Sydney responded, Jacob stepped forward. "Answer me, goddammit!"

Grayson growled warningly as Jacob took another step toward Sydney.

"Tell me, Tobias," the man in the pinstripe suit said, "does your client always have this much trouble controlling his temper?"

When Jacob looked at him, nostrils flaring, the man smiled thinly. "It hardly seems like a suitable environment for a child to be raised in."

"What did you just say?" Jacob asked angrily before his lawyer pulled him away.

"Jacob, let's go. Right now." He dragged Jacob down the steps. Sydney released her breath in a shuddering sigh, and Grayson squeezed her waist.

He bent his head, putting his mouth to her ear. "Are you okay?"

She shivered at the feel of his warm breath. "Yes."

The man in the pinstripe suit smiled at her and held out his hand. "I don't believe we've been properly introduced, Ms. Wright. My name is Martin Thompson. I'm your new lawyer."

* * *

"Have you decided on something to eat, Sydney?" Martin asked.

Sydney looked up from the menu. Martin and Grayson had taken her to one of the nicer restaurants in town, and she was desperately scanning the menu for something she could afford. She had exactly ten dollars left, and even a salad cost more than that.

"I'll have the starter soup. I ate a big breakfast," she fibbed.

"You need to eat more than just soup," Grayson said.

"Soup is fine," she said.

Martin smiled at her. "Please, order something else. It's on me." He paused and winked at her. "Well, actually, it's on Grayson since I'll be billing him for the lunch."

Sydney smiled weakly at him and ordered the soup to start and the rice and chicken dish. Martin and Grayson ordered their meals, and as the waitress walked away, she leaned back in the booth and stared at the two men sitting across from her.

"Would one of you please tell me what's going on?"

Martin glanced at Grayson. "Grayson stopped by my office this morning and asked me to represent you in your child custody case. I agreed."

"Yeah, that's what I thought," she said. "Mr. Thompson, I appreciate -"

"Call me Martin."

"Martin, I appreciate your help but can't afford a lawyer. I'm unsure what Grayson told you, but I cannot pay you."

Martin reached across the table and patted her hand. "My dear, Grayson has already paid me a sizeable retainer. It will be more than enough to cover my fees."

Sydney glared at Grayson. "No way. This has gone far enough."

Grayson frowned. "What are you talking about?"

"I already owe you for the hospital bill from the weekend."

"Oh, that reminds me. I picked up your antibiotics." He pulled a small paper bag from his pocket and pushed it across the table towards her. "You should probably take one now."

She gritted her teeth. "I owe you for the hospital bill *and* my antibiotics. I am not racking up more debt to you in the form of a lawyer."

He shrugged and smiled boyishly at her. "It's too late. Martin's already deposited the cheque."

"It's true." Martin laughed and took a sip of wine.

"I still can't accept -"

"Sydney, you want Emma back, don't you? This is the first step toward getting her back. You need a lawyer to help you. This isn't something you have to repay me for. It's a gift. It's my way of saying sorry for all the times I've been a rude bastard to you in the last two weeks. Okay?" Grayson said.

"You have been an asshole," she said.

Martin laughed again. "I like her."

Their appetizers arrived, and, her stomach rumbling, Sydney picked up her spoon and began to eat as Martin leaned forward. "Okay, Sydney. Tell me everything."

* * *

"WELL, WHAT DO YOU THINK?" GRAYSON ASKED MARTIN. After finishing lunch, Sydney left for the bookstore. Barb had told her to come in for a half shift in the afternoon, and she'd agreed to meet Martin tomorrow afternoon at the bookstore once her shift was over. She had hurried off, her head bent against the cold wind and Martin's business card in her pocket.

"I think for such a tiny slip of a thing, she's got the biggest appetite I've ever seen," Martin laughed. "Where do you think she puts it all? Hollow leg?"

Grayson grinned. "She does enjoy her food." He groaned and slapped himself on the forehead.

"What?" Martin asked.

"Nothing. I just figured something out." He couldn't believe how stupid he was. Sydney didn't have anorexia – she couldn't afford to buy groceries.

Martin was speaking, and he forced himself to concentrate on the older man. "What was that?"

"I said, it's not terrible, but it could be better. Sydney seems to have done well at proving that she's a good mother and responsible since the incident where she took Emma, but I'm not sure that will be enough. We've got Judge Hawkins, and he's notoriously tough regarding children's cases."

Martin finished his glass of wine. "Sydney has done everything Child Services and Jacob have demanded for the last three years, but I'm still not positive it will be enough. Not for Judge Hawkins, anyway. Emma has a stable home life with Jacob. His parents are very involved in her life. Jacob owns his own home, is highly respected in the community, and has a steady source of income. He's engaged to a nice woman who, Sydney tells me, loves Emma as much as she and Jacob do."

He gave Grayson a frank look. "Sydney, on the other hand, has no family, she rents a guesthouse from your grandmother, makes minimum wage working at a bar, and there's a history of mental illness in her family. Despite all the progress she's made, my guess is that Tobias will play up all those negatives, and Judge Hawkins will deny her unsupervised overnight visits."

Grayson swore softly. "Isn't there anything we can do?"

Martin shrugged. "I don't think we should drag Jacob through the mud. I could try to dig up some dirt on him in the next couple of days, but I think it's a waste of time. Sydney says Jacob is an excellent father, and Emma loves him very much. I think our best chance is if we concentrate on showing all the progress Sydney has made and that she realizes that Jacob is a good father and she isn't trying to take Emma away from him."

He stared thoughtfully at Grayson.

"What?" Grayson asked.

"How close are you and Sydney?"

"What do you mean?"

"I mean, are you sleeping together? Dating? In a committed relationship?" Martin asked.

Grayson shook his head. "We're just friends, why?"

Martin shrugged. "Your grandmother and you, by association, are well-loved in this community. If Sydney were a part of your family, even just by dating you, it would probably help her case."

Grayson stared at him as an idea began to form in his head. He leaned forward. "Martin, I think I have an idea."

He told his plan to Martin, who stared at him incredulously. "Grayson, what you're suggesting is considered committing perjury."

"Technically, it isn't," Grayson argued.

Martin rolled his eyes. "Yes, it is. Besides, Sydney will never agree to it."

"Let's keep it as Plan B," Grayson said. "If you think you're losing the case on Friday, we'll switch to my idea, okay?"

Martin shook his head. "This is crazy. You still haven't told me how you'll convince Sydney to go along with it."

"I don't think we should tell her."

Martin opened his mouth to argue, and Grayson hurried on. "We may not even have to go to Plan B, right? If you can convince the judge that Sydney should be allowed unsupervised visits with Emma, then we won't have to worry about it."

Martin frowned. "Grayson, this isn't a good idea."

"It will destroy Sydney if she doesn't get to have Emma on the weekends. I promise you, if we have to go to Plan B, no one will ever know it isn't real."

"Fine," Martin said. "But let's hope it doesn't come to that."

"Thank you, Martin. Listen, I've got to go." Grayson slid out from the booth.

"Where are you off to?" Martin dropped some bills onto the table and waved to the waitress as he followed Grayson out of the restaurant.

"I have some grocery shopping to do," Grayson said.

# CHAPTER 9

S ydney dropped her keys and purse on the kitchen table and kicked off her shoes with a weary groan. She sat down on the chair and placed her head on the table. She was tired, and her abdomen and hip were aching and throbbing. She should have been happy. She had a lawyer now who would help with her fight for Emma, but she felt blue and depressed.

Her stomach ached with hunger despite her large lunch, and with another sigh, she stood and walked to the fridge. At least she still had some leftovers from Sunday night. She opened the fridge and stared silently into it, her mouth dropping open. Her previously empty fridge was now overflowing with food.

She reached out and touched a package of fresh, green salad mix. Her fingers trembled slightly as she started opening the crispers. There was cheese and fruit, fresh vegetables and eggs, milk and three different kinds of juice.

Feeling like she was dreaming, she closed the fridge and opened the freezer. It was filled to the brim with meat packages and bags of frozen vegetables.

"What the hell?" she said.

She opened the pantry, her mouth dropping open again at the soup cans, pasta bags, and potatoes. There were jars of tomato sauce, cans of beans, a jar of peanut butter and a loaf of bread. A large bag of rice was in the bottom half of the pantry, along with two boxes of cereal, and spices and condiments were lined up in neat rows on the very top shelf. One shelf had been filled with baking ingredients, and she smiled a little at the box of cookies tucked into the back of the shelf.

"Grayson." She dropped back into the chair, her head spinning.

She sat for a few more minutes, feeling a weird combination of shame and gratefulness before her stomach growled loudly. Sighing, she stood and began to cook dinner.

\* \* \*

"OH, FOR GOD'S SAKE, WHERE IS IT?" SYDNEY BLEW HER breath out in frustration. She had been through her meager amount of clothing three times now, and she still couldn't find her damn bra. It was Thursday, and she had to leave for her shift at the bar in less than an hour. She had very little clothing, but somehow, she'd mysteriously lost the push-up bra she had bought specifically to wear at the bar.

"Where could it be?" She sat on the edge of the bed and thought back to when she had it last. She had been wearing it Saturday night, and it –

Her eyes widened with horror.

"Oh shit." She had a clear vision of Grayson shoving her bra into his jacket pocket at the hospital. Jesus, neither of them had remembered it was there. He had to have been carrying it around with him ever since.

She reached for her everyday plain white bra and hesitated. Her tips had nearly doubled since she'd started wearing the push-up bra. With a soft groan, she threw her work tank top on and headed for GG's.

"GG?" She knocked and entered the old farmhouse.

"In here, honey," GG called from the kitchen.

"Hey, GG, is Grayson around?" She hadn't seen him since the meeting with Martin on Tuesday, and although she hadn't been specifically avoiding him, she hadn't actively looked for him either. She was still embarrassed that he had stocked her kitchen with food, and although she knew she would have to thank him sooner or later, she hadn't yet worked up the nerve.

"He's upstairs taking a nap. He was out most of the day repairing the fence in the west field. That crazy boy is thinking about starting a cattle farm again," GG said. "Although I admit, I'm a little excited about having the farm up and running again."

She smiled at Sydney. "Do you need to speak with him?"

"Well, not exactly. He has something of mine that I need for work. I think it's in his jacket pocket." She looked at the coat tree at the front entrance, but Grayson's jacket wasn't hanging on it.

"Oh, I think he was still wearing his jacket when he went upstairs. It's probably in his room. You can just run up there and grab it."

"I'd better not. I wouldn't want to wake him."

GG laughed. "Honey, that boy could sleep through an earthquake. Trust me – tiny little you won't wake him up. Go on now. You know which room is his."

Sydney hesitated and then nodded. "Okay, thanks, GG."

Feeling oddly nervous, Sydney climbed the stairs and crept down the hallway. She eased opened Grayson's bedroom door, and peeked in. He was lying on his back in the bed, breathing evenly and deeply.

She quietly closed the door and looked for his jacket. It

was draped across a chair beside the bed, and she walked softly across the room. She glanced at Grayson. His eyes were closed, and she could see his broad chest still rising and falling evenly. She had a sudden urge to reach out and thread her fingers through the hair on his chest. Instead, she curled her fingers into fists, silently berating herself before reaching into his jacket pocket and pulling out her bra.

She turned to leave when a hard hand wrapped around her wrist. She dropped her bra and let out a soft shriek of surprise as she was jerked backward onto the bed. Grayson pinned her hands above her head and threw one muscular leg over her thighs before leaning over her.

He stared down at her, his eyes sleepy and unfocused. "Why are you in my room?"

"I – I needed my bra," she squeaked.

He frowned. "Your bra?"

"From the night in the hospital. It was in your jacket pocket."

"Right – the hospital."

He studied her abdomen. "How is your stomach, by the way?"

"It's fine. Much better." She cleared her throat. He still held her hands captive above her head, and she tried to ignore the way it made her pulse speed up.

"Let me see." Keeping one hand around her wrists, he used his other hand to lift her white tank top. He ran his hand over the healing cut on her stomach and then tugged the waistline of her jean skirt down until he could see her hip. He inhaled sharply at the sight of the large and sprawling bruise.

"Jesus," he said.

"It's fine," she said.

Without speaking, he leaned over and licked her bruised skin. She moaned and twitched against him.

He looked up at her. "Did that hurt?"

"N-no."

He bent his head again, and she squirmed against him. "Stop that."

"Stop what?"

"Licking me!"

"You licked me."

"I did not," she said.

He grinned. "You did. The night I brought you home from the hospital, you asked me to stay and keep you warm, and then you licked me."

She gave him a look of horror. "I don't believe you."

He dipped his head to her neck. "You licked me right here." He used the tip of his tongue to lick her soft skin, and she wiggled beneath him. He licked along her jawline and then licked her mouth until her lips parted, and she moaned again.

He pulled his head back and stared at her mouth for a long moment before his eyes dropped to her breasts. Her arousal was evident, her nipples hard and straining against the thin material of her shirt, and his nostrils flared in response.

"Please, Grayson," she said. "Let me go." She tried to free her wrists from his hand, and he pressed them down further into the soft mattress.

"You're so little, so helpless against me." His voice had deepened with desire, and Sydney felt a flare of heat deep in her pelvis in response to the raw need in his voice.

"If I wanted to kiss you right now, I could, and you wouldn't be able to stop me." He reached down and pushed her thighs apart, shoving his hard thigh between hers.

Sydney groaned and shuddered against him. He trailed kisses across her jaw and placed his mouth just above hers. His warm breath made her lips tingle with anticipation.

"But you want me to kiss you. Don't you, Sydney?"

"Yes," she said.

"Good." He kissed her hard on the mouth. His tongue probed at her lips, and she parted them, giving him access to the warmth of her mouth.

He flicked his tongue into her mouth, darting and tasting and driving her crazy. He tugged lightly on her bottom lip with his teeth and then sucked hard on it, making her moan and writhe against him.

He kissed her slowly, taking his time exploring every nook and cranny of her mouth. He gave her no break from his relentless tongue, sliding it against hers, tracing it along her teeth as he pushed her deeper into the pillow until they were both gasping and shuddering. He pulled his mouth free and stared down at her. Her full lips trembled, and he nibbled lightly, first on her top lip and then her bottom.

"You have the most beautiful mouth. Did you know that, Sydney?"

She moaned when he traced the low neckline of her tank top with one warm finger.

She pulled at his hand again, and he tightened his grip on her wrists. "Do you want me to let you go?"

"Y-yes," she lied. Something about the way he so easily held her captive in his bed was turning her on to the point of embarrassment. She glanced upward, her face flushing at the sight of her small hands held in Grayson's large one.

He could do whatever he wanted to her, and she couldn't stop him. The thought should have alarmed her, but instead, it brought on another large wave of desire that made her entire body shudder against him.

"Are you sure?" He smiled and kissed her again, sucking roughly on her bottom lip until she gasped.

He dropped his gaze to her body once more. The way he held her arms above her head made her slender body arch, and her small breasts, their nipples jutting out against the thin fabric, were practically calling his name.

She stared wide-eyed at him. He hadn't shaved this morning, and his stubble had left red marks on her skin and mouth that tingled pleasantly. His hazel eyes had darkened until they were nearly brown, and she moaned loudly when he bent his head and trailed kisses along her upper chest.

He hooked his fingers into the neckline of her tank top and tugged it down until her breasts were bared. He admired them for a moment, watching how her nipples grew harder in the cool air. He licked her right nipple with the tip of his tongue, making her cry out, and then sucked it into his mouth. She arched her back, pulling frantically at his hand as he licked and pulled on her hardened nipple.

"Grayson, please," she begged as he switched to her left nipple and grazed it gently with his teeth. Her nipples were extremely sensitive, and just the wetness of his mouth and tongue was driving her crazy.

"Does that feel good, Sydney?" he asked.

"Yes," she moaned again. She couldn't stop herself from rubbing against his hard thigh, feeling the delicious friction of his rough hair against her smooth skin. His cock was hard against her thigh, and she gasped again when he bit lightly on her nipple.

She pulled again at his hand, and he let her go this time. She immediately clutched his head, twisting her fingers through his short, dark hair and pulling on it. He lifted his head, and she mashed her mouth down on his, desperate to taste him again.

He kissed her, his tongue stroking her upper lip with delicate movements that had her shuddering against him. He cupped one breast in his large hand and ran his thumb over her nipple before he pinched it lightly with his thumb and forefinger.

She wrenched her mouth free and stared up at the ceiling as he slipped his hand behind her neck and cupped it firmly. He trailed kisses down her neck and across her collarbone before kissing the base of her neck. He flipped onto his back, pulling her small body on top of him and sliding her into a straddling position. He sat up and abruptly yanked her tank top over her head.

He stared greedily at her, and suddenly feeling shy, she crossed her arms over her breasts. "Grayson, maybe we should – "

He pulled her arms away roughly and took one nipple into his mouth again. He sucked hard on it, and she thrust her pelvis helplessly against him, her fingers clutching and pulling at his broad back. He was wearing just a pair of boxer briefs, and she could feel his cock against her warm core. He wrapped his large arms around her, curling his hands into her mass of hair and pulling until she stared at the ceiling. He kissed her throat, then her breasts and upper chest, licking and nipping until she thrust frantically against him. He groaned against her breast, grabbed the hem of her jean skirt and pushed it up around her waist.

He was reaching between her legs, wanting to slip his fingers under the soft material of her panties and explore her warm flesh, when GG's voice made them both freeze.

"Sid, did you find what you were looking for?" she called softly up the stairs.

"Sydney stared at him, her eyes wide and her small chest heaving for air. She swallowed hard. "Yes, GG, I did. I – I'll be right down."

She tried to slide off his lap, and he frowned and tightened his grip around her.

"I have to go," she said. "I'm supposed to be at work in -" she looked at his alarm clock. "Shit! Twenty minutes! Let me go!"

She tried again to wiggle free, and he slid his hands back into her hair and forced her mouth down on his. He kissed her deeply, tightening one hand in her hair and sliding the other down her bare back. He pressed her against his chest, and Sydney moaned at the feel of his rough hair against her nipples. Still kissing her, he fell back onto the bed. Her skirt was still up around her waist, and he moved his hands to her ass, squeezing her bare cheeks and pressing her down against his cock.

She gasped and tore her mouth from his, bracing her hands against his chest and shoving. "Grayson, seriously – I have to go to work."

"Call in sick," he demanded. He rubbed her against his crotch, and they both moaned.

"I can't." She tried to wrench herself free and cried out when she twisted too far, and the stitches pulled at her skin.

He let go of her immediately and sat up, placing gentle hands around her hips and easing her off his lap.

"I'm sorry," he said. "Did I hurt you?"

"No, the stitches just pulled a little."

He studied the cut carefully and then ran his hand over it. A pulse of pleasure went through her at his warm touch.

"Jesus, Grayson. Stop touching me – I have to go," she said irritably.

She scrambled off the bed and grabbed her bra. Grayson reclined on the bed and watched as she pulled her skirt back into place, quickly put on her bra and slipped her shirt over her head. She glanced at him, and he grinned when her eyes flickered down to his crotch. He was still hard as a rock, and he winked at her as he slipped his hand inside his underwear and slowly stroked his cock.

"Are you sure you don't want to call in sick, Sid?"

She swallowed hard and made herself look away. "I'm

sure." She paused at his bedroom door and said quietly, "Thank you for the groceries."

She slipped out of the room before he could reply.

\* \* \*

"WHERE ON EARTH ARE YOU GOING, GRAYSON?"

GG looked at her watch. It was just after midnight, and she had been heading to bed when Grayson shrugged into his jacket.

"I don't trust that Sydney's car will start, and I still haven't given her my cell number. I don't want her to be stranded at the bar."

"That's awfully nice of you." GG didn't bother to hide her smile.

Grayson hesitated. "Speaking of Sydney – GG, you care for her, right?"

She nodded. "I do. She's like a daughter to me."

"You know that tomorrow is the hearing to see if she can have Emma for overnight visits?"

GG nodded again. "Yes, Sydney and I have talked about it. She told me you hired Martin Thompson to be her lawyer."

He reached out and took his grandmother's hand. "Sydney doesn't know this, but Martin doesn't think she has much chance of getting the overnight visits approved."

GG sighed. "That poor child."

He squeezed her hand. "There may be a way that you can help her win overnight visits, but it, well, involves a bit of stretching the truth."

He waited. GG was a devout Catholic, and he seriously doubted she had ever told a lie in her life.

She gave him a curious look. "Tell me what it is."

\* \* \*

SYDNEY FORCED HERSELF TO SMILE AT THE TABLE OF YOUNG men she was waiting on. Her side was aching and throbbing, and although Wayne had given her a smaller section to work, it had been a mistake to return to work so soon. She could feel the stitches pulling with every tray of drinks she lifted.

To add to her misery, she had a terrible headache. The pain was like a living thing behind her eye, and it pulsed steadily with the beat of the music that was blaring out from the dance floor.

*At least I'm not hungry.*

Not that she could eat right now, anyway. The combination of the throbbing in her side and in her head had made her nauseous. All she wanted was to be in the blessed quietness of her home, curled up in her bed with the covers pulled over her head.

The man closest to her put his arm around her and squeezed her hip as he placed his order. She flinched as he pressed on the bruise there, but he was too drunk to notice. As his hand wandered down to her ass and squeezed, she eased away from him and made herself give him a flirty little grin before escaping to the bar. She gave the drink orders to Greg and then slipped down the hallway towards the bathrooms. It was marginally quieter in the hallway, and she leaned against the wall, one hand rubbing her side and the other rubbing at her aching forehead.

She took deep breaths and focused on the fact that she only had half an hour to go, and then she could go home. "You can do it, Sydney. Keep it together," she whispered to herself.

"Do you let all your customers grab your ass or just the ones who give large tips?" A familiar voice spoke angrily behind her, and she jerked in alarm, wincing and grabbing at her side.

"Hello to you too, Grayson," she said wearily.

He didn't reply. She could hear him breathing heavily behind her. He sounded like an angry bull, and she rolled her eyes.

"Well, do you?" he demanded.

"What I do at work is none of your business."

"So, it doesn't bother you to flirt with them. Let them grope you, as long as it means you'll get more money?"

She could hear the judgement in his voice. Suddenly, her blood was boiling, and she was completely and utterly furious with him. She turned on him. "Fuck you, Grayson O'Reilly."

"You had your chance earlier this afternoon, remember?" he said icily.

"I remember, and believe me – I'm very happy I didn't," she spat at him.

"That makes two of us."

"Bullshit," she sneered. "You were practically begging me to sleep with you."

"It was nothing more than a momentary lapse in judgment. I can assure you it won't happen again," he retorted.

Hurt rippled through her at his words. "What are you even doing here? You're like my goddamn stalker."

"You weren't complaining when I saved you from being trampled or when I picked you up from the side of the road after your piece-of-shit car broke down again."

She sighed angrily. "You know what, Grayson? Why don't you do us both a favour and stay away from me? I don't need you playing macho man at my place of employment. In case you haven't noticed, I don't exactly have money dripping out of my ears. I need this job, and you seem hell-bent on getting me fired."

"How am I doing that?" he sputtered angrily.

"Have you forgotten that you threatened to rip Ron's arm

from his socket if he so much as looked at me? Ron's a regular and a good friend of Wayne's." She glared at him.

"I don't care who he is. He's an idiot, and he got you hurt."

"It was an accident," she snapped. She glanced at her watch and tried to move around him, but he blocked her path.

"Grayson, listen, I appreciate everything you've done for me, but you have to stop acting like I'm helpless. I am more than capable of taking care of myself."

"Oh really?" He raised his eyebrow at her. "Because by my count, if it weren't for me, you'd be starving to death, still be picking shards of glass out of your stomach and not have even a chance in hell of getting your daughter for overnight visits."

She froze, the colour draining from her cheeks and emphasizing the dark circles under her eyes. She could see the immediate regret in Grayson's eyes as she raised one shaking hand and rubbed at her forehead.

"You're right," she said. "I apologize for not being grateful enough."

"Sid, no – I'm sorry. I didn't mean it like that." He reached for her, and she twitched away, wincing and resting her hand against her side.

"Thank you for everything you've done, Grayson, but please leave me alone now."

He grimaced. "Sydney, don't -"

She shook her head. "I'll call Martin tomorrow and tell him I no longer need him to represent me. Hopefully, he hasn't used much of the retainer you gave him. Just tell GG how much I owe you for the hospital bill and the lawyer fees, and I'll start paying you back."

She brushed past him, and he reached for her. "Sydney, please don't ask Martin to stop representing you."

She shook off his hand. "Goodbye, Grayson."

# CHAPTER 10

S ydney smoothed her hands nervously down her skirt as she entered the courtroom. Her stomach was churning with nerves, but she stood straight and walked boldly through the swinging gate to sit at the table.

Early this morning, she had called Martin Thompson's office. His secretary had told her that he was in a meeting. She left him a voicemail thanking him for his time but informing him she would no longer require his services. She felt like she had made a huge mistake the moment she ended the call, but she shook off her feeling of doom. She could do this.

She nodded nervously to Jacob and his lawyer. She could do this, she reminded herself. She just had to –

A hand touched her elbow, and she stared blankly at Martin Thompson.

"Hello, Sydney. Are you ready?"

She blinked at him. "Martin, I – I'm sorry. Did you not get my voicemail this morning?"

"I did." He smiled cheerfully at her. "I ignored it."

"Martin I – "

"Sydney?"

She turned around to see both GG and Grayson standing behind her.

"Hi, honey." GG kissed her on the cheek and sat directly behind Sydney and Martin in the first row.

"What – what are you doing here?" She frowned at Grayson, but he ignored it and leaned over the railing. He took her completely by surprise when he hugged her.

As Martin crossed to the table where Jacob and his lawyer sat, shaking Tobias' hand while blocking their view of Grayson and Sydney, Grayson took her left hand.

"Put this on," he murmured.

He slipped a silver ring with a large diamond surrounded by small, round pearls onto her third finger. It was too big, and as she reached to pull it off, he closed her fingers in his large one.

"No, leave it on for now, Sydney. Please." He squeezed her hand as Martin walked back to the table.

"Grayson, I don't understand what -"

He surprised her again by kissing her warmly before whispering in her ear. "Good luck."

As the judge entered the courtroom, he stood beside GG, and Martin gently turned Sydney forward.

"Good afternoon, ladies and gentlemen." Judge Hawkins nodded as he sat down. "Let's begin."

\* \* \*

JUDGE HAWKINS FOLDED HIS HANDS TOGETHER BEFORE STARING at Sydney. "Ms. Wright, I am impressed by your growth and your willingness to do what it takes to spend more time with your daughter. While I am tempted to allow you overnight visits with your daughter, I have some reservations."

"Your Honour," Martin cleared his throat. "Ms. Wright

understands how important it is for her daughter to have stability. She's been living in the same house for nearly a year, and it has a second bedroom ready and waiting for Emma. She's working two jobs and earning a steady income and – "

"She works part-time at a bookstore and weekends as a waitress at a bar," Tobias interjected.

"Are you suggesting that because she works at a bookstore and a bar, she is an unfit mother?" Martin raised his eyebrow at Tobias.

"No, but I would hardly consider that steady income. Who will look after Emma while she's working as a waitress? Plus, her history has shown that she will take off at the slightest provocation. Your Honour, she's a flight risk. She has no family in town, nothing to keep her here. If she wants to leave with Emma, there's nothing to stop her from doing so," Tobias replied.

Judge Hawkins sighed irritably. "Gentlemen, I heard both of your arguments earlier. I don't need to listen to them again. I am well aware of her lack of family support. In fact, it's my biggest concern in allowing Ms. Wright to have overnight visits with her daughter. Ms. Wright, do you understand how important family can be in raising a child? You haven't lived with Emma since she was a year old. Being a single mother is a very difficult job, and I'm not entirely sure you're ready for that responsibility. Because of that, I feel it is best if -"

"Your honour, Ms. Wright does have family support," Martin spoke quickly.

Judge Hawkins frowned. "What do you mean?"

Martin turned and pointed to Grayson and GG sitting in the front row. "Ms. Wright is engaged to Mr. O'Reilly."

"Like hell she is!" Jacob burst out.

Looking back, Sydney thought it was extremely fortunate

that the judge turned toward Jacob at his outburst. Her mouth had dropped open so far that Martin muttered, "Close your mouth," and squeezed her arm firmly.

She closed her mouth with a snap as the judge swung his gaze back to her. Martin still held her arm in a death grip, and as the judge eyed her, she turned and glanced at Grayson. He stared at her calmly and gave her a small nod and a smile.

"Ms. Wright – is this true? Are you and Mr. O'Reilly engaged?" the judge asked.

Sydney swallowed and glanced down at her left hand. The ring Grayson had placed there sparkled softly. Martin was squeezing her arm so tightly that the entire length of her forearm and hand had gone numb.

"Ms. Wright?" The judge prompted.

She swallowed again. "Yes, Your Honour. We are."

"Are you kidding me?" Jacob stood up angrily. "Your Honour, she's lying! Grayson O'Reilly's been back in town for less than a month. You can't tell me they fell in love and got engaged in less than a month."

"Mr. Yewn, sit down!" The judge rolled his eyes before staring at Grayson. "Mr. O'Reilly, come forward, please."

Grayson stood and stepped past the gate, slipping behind Martin to stand on the other side of Sydney. He rested his hand on her shoulder, smiling reassuringly before squeezing it gently.

"Is it true, Mr. O'Reilly? Have you been in town for less than a month?"

"Yes, Your Honour."

"And yet you're now engaged to Ms. Wright?"

Grayson shrugged. "What can I say, Your Honour? I'm a hopeless romantic."

There was a soft wave of laughter from the people sitting and waiting for their cases to come up.

"Your Honour, Mr. O'Reilly and Ms. Wright live together in the guesthouse. The guesthouse is only steps away from Mr. O'Reilly's grandmother's home, and she has plenty of experience with children," Martin said.

The judge craned his head to look past Martin at GG.

GG grinned and waved at him. "Hello, Ricky!"

The judge blushed as another wave of laughter went through the crowd. "Hello, Eleanor."

"Together, the three of them are more than capable of caring for Emma," Martin continued. "Both Mr. O'Reilly and his grandmother are anxious to get to know Emma better. And obviously, Ms. Wright will be less inclined to 'take off' if her fiancé is waiting at home for her."

"There's still the matter of Ms. Wright working nights at the bar. How is she supposed to look after Emma when she's working?" Jacob's lawyer said with a hint of desperation in his voice.

"Ms. Wright has asked to have Emma on Sunday and Monday. She doesn't work either of those days at Dawson's or Barb's Bookshelf," Martin said.

"Eventually, Emma will be in school. She'll have to switch to weekends if she wants to see her daughter. Who will look after Emma?"

Martin rolled his eyes. "Obviously, Mr. O'Reilly or his grandmother would be happy to help look after Emma if Ms. Wright is working. Although I think we're getting ahead of ourselves. Don't you, Tobias?"

Before Tobias could reply, Grayson cleared his throat. "Your Honour, Sydney will only work at the bar until the new year. Once January arrives, she'll return to college to complete her teaching degree."

Sydney kept her mouth shut this time but stared up at Grayson, her eyes wide with surprise. He smiled down at her before bending and kissing her forehead.

Judge Hawkins pulled on his bottom lip thoughtfully while he stared at Grayson and Sydney. Sydney, her stomach twisting and turning, began to tremble lightly.

"I've made my decision," Judge Hawkins said.

Sydney stumbled to her feet as Martin, Jacob, and Tobias stood. Her knees were shaking so badly she thought she might collapse. She didn't object when Grayson put one strong arm around her waist and held her against him.

"Based on what I've heard today, I'm allowing Ms. Wright overnight visits with her daughter."

Sydney stared in shock at the judge, uncertain if she had heard him correctly. It wasn't until Grayson squeezed her tightly and kissed the top of her head that she released her breath in a harsh rush.

"This is on a trial basis. Ms. Wright? Do you understand?" The judge stared at her sternly.

"Yes, Your Honour. Thank you," she said weakly.

The judge turned to Jacob. "Starting this Sunday, you will allow Ms. Wright weekly overnight visits with her daughter."

"Ms. Wright, you will pick Emma up at ten a.m. on Sunday and bring her back to her father's home no later than seven p.m. Monday night. Do both of you understand the rules?"

As Jacob and Sydney nodded, the judge closed the file folder before him. "Good, we'll meet again in three months. As long as there are no problems in the three-month period, we'll look at extending your visitation rights at that time."

He reached for his gavel and banged it briskly. "Case dismissed."

* * *

"I just committed perjury," Sydney said.

Martin glanced around the diner. "Sydney, keep your voice down."

She stared first at him and then at Grayson. "What the hell just happened?"

GG squeezed her hand. "You got your Emma for overnight visits – that's what happened."

She looked at GG and whispered, "You lied to the judge."

"I did not," GG said indignantly. "He never specifically asked me if you were engaged to my grandson. Besides, you're wearing my great-grandmother's ring, aren't you? I wouldn't let anyone who wasn't a family member wear it."

Sydney looked down at the ring. "Oh my God," she said. "GG, I'm sorry. I shouldn't be wearing this."

She started to pull off the ring, and Grayson reached out and put his hand over hers. "Leave it on, Sydney."

"It's too big. What if I lose it? I'd never forgive myself."

"We'll get it sized to fit your finger," he said dismissively.

"The women in my family have always had big hands," GG grinned. "You'll have to get it moved down quite a few sizes."

"GG," Sydney said softly, "there's no need to get it sized. Grayson and I are not getting married. You understand that, right?"

She glared at Grayson and Martin. "You did tell her this is all one big fat lie, didn't you?"

"Seriously, Sydney. Keep your damn voice down," Martin repeated in a low voice.

"You've all gone completely mad. Do you realize that?" Sydney squeezed the edge of the table until her knuckles turned white.

"We'll never be able to pull this off. When the judge finds out I lied, he'll take Emma away forever."

"Sydney, that's not going to happen," Grayson said, and she glared at him.

"Why are you even doing this? You barely know me. In fact, I'm pretty sure you hate me, and frankly, I'm not that fond of you."

"I don't hate you," he protested. "Sydney, this was the only way to get Emma for overnight visits. I thought you would be happy."

"I am happy," she said. "But you don't seem to realize the magnitude of this lie. You told them we're *engaged* and living together, for God's sake! You saw the look on Jacob's face – he doesn't believe it. You don't know him the way I do. He's a goddamn control freak who thinks I'm an unfit mother, and he'll stop at nothing to prove that I'm lying. Do you get that, Grayson? Do you?"

She was sweating, her face pale, and her body trembling, and Grayson gave Martin and his grandmother an alarmed look before sliding across the seat. He took her cold hand in his. "Honey, calm down. Everything will be fine."

"No, it won't," she said. "Jacob will find out and -"

He's not going to find out. All we have to do is pretend we're engaged for a while. It'll be easy."

She rolled her eyes. "You realize that engaged people eventually get married, right, Grayson?"

He shrugged. "Yeah, but people have long engagements all the time. No one will find it weird if we're engaged for a few years."

She stared at him, her eyes nearly bugging out of her head. "A few years? You *have* gone mad!"

Martin leaned forward. "Sydney, it won't take a few years. Trust me on this. In three months, six at the most, I bet you'll have earned back partial custody of Emma, and you won't need Grayson after that. You can quietly end your engagement, and no one will be the wiser."

"Martin, this is -"

"It's a good plan, Sydney," Martin said firmly. "And

Grayson is right – it was the only way to get you access to Emma. All you have to do is pretend to be engaged around other people."

"And live together." She frowned.

Grayson shrugged. "Have you never lived with a room-mate before?"

"It's not the same, and you know it," she said tightly. She could feel her stomach twisting at the thought of living in the same house as Grayson. Even just having him sit beside her in the booth made her overheat. After what he said to her last night, she should be punching his face in, not considering living with him and wondering how long it might take to convince him to fuck her.

She dropped her head in her hands, rubbed at her fore-head and then stared at the others around the table. "Am I the only one who sees this for how crazy it is?"

When they didn't answer, she sighed and glanced at her watch. "I have to go to work."

Grayson frowned. "You shouldn't be going to work, Sid. You heard what the doctor said about taking it easy for a week. You looked terrible last night."

"Gee, thanks. Maybe it was because someone was being an asshole to me," she said sarcastically.

He flushed. "You should call in sick and go home to bed."

"He's right, Sydney," GG said gently. "You look very pale and tired."

"I'd love to call in sick, but apparently, I'm going back to college in January, and I need to find some way to pay for it," she said.

"Sydney about that…" Grayson took her arm as she was sliding out of the booth.

"If you tell me that you'll pay for it and I can pay you back, I swear to God I will punch you in the face," she warned him.

He hesitated, and she snatched her arm free and slid the rest of the way out of the booth.

"Sydney, wait!" Grayson unfolded his lean body from the booth and took her arm again. "At least let me drive -"

"Why, Grayson O'Reilly, we just keep bumping into each other, don't we?"

Sydney groaned. Mary and Erin had entered the diner, and the two women gave Grayson identical inviting smiles.

"Ladies, it's nice to see you again," Grayson said politely.

Sydney rolled her eyes as the women ignored her completely and stepped closer. Ivan was standing behind the counter, and she caught his eye and made a very childish face. He grinned and winked at her before disappearing into the kitchen.

"When will you take us up on our offer to cook dinner for you, Grayson? Both Mary and I are excellent cooks. Why don't you pop by my place tomorrow night?" Erin smiled at him.

Sydney's temper, already stretched to the breaking point, suddenly snapped, and she cleared her throat loudly.

"Oh, I'm sorry, ladies. Haven't you heard? Grayson and I are engaged." She stuck her hand out in front of their faces, watching with smug enjoyment as their mouths dropped open at the sight of the ring on her third finger.

"You're joking," Mary breathed.

"Oh, I can assure you I'm not." Sydney smiled coolly. Before either woman could say anything else, she turned to Grayson, grabbed his head between her hands, and tugged it toward hers.

"I'll see you after work, honey." She tried to speak seductively, but her voice sounded decidedly squeaky.

*Fuck it.* She embraced the madness and mashed her mouth against Grayson's, feeling his teeth scrape her lower lip. He stiffened in surprise when she shoved her tongue into his mouth. After a few seconds, she released his mouth and squeezed his ass. He jumped a little, and she grinned and squeezed his ass again. *A girl could get used to this.*

"Until tonight, cowboy," she said huskily before turning and winking at the women standing before them. She left the diner, leaving the five of them to stare after her.

# CHAPTER 11

"Hey, look – your tall glass of water is back." Belinda nudged Sydney and pointed towards the door.

Sydney groaned inwardly and continued to count out her cash. The bar had closed half an hour ago, and she was tired and in no mood to deal with him.

Grayson paused to speak to Frank before making his way towards the bar. "Ready to go home, Sid?"

She looked up at him. "I have my car here."

"I'll bet you ten dollars it doesn't start." He grinned at her.

"Ha, ha," she said sourly. "It'll start."

He shrugged and leaned down. She realized he meant to kiss her, and she dropped some bills on the floor, ducking to pick them up before he could kiss her. He gave her a decidedly wicked grin, and she suddenly had a very bad feeling that he was about to get payback for her little stunt in the diner.

"I don't believe we've formally met. I'm Grayson O'Reilly, Sydney's fiancé." He held his hand out to Belinda, who gaped at him before taking his hand.

"Uh – I'm Belinda," she said weakly as he shook her hand.

Grayson smiled, his white teeth flashing in the dim light, and put his arm around Sydney's waist. He dropped an affectionate kiss on her head, and she elbowed him in the stomach.

He didn't even flinch, and with an exasperated sigh, she wiggled free as Belinda stared at her.

"Sydney, you're – you're getting married?"

"You didn't tell her, honey? I'm shocked. You were so excited when I asked you." He took her left hand, frowning down at it. "Where's your ring?"

"I told you, *sweetie*, it's too big, and I'm afraid I'll lose it. It's in my pocket," she said through gritted teeth.

"Show Belinda. I'm sure she'd love to see it, honey." He smiled as she wondered if using her mind to strike down a person with lightning was possible.

"I absolutely want to see it!" Belinda suddenly shrieked. She looked around the bar. "Wayne! Frank! Sydney and Grayson are getting married!"

"Belinda, be quiet!" Sydney said, but it was too late. Wayne and Frank were coming over, and she smiled politely and allowed them to hug her. Grinning hugely at her, Grayson shook their hands as Belinda urged her to bring out her ring.

She pulled it from the pocket of her jean skirt and slipped it onto her finger. Belinda oohed and aahed over it as Wayne and Frank dragged Grayson to the far end of the bar for a celebratory whiskey.

"It's so beautiful." Belinda smiled at her. "Did you pick it out together, or did he surprise you?"

"It was GG's great-grandmother's ring," Sydney said.

"How romantic," Belinda sighed. She paused. "Listen, Sid, I don't mean to be nosy, but this seems fast. Grayson's only been back in town for what, a month?"

Sydney smiled at her. "I know it's pretty quick, but we'll

have a fairly long engagement. Sometimes, when you fall in love, you just know it's the right thing, you know?"

She groaned to herself. She sounded incredibly lame and reminded herself to come up with a better reason for why their engagement was so quick and then practice making it sound convincing.

Belinda, however, shrugged and then hugged her. "Yep, I know. I only knew Bill for a few months before I knew he was the one for me. Have you been dress shopping yet?"

Sydney laughed. "No, Belinda. He just asked me to marry him. I haven't made any wedding plans yet."

Belinda hugged her again. "Are you moving into the house with him?"

"No. He's moving into the guesthouse."

"I guess it would be kind of awkward to be having sex with him while his grandmother is sleeping in the same house." Belinda wiggled her eyebrows at her and then laughed when Sydney blushed brightly.

Belinda glanced at the bar before lowering her voice. "Spill your guts, girl. Are the rumours true about how good he is in bed?"

Sydney blushed again. "What rumours?"

"Were you a monk in high school, Sydney? Christ – Donna used to go on and on about how good he was in bed."

"I was three years younger than Grayson and Donna. I hardly even remember Grayson from high school." She decided she was getting entirely too good at lying.

"Yeah, well, it wasn't just Donna. Do you remember Alison Moore?"

Sydney shook her head. "Vaguely. Wasn't she the girl who ran off with that rodeo guy?"

Belinda nodded. "Yep. But before that, she and Grayson dated off and on for a couple of years. According to Mandy Benson, Alison's best friend for years, Alison wanted it to be more, but Grayson kept her at a distance. Anyway, Alison wasn't shy about sharing details of Grayson's," she paused, "abilities in bed."

"So? Are the rumours true?" Belinda asked again.

Sydney was saved from answering by Grayson's deep voice behind her. "Ready, Sid? I have a feeling I'm about to win ten bucks."

\* \* \*

"I'M STILL NOT ENTIRELY SURE YOU DIDN'T SABOTAGE MY CAR," Sydney said grumpily as Grayson turned into the farm's driveway.

He laughed. "I swear I didn't break your car so that I could win a ten-dollar bet."

"Whatever," she muttered.

She breathed a sigh of relief when he shut off the truck, and she hurriedly opened the door and slid out to the ground. Her side was aching miserably, and she wanted a hot shower, a quick bite to eat and to crawl into bed.

"Thank you, Grayson. Good night!" She called over her shoulder as she moved quickly up the stairs to the front door. She turned the knob, frowning when it was locked and reached into her purse for her keys. She was sure she hadn't locked it when she left this morning.

She gave a soft scream when Grayson suddenly spoke behind her. "I told you to keep it locked."

He reached around her and, using his key, unlocked and opened the door.

"Thanks again. Good night." She slipped into the house, but he walked in before she could shut the door. He stood on one foot and pulled off one boot before switching legs and pulling off the other. He lined them up neatly in the hallway and shrugged out of his jacket.

"Grayson, what are you doing?"

"Taking off my jacket?" He arched his eyebrow at her.

"I mean, why are you in my house?"

"Our house, remember?" He corrected before walking into the kitchen.

She trailed after him as he flipped on the kitchen light and poured himself a glass of water.

"Grayson -"

"Don't tell me you've forgotten we're living together?" He took a drink of water and unbuttoned the top button of his shirt.

"No, I haven't forgotten, but I thought -"

"I moved in my stuff this evening while you were at work." He smiled at her and unbuttoned another button. I also moved the bed from my room at the farm into the guest bedroom here. Emma can use it to sleep in. We'll have to decorate the room and make it more child friendly, but I thought we would ask Emma to help decorate it. Would she like that, do you think?"

"Yes, she'd like that," she said faintly. "I'm going to go have a shower." She nearly ran from the kitchen.

\* \* \*

"I THINK WE NEED TO SET SOME GROUND RULES." SYDNEY pushed her empty plate away and folded her arms nervously over her torso.

After her shower, her plan to hide in her bedroom was ruined when Grayson insisted she eat the dinner he'd prepared earlier. He'd carefully piled a plate with leftovers, and she had to admit that the chicken, potatoes, and steamed broccoli smelled delicious.

Although it was nearly two in the morning, he showed no signs of retiring for the night and sat at the table with her while she ate.

"Ground rules?" He repeated politely.

"Yes, ground rules. When we're not around people, we treat this strictly like a roommate thing. You can sleep in Emma's room when she's not here, and when she is here, I'll sleep on the couch, and you can have my room."

"I'll take the couch."

"Nope. You're only doing this because of me, so I'll take the couch. I'm smaller and fit better on it."

He shrugged. "Whatever you say, Sydney."

"Why are you doing this anyway?" She asked without warning. She bit nervously at her bottom lip as she waited for his reply.

Thrown off by her question, he cleared his throat and tried to think quickly. "Because GG cares for you and wants to help you."

She stared at him suspiciously. "You're doing this because of GG?"

"Yes."

"It's an awful lot to do just because your grandmother feels bad for her tenant."

He grinned. "What can I say? I'm a nice guy."

She snorted softly, and he made a wry face. "Okay, I'm a nice guy most of the time."

She hesitated, smoothing her hands down the pants of her flannel pajamas. "Also, I know we had a… thing earlier in your bedroom, but I think we can both agree that it was a huge error in judgment on both our parts. I would prefer, and I know you do, too, that we keep this strictly platonic. I have a lot on my plate and don't need any added complications. Emma is my number one priority."

He stared at her, and she stuck her hand toward him. "A fake engagement on the outside and just friends on the inside. Agreed?"

He reached out and swallowed her small hand in his large one. She could feel his rough calluses against her smooth skin and fiercely suppressed the shiver of need that went through her.

"Agreed," he said.

She pulled her hand free and smiled nervously at him. "Great! I'm going to bed."

She stood up, and he frowned as she walked to the thermostat and lowered the heat. "It's already cold in here. Are you trying to freeze me out of the house?"

She blushed. "I'm keeping costs low. There are extra blankets in the hall closet."

He stood and stared down at her. After her shower, she returned to the kitchen wearing a shapeless and faded pair of blue flannel pajamas. It was probably the least sexy pair of pajamas he had ever seen, but his groin had still twitched at the possibility that she was naked underneath them.

"Well, that explains the flannel," he said dryly, reaching over her and turning up the thermostat.

"Hey!" She scowled and reached for the thermostat, but he stepped in front of it.

"You've given me your ground rules. How about you hear mine?" He smiled at her, and she looked at him warily.

"What do you mean?"

He shrugged. "I have a few of my own ground rules. First – no more driving your piece-of-shit car. Either I'll drive you to where you need to go, or you can borrow my truck. Second – we keep the damn heat at a reasonable level."

"I am not paying a giant heat bill just because you get cold easily," she said.

"Sydney, I'm living in the house now. GG won't charge you rent, and I'll pay half of the utilities."

"What?" She sputtered. "I can't – I mean - I'm not taking advantage of GG like that. I can at least – "

He shook his head firmly. "No. She and I have already discussed it. You can stay here for free as long as I live here."

He could see her starting to protest, and he sighed with annoyance. "Think of it as a way to help save for college in January."

"Fine," she muttered. She turned to leave the kitchen, stopping when Grayson continued to speak.

"Third – no more letting the idiots at the bar grope you."

She spun around to face him. "Nope. You do not get the right to tell me what I can and cannot do at work, Grayson O'Reilly."

He glowered at her. "In case you've forgotten, we're engaged now. I hate watching those idiots grab your ass."

She smiled sweetly at him. "In case *you've* forgotten, we're fake engaged. Stop stalking me at work if you don't want to see it happen. Besides, the ass-grabbing is a rare occurrence. Trust me, Belinda and Lisa have to side-step the wandering hands more than I ever will."

She yawned tiredly. "Are we done? I'm very tired."

"Yes. Good night, Sydney," he said.

"Good night, Grayson."

* * *

"IS GRAYSON PICKING YOU UP TONIGHT?" BELINDA ASKED AS she helped Sydney wipe down the tables. Frank and Mark were ushering the last of the customers out, and Lisa was helping Greg clean and refill the bottles at the bar.

"Yes. Apparently, I'm not allowed to drive my car anymore. He thinks it isn't safe."

Belinda laughed. "He's right. Are you excited about getting Emma tomorrow?"

"So excited!" Sydney crowed. "Can you believe I get to have her for two whole days? I can't wait!"

Belinda hugged her. "I'm so glad, Sid." She ducked behind the bar and plucked from under the counter a large red box with a black bow wrapped around it. "I bought you an engagement present."

She handed the box to Sydney, beaming brightly at her.

"Belinda! You didn't have to do that," Sydney protested.

"I wanted to." She glanced around to make sure the others weren't near them. "Open it."

Smiling, Sydney untied the bow and pulled the lid off the box. She let her breath out in a soft little whoosh and could feel the blush starting in her chest. It rose through her face, making her ears tingle, and her cheeks burn.

"Belinda!" She gave her a look of shock, and Belinda laughed and kissed her forehead.

"Oh my God, Sydney. I've never seen anyone turn so red in my life!"

Sydney stared at the gift. The collar, scarves and feather from the 'Naughty Little Secrets' store were nestled in the tissue paper. They were resting on top of the red corset.

Her heart thudded loudly, and she couldn't stop staring at the collar and scarves. The same image of Grayson using those red scarves to tie her to the bed flashed through her mind, and she squeezed her thighs together as pleasure surged in her belly.

She glanced up at Belinda. "Thank you, Belinda.

"You're welcome, honey. Hey, Grayson."

With a horrified squeak, Sydney lunged for the box lid. She jammed it downward, trying to stuff the tissue paper and the feather, which had bits sticking over the side, under the lid.

"Hi, Belinda." Grayson peered over Sydney's shoulder. "What's in the box?"

"Oh, it's just a little engagement present for Sydney.

Well...maybe it's more for you." Belinda winked. "Have fun, you two."

Giggling, she headed for the front door as Grayson reached to open the box. Sydney snatched it away, her heart thumping madly and her cheeks flaming.

"What?" He gave her a quizzical look. "Can't I see it?"

"No, definitely not. It's a joke gift, okay?"

"Belinda said it was for me, too," he said.

"It isn't. Listen, can we go? I want to get as much sleep as possible before I pick up Emma in the morning."

"Sure." He led her toward the door, one hand resting lightly on the small of her back.

She knew he was curious about what was in the box, but she appreciated that he didn't press her on it. They drove to the farm in silence. After watching her shift in the truck seat a few times, Grayson finally asked if she felt okay.

"What? Yeah, I'm fine. Why do you ask?" she said nervously.

"You just seem very on edge," he said.

"No, everything's good." Sydney took a deep breath and forced herself to sit still. She had never felt so horny in her life. Every time she thought she had herself under control, she would glance over at Grayson, picture him buckling the collar around her neck, wrapping the soft scarves around her wrist and using the feather to tease and torture her.

She was going straight to bed as soon as she got home. She would touch herself and get rid of some of the aching need coursing through her body. She would forget her friendship ground rule and attack Grayson if she didn't.

She cursed Belinda in her head as Grayson turned into the farm's driveway.

"Sydney?" He looked at her, frowning a little. "Are you sure you're -"

"Look out!" she shouted.

He slammed on the brakes, and she was thrown forward, her seatbelt locking painfully against her chest as one of GG's barn cats, a dead mouse clamped firmly in its jaws, froze in the glare of the headlights before sauntering away.

She blew her breath out in a trembling rush and undid her seat belt. "Stupid cat," she muttered.

Her mouth dropped open with horror when she realized the sudden stop had thrown the present off the seat beside her and onto the floor. The lid had popped off, and the contents had spilled onto the truck's floor. Grayson, his face carefully neutral, reached for it.

She scrambled to grab the stuff first. Shoving his hands aside, she grabbed the box and tossed in the scarves and corset. The feather was next to his foot, and she grabbed it and chucked it into the box.

The collar? Where was the damn collar? She looked frantically around the truck floor before, with a sinking feeling in her stomach, glancing up at Grayson. He held it in his hands, his fingers rubbing the soft leather. He looked at the collar for a long moment before looking at her, his eyes dark and unreadable.

She gave him a weak smile. "I told you it was a joke gift." She reached for the collar, but he pulled it away, his thumb still stroking the leather.

"A joke gift," he repeated.

"Yes," she said. "Please, may I have it back?"

He nodded silently and held it out to her. She reached for it, her fingers sliding around the warm leather, and gasped in surprise when he latched on to her wrist, his hand holding her tightly. He slid across the seat, cupped the back of her neck with his other hand and kissed her hard on the mouth.

She moaned into his mouth as he thrust his tongue between her lips. The way he had kissed her in his bedroom was nothing like the way he kissed her now. Those kisses had been gentle and coaxing. These were rough and demanding, and she gasped again when he wound his fingers through her hair and pulled her head back. He nipped his way across her throat to her ear.

He sucked on her earlobe before biting it. "I know we're just friends, but I want to fuck you, Sydney."

She responded by rubbing his cock through his jeans. He jerked against her, his hands tightening almost painfully in her hair before he suddenly pulled her tank top over her head. He dropped it to the seat and reached behind her, undoing her bra with one hand. He yanked it free and then groaned loudly and arched his back when she wiggled her hand into his jeans and wrapped her fingers around his thick cock, rubbing and stroking firmly.

He cupped one breast in his hand and bent his head to lick and kiss the other one. He sucked hard on her nipple before scraping his teeth across it. He made a guttural noise of pleasure when her fingers tightened around his cock in response, and he pulled his mouth away from her breast.

He pulled her hand out of his pants and pushed her away from him. She stared at him, her mouth swollen and trembling. "Grayson, what's wrong? Did I do something wrong?"

"Take off your panties," he said hoarsely.

He pulled off his shirt and started to unbuckle his belt. When she hesitated, he growled, "Take them off now, or I'll rip them off you."

A spasm of pleasure, so strong it nearly hurt, rippled through her and she reached under her skirt and tugged down her panties. Beside her, she could hear Grayson lowering his zipper and the rustle of a wrapper. By the time she had untangled her underwear from her feet, he had pulled his jeans down to his knees, smoothed the condom on and was staring at her impatiently.

"Straddle me," he demanded.

She eyed the size of his cock with some trepidation. He was much bigger than Jacob, and as turned on as she was, she wasn't entirely sure he would fit inside of her without some pain.

"Straddle me, Sydney," he repeated, holding his hand out to her. "C'mon."

She took his hand, swinging her leg over his lap until she was straddling his thighs. She started to lower herself down, but he put one arm around her waist and stopped her.

"Wait, I want to make sure you're wet enough."

He pushed her skirt up around her waist and then reached between her legs. She cried out at the first feel of his calloused fingers against her clit. He rubbed it roughly before sliding two fingers deep inside of her.

She clutched his shoulders, arching her back and moaning as he slid them in and out of her.

"You're definitely wet enough." He smiled with satisfaction.

She blushed with embarrassment, but he used his thumb to rub back and forth over her clit, and her embarrassment quickly turned to pleasure.

"Spread your legs wider," he said. When she obeyed him immediately, he smiled again and kissed her.

"Good girl. But just a little more," he said, spreading his legs and forcing hers apart a few more inches.

She was completely open to him now, and he used one hand to grip his cock and the other to cup the back of her neck. He guided his cock to her wet slit and then pushed her down. He slid into her wet pussy easily, and they gave mutual groans of pleasure as he sunk completely into her.

Sydney squeezed her fingers into the hard muscles of his shoulders. She felt stretched and full to the brim and waited a moment before rocking experimentally on top of him.

He groaned again, his fingers digging into the back of her

neck before he pulled her forward and kissed her, pushing his tongue deep into her mouth as he put his other arm around her waist. He held her tightly and thrust hard into her.

"Grayson," she moaned into his mouth.

He licked her upper lip. "It feels so good to fuck you, Sydney."

She shuddered again at his words and lifted her head so he could kiss her throat. Before he could thrust into her again, her purse on the seat beside them rang faintly.

"Ignore it," he muttered.

"I can't," she gasped. "It's Jacob's ring."

She reached for her purse, pulling her phone out with shaking hands as Grayson sighed with frustration beneath her. She cleared her throat, trying to ignore both the way Grayson was stroking her bare thighs and how hard his cock still was inside of her.

"Hello?"

Grayson leaned forward to kiss her throat, stopping when she made a soft sound of distress.

"Hurt? How? What happened?"

She listened for a few minutes and then said. "I'll be right there."

She hung up and stared down at him. "I need to go to the hospital. Emma's broken her arm."

# CHAPTER 12

"Where is she?" Sydney asked frantically.

Standing next to the nurse's desk in the waiting area of the emergency room, Jacob looked her up and down. "Jesus Christ, Sydney. What kind of outfit is that?"

"I just finished work," Sydney said impatiently. "Jacob, where is Emma?"

"She's fine. They finally put a cast on her. We've been here since goddamn eight o'clock." Jacob grumbled.

"I want to see her," Sydney demanded as Grayson took her cold hand in his and squeezed it gently.

"She's in the back." He glanced at Grayson. "I think it should just be family, Sydney."

"Grayson is family," she snapped. Still holding Grayson's hand, she followed Jacob into the emergency department.

Jacob led her past a few curtained-off sections before stopping at the last one. They ducked behind the curtain, and Sydney dropped Grayson's hand and ran to the bed. Looking very small and pale, Emma was lying in bed with her left arm encased in a bright pink cast.

"Hi, Mama," she said solemnly.

"Hi, baby," Sydney said. She sat on the side of the bed and kissed Emma's face before stroking her hair. "How are you feeling?"

"I hurt my arm."

"I know you did. I'm sorry, Emma."

"It hurt a lot," she sighed. "It feels better now."

"The doctor gave her some meds for pain," Jacob said.

Sydney glanced behind her. Monica, her face completely devoid of colour, stood beside Jacob. He put his arm around her, and she gave him a small, sick smile.

"How did it happen?" Sydney asked.

Jacob hesitated, and Monica, wiping tears from her face, said softly, "It's my fault, Sydney. Emma wanted to try out the top bunk of her bed. I put her in there, then left the room for a minute, and she tried to climb down herself. She fell off the ladder."

She swallowed back a sob. "I'm really sorry."

"It's fine, Monica. Accidents happen," Sydney said gently.

"Am I going to your house now, Mama?" Emma asked.

"Not just yet, baby."

"Actually," Jacob sat down on the other side of Emma and rubbed her blanket-covered leg. "Maybe you should stay home this weekend, Emma. With your sore arm, it's probably better if you stay with Daddy and Monica."

Sydney bit back a protest as her stomach twisted painfully. She had been so looking forward to having Emma to herself this weekend.

Emma stared at Jacob, her lower lip trembling. "I'm not going to Mama's?"

"You will, honey. Just not tomorrow," Jacob said, giving her a small smile.

Emma wailed loudly, and Jacob winced as Sydney tried to soothe her. "It's okay, baby girl, don't cry."

"I want to go to Mama's house," Emma sobbed. "You said

I could go to Mama's house!" She started to cry harder, and with a frantic look at Monica, Jacob rubbed Emma's leg again.

"Okay, sweetheart, okay. Don't cry. You can go to your Mama's house tomorrow, okay?"

She continued to cry. Emma was an easy child, not prone to temper tantrums or crying, and faced with the alien sound of her sobs, Jacob could do nothing but continue to rub her leg helplessly. Sydney slipped around to the other side of the bed and crawled in beside Emma. She put her arms around the little girl and cradled her gently.

"Shh, baby girl, shh." She rocked her quietly back and forth until Emma's crying had subsided.

"Will you stay with me tonight?" the little girl asked.

"Of course I will, baby." Sydney kissed the top of her head, inhaling her sweet smell.

Half an hour later, Emma had fallen asleep, and Jacob stood and gave Monica a quick hug. "You should go home and try to get some sleep."

She nodded and then hesitated, tears welling up in her eyes again. "I am so sorry, Sydney. I feel so terrible about this."

Sydney reached out and squeezed her hand gently. "Monica, stop blaming yourself. It could have easily happened with Jacob or me. Emma will be okay."

"Thanks, Sid," Monica said.

"I'll walk you to your car." Jacob put his arm around Monica's waist and led her from the room.

Grayson sat on the side of the bed next to Sydney. "That was nice of you to say."

Sydney shrugged. "I mean it."

She gazed at Emma's sleeping face. She had meant it. Despite her issues with Jacob, Monica had always been pleasant and friendly to her. She knew how much Monica loved Emma and, more importantly, how much Emma loved Monica.

She looked behind her at Grayson. "You should probably go as well. I'm sure you're tired."

"I'll stay."

"It's okay. Go home and get some sleep. Can you pick us up in the morning, though?"

He nodded. "Of course I can. I'll come by early, but I don't mind staying."

"I appreciate that, but it's not necessary." She hesitated. "Could you bring some other clothes for me? Just a t-shirt and a pair of jeans would be great. There should be some in the bottom drawer of my dresser."

"No problem." He gently touched her hip, leaned over, and kissed her as Jacob ducked back into the room.

Sydney immediately felt a shiver of desire course through her. His kiss was gentle and close-mouthed, but she could feel the hunger beneath it. Even just the brush of his lips against hers was enough to make her remember how it had felt to have him inside of her.

Jacob cleared his throat, and Grayson ended the kiss but cupped her face warmly. "I'll be back in the morning, but call me if you need anything, okay?"

She nodded, and he kissed her again before standing and leaving without looking at Jacob.

\* \* \*

"Are you getting tired, sweetie?" Sydney ran her hand through Emma's blonde hair before kissing the top of her head.

The little girl leaned against her and sighed. "A little."

"Why don't we get you ready for bed? It's almost time to take your medicine for your arm, and that will make you moments, Emma's shaking stopped, and she stared at Sydney.

"Where's Grayson?"

"He's in bed, honey. It's very late. In fact, why don't you crawl back into bed so you can fall asleep again."

The little girl shook her head. "I want to sleep with you and Grayson."

"Oh, honey, that's not a good idea," Sydney said. "But I'll sleep in your bed with you. Would you like that?"

"No." The little girl's face crumpled. "I want to sleep in your bed with you and Grayson. Daddy lets me sleep with him and Monica when I'm scared at home. I promise I'll be good and won't wet the bed."

Sydney hesitated, and Emma sniffed loudly. "Please, Mama."

"Okay, honey. But Grayson is sleeping, so you have to be very quiet and go to sleep, okay?"

Emma nodded eagerly, and Sydney carried her out of the bedroom. "Do you have to go to the bathroom?"

She shook her head and snuggled into her. "No, Mama."

Sydney put her finger to her lips as she stopped in front of her bedroom. "Remember, very quiet. Okay, baby?"

"Okay," Emma whispered loudly.

Sydney eased the door open, wincing as it squeaked on its hinges, and entered the bedroom. Grayson was a sleeping lump under the blankets, and she moved silently to the bed. She pulled back the blankets and carefully eased Emma into the bed.

As she slid the little girl to the middle of the bed, Grayson's deep voice made them jump. "Can't sleep, Emma-Lou?"

"Hi, Grayson!" Emma said excitedly. "I had a bad dream, and Mama said I could sleep with you guys in your bed. Isn't that nice of her?"

even sleepier." Sydney stood, and Emma followed her into the guest house's kitchen.

"Where's Grayson?" she asked suddenly.

"I told you, baby, he went with GG to visit friends. He'll be back later." She smiled at Emma.

It had only been one day, but Emma was already quite taken with Grayson. He had picked them up from the hospital Sunday morning and driven them back to the farmhouse. Once there, he held Emma gently and carried her into the barn, showing her the horses and the new litter of kittens hiding in the hayloft. Next, he took her to meet GG, and the four of them enjoyed lunch together in the farmhouse's kitchen.

Grayson had played with Emma all afternoon. He had carried her back to the barn at her request so she could see the kittens again. He had shown her how to brush the horses and promised to take her riding once her arm healed.

Sydney had been surprised at how sweet and gentle he was with Emma, and she had no sense that he was being kind to her daughter to win her favour. He had genuinely seemed to enjoy Emma's company and had even sat in the kitchen with her after lunch. He patiently stirred the cookie batter while GG showed Emma how to make cookies.

The little girl pouted and collapsed dramatically into one of the kitchen chairs. "I want Grayson to read me a bedtime story."

"I don't think he'll be back in time to read to you, honey. I'm sorry," Sydney said. "How about I read you one instead, and when Grayson gets home, I'll tell him to go in and kiss you goodnight."

"Okay," Emma said. "I like Grayson, Mama. He's nice."

"I'm glad, honey. Come on, let's get you into your pajamas and into bed."

* * *

GRAYSON SLIPPED QUIETLY INTO THE GUESTHOUSE. BARB HAD kept him and GG for much longer than he had wanted. He was barely able to disguise his impatience to get back to Sydney and Emma, and finally, when it was nearly ten, he had stood and given GG a pointed look.

She smiled and took the hint, standing and collecting her things before hugging Barb goodbye. They had left with apple pie and promised to bring Sydney the next time. He had forgotten how fast information travelled through his hometown. He had been briefly surprised when Barb had squealed and told him congratulations the minute he walked through the door.

He nodded his thanks and breathed a sigh of relief when GG immediately changed the subject before Barb could ask questions. He would have to speak with Sydney so they could get their stories straight about their engagement.

The house was quiet and dark, and he slipped off his boots and crept towards Sydney's bedroom. It was stupid, but he hoped that Sydney would have thrown out her ground rule about being just friends after what happened between them in the truck. His cock hardened a little at the thought of her waiting for him in the bed. Her skin would be soft and warm, and he let himself imagine how good it would feel to lay her back on the bed, spread her legs and sink into her tight warmth.

He opened the door of the bedroom and peered hopefully at the bed. It was empty, and he gave a harsh sigh of frustration before heading to the attached bathroom. It had been stupid of him to think Sydney would be waiting for him. It was her first night with Emma. She was probably in the bed with her.

* * *

SYDNEY'S BREATHING QUICKENED WHEN SHE HEARD GR entering the guesthouse. She burrowed a little further u the covers of the makeshift bed she had created on the co and tightly clenched her hands.

She had been in the middle of a sweet little fantasy wh Grayson had come home and discovered she wasn't in t bed. He had walked into the living room and carried her the bed, ignoring her feeble protests. Fantasy Grayson ha just finished peeling off her shapeless flannel pajamas and was placing her on her hands and knees on the bed so he could take her from behind when she heard the soft click of the front door.

Her stomach twisting, she held her breath when he walked by the living room and into the bedroom. She waited breathlessly, refusing to admit that she was hoping her little fantasy was about to come true. After about ten minutes, the light under the bedroom door went out, and there was the sound of Grayson climbing into the bed. It creaked loudly under his weight.

She blew her breath out in a frustrated little rush and reminded herself that she had set the ground rules. He was simply following them. She tossed and turned before finally falling into a light doze that was woken by Emma's soft crying only a few hours later. She slipped off the couch and ran into the second bedroom.

"Emma? Baby, what's wrong?"

The little girl sat up and reached for her with one arm. "I had a bad dream, and now my arm hurts."

She gathered Emma onto her lap and rocked her gently back and forth. "I'm sorry, honey. You're okay." She kissed Emma's face and hummed quietly to her. After a few

"Very nice of her," Grayson rumbled. He turned over and smiled at Emma. "Make sure you don't hit me with your cast in the middle of the night."

She giggled. "I can't, silly. I'm wearing my hammock."

"It's called a sling, honey," Sydney said. She stood beside the bed and rubbed her hands together anxiously.

"Where are your pajamas, Grayson?" Emma stared at his naked chest curiously.

"I just wear shorts to bed, Emma," he said.

"Oh. Daddy wears pajamas." She relaxed on her back and looked at Sydney. "Get into bed, Mama."

"Yeah, get into bed, Sydney," Grayson repeated softly.

She smiled nervously before climbing into the bed. She curled up next to Emma, putting her arm around the little girl's waist and kissing her cheek.

"Go to sleep, Emma, okay?"

"Okay, Mama. I love you."

"I love you too, baby girl."

"Good night, Grayson," Emma said.

"Good night, Emma-Lou. Sleep tight, don't let the bedbugs bite."

The little girl giggled softly as Grayson reached across her and stroked Sydney's hip. "Good night, Sid."

She cleared her throat. "Good night, Grayson."

# CHAPTER 13

S he woke the moment he put his arm around her. She squinted in the early morning light as Grayson cupped her throat gently and buried his face against her flannel-covered back. He was pressed up against her from head to toe, and she could feel his morning wood pushing against her ass.

Emma, where was Emma? She looked around the bed, her fingers tightening on the covers and her heart speeding up when there was no sign of her. She breathed a sigh of relief when she heard the television turn on and the familiar sound of cartoons. Emma laughed loudly, and Sydney let go of the covers. She was fine. Up until two days ago, there would have been no TV for Emma to watch, but Grayson had arranged to have the cable hooked up. She didn't watch much TV but was grateful for it now. Emma was used to watching her cartoons at Jacob's house, and she wanted to keep the same sort of routine for the little girl.

She closed her eyes for a moment. Grayson was still holding her firmly against him, and she enjoyed the feel of his hard body against hers. Enjoyed it a little too much.

Already, her nipples had hardened, and the familiar throbbing was starting up in her pelvis.

She groaned to herself and tried to untangle her body from his. He muttered low in his throat and burrowed deeper into her back. She gasped as his cock pressed firmly against her. She pulled on his arm, and snorting softly, he moved his hand down and cupped her breast through her pajamas. His thumb rubbed familiarly across her hard nipple, and she was helpless to stop her soft moan. His hand tightened in response to her moan, and then his fingers were unbuttoning her shirt.

"Grayson!" She slapped at his hand.

He ignored her and deftly unbuttoned her shirt completely before pushing it open. Her nipples puckered into tight points, and he made a soft growl before slipping his other arm under her slender body. He cupped both her breasts and pulled her back against his hard chest, tugging roughly on the nipples until they had darkened to a deep rose colour.

She moaned softly. "Grayson, we can't. Emma is here."

"She's watching cartoons. If she comes in, I'll stop." He nuzzled her hair out of the way and nipped at her earlobe.

"She's going to catch us," she whispered as he reached under the covers and pulled the back of her pajama bottoms down, exposing her ass. He shoved his shorts down and nestled his cock between her ass cheeks before rubbing his pelvis against her.

"No, she won't." He cupped her breasts again as she tried to wiggle free.

"Grayson." She turned her head to look at him, and he kissed her hard. She moaned and gave up on her half-hearted protests. Grayson's hard body and hot tongue had pushed all thoughts of Emma from her mind, and she pressed her ass against his cock, liking the way it made him groan into her mouth.

He slipped his hand down the front of her pajama bottoms and cupped her warm sex. His fingers quickly found her clit, and he rubbed it firmly as it swelled under his touch.

"You have no idea how many times I've wondered if you were naked under these damn flannels." His hot breath tickled her ear, and she drew in a deep shuddering breath as he probed at her pussy with one hard finger. He slipped it inside of her and tweaked her clit with his thumb.

Desire burned in her belly and made her limbs tremble. Grayson was still using one hand to cup and play with her breasts, and her nipples were throbbing and pulsing from his gentle touch. She thrust her pelvis against his hand and spread her thighs so his cock slipped between them. He groaned and moved his hand so that he could rub his cock up and down her pussy until he was coated in her juices.

"Sid," he whispered urgently, "do you have any condoms here?"

She groaned with frustration. "No."

"Fuck," he muttered.

"I'm on the pill," she panted. "And Jacob's the only guy I've ever slept with. I was tested a few years ago, and the results were normal."

The head of his cock rubbed against her clit, and she gasped with pleasure as he whispered, "I was tested last year, and I'm infection free. I haven't slept with anyone since then. I can show you the results later, I promise."

When she didn't reply, he groaned. "I swear to God I'm going to start carrying the damn results around in my pocket."

She giggled. "Maybe you should just carry a condom."

"I did." He kissed her neck, his tongue sliding against her sensitive skin. "We used it in the truck. Remember?" He plucked at her nipple, and she jerked against him as the memory of straddling him in his truck flickered through her.

"I remember," she said breathlessly.

He was still sliding his cock up and down her pussy, and as he brushed it past her opening, she twisted her hips so that the head of his cock slipped into her tight opening. He inhaled sharply and then thrust deeply into her. She pushed back against him as her pussy stretched around him.

"Are you sure, Sid?" he muttered into her ear.

"Oh God, yes," she whispered. "Please, Grayson, fuck me."

She felt his entire body shudder at her words, and then he pushed her pajama bottoms down to her knees and shifted downward until he could easily slide in and out of her. He pushed one hand under her flannel shirt and rested it on her back before moving his other hand on her hip. He held her firmly, his fingers digging into her soft skin as he moved his pelvis back and forth. Her pussy was so tight and wet that he was already embarrassingly close to coming.

Sydney moaned and gasped softly, barely feeling the sting of his fingers against her hip as the feel of his cock consumed her. With every thrust, he filled her, and she pushed back against him with a ferocity that surprised her.

She had enjoyed sex with Jacob and had found it pleasant enough, but for the first time in her life, she finally understood why sex could be so addictive. Her entire body felt like it was on fire. Each nerve ending throbbed and tingled with unabashed delight. Every stroke of Grayson's cock sent an almost unbearable surge of pleasure through her, and as the tingling started to move down her spine and towards her pelvis, she panted and dug her fingers into the soft mattress. She was so close, she could feel –

Grayson suddenly pulled out of her, and he yanked up her pajama bottoms and shoved her shirt closed before she could even open her mouth to protest. As he pulled up his shorts, she gave him a look of confusion. "Grayson, what's wrong?"

"Emma's coming," he muttered.

Her eyes widened, and she reached for her shirt buttons just as Emma's head peered into the bedroom.

"Mama? Are you awake?" she said in a loud whisper.

"I am, honey." Sydney cleared her throat and quickly finished buttoning her shirt under the covers.

She sat up. "What's wrong? Does your arm hurt?"

"Yeah. And I'm hungry." The little girl approached the bed and held up her one good arm. Sydney leaned over and picked her up carefully, kissing her soft cheek before setting her on the bed beside her.

"We'll give you more medicine for your arm and make some breakfast. Okay?"

"Okay." Emma stared at her for so long that Sydney blushed.

"What, honey?"

"Your hair is really big," she said solemnly. "It's the size of a watermelon."

Sydney burst out laughing. "That's what happens when you have curly hair, honey. You get crazy bedhead."

Emma touched her own straight, blonde hair. "How come my hair isn't curly, Mama?"

"Luckily, you got your father's hair and not your mama's." Sydney grinned at her.

Grayson sat up behind her and tugged gently on one corkscrew curl. "I like your curly hair."

"Hi, Grayson!" Emma's eyes brightened, and she crawled closer, leaning over Sydney to pat his arm with her small hand. "Did you sleep tight?"

He grinned. "I did. And not a single bed bug bite. How about you?"

She nodded, "Yes. Will you watch cartoons with me?"

"I will. But first, let's make you breakfast. What do you think about pancakes?"

"I like pancakes," Emma said, patting his arm again.

Sydney kissed the top of Emma's head. "Come, my love. We'll get you some juice to take your medicine with."

She slid out of the bed and picked the little girl up, snuggling her close and inhaling deeply. The little girl wiggled against her. "I want Grayson to carry me."

Sydney hesitated as Grayson threw back the covers and climbed out of the bed. She avoided looking at his hard, tanned chest and at the way his muscular thighs flexed as he walked toward her. He was gorgeous, and she could feel her pussy throbbing in response. She nervously smoothed down her wayward hair as he approached them.

He plucked Emma from her arms and kissed the little girl on the forehead. "Come on, Emma Lou. We'll get the pancakes started while your mama showers."

She slung her good arm around his neck, tangling her tiny fingers in his hair. "Okay."

He hesitated and then brushed his lips across hers. "Good morning, Sid."

She smiled weakly at him. "Good morning."

He winked at her and left her bedroom, Emma chatting happily at him. Sydney blew her breath out and practically ran for the bathroom. She stared at herself in the mirror, groaning miserably at the sight of the pillow wrinkles on her face and her out-of-control hair. Emma was right – her head *was* the size of a watermelon.

What the hell did Grayson see in her, she wondered. Forget that look-wise, she was the complete opposite of what he usually dated, she was also a broke college dropout, deeply in debt, a single mom, and worked two part-time menial jobs.

Maybe it was because she was so different, she mused.

They did say that opposites attract. She snorted softly to herself. She and Jacob had been completely different, and look how well that had turned out.

She squirted toothpaste onto her toothbrush and brushed her teeth vigorously. Of course, Jacob had never made her feel like she would explode just from his touch alone. Jacob had never been so demanding and confident in bed. She sighed at the memory of Grayson's hard hand holding hers captive above her head. She couldn't believe how turned on the thought of being helpless against him made her. She bent and spit into the sink, rinsing her mouth before staring at herself in the bathroom mirror again.

She thought about the collar and the scarves tucked securely away and wondered if Grayson had liked them, wondered if he had enjoyed the idea of her wearing the collar around her neck and the red corset on her too-thin body. She swallowed hard. He must have liked it. His reaction in the truck had been hot and immediate.

She turned on the shower and stepped into the tub, wetting her hair before pouring shampoo into the palm of her hand. Maybe she could put the lingerie on, buckle the collar around her neck, and surprise Grayson. Tonight, after Emma had returned to Jacob's, she could –

She stopped, her curly hair a mass of suds, as a feeling of shame swept through her. This was the first time in three years that she had finally gotten Emma to herself, and all she could think about was getting Grayson O'Reilly to fuck her.

She scrubbed angrily at her hair. What the hell was wrong with her? Emma was the most important thing, the *only* thing that mattered to her. At least, she used to be until Grayson showed up. Shameful tears rolled down her cheeks as she ducked her head under the hot water spray.

Jacob was right – she was an awful mother. She had nearly been caught having sex with Grayson by her daughter.

She had been so wrapped up in what he was doing to her that she hadn't even heard Emma. Emma would have walked right in on them if it hadn't been for Grayson.

Her face paled. Or worse – something could have happened to her while her mother was spreading her legs for her goddamn neighbour. What if Emma had decided to try to cook breakfast on her own? What if she had left the house?

Sydney let the hot tears fall as she stood under the spray of water. It didn't matter how much she wanted Grayson. Now was not the time to indulge in her decades-old crush on him. She couldn't do anything that would jeopardize her ability to earn partial custody of Emma. Jacob would ensure she never had Emma alone again if something happened to her while she was with Sydney. The thought filled Sydney with a wordless horror, and she rubbed at her forehead wearily.

She would have to tell Grayson that she couldn't do this with him and that she needed to concentrate on Emma. He would understand. He would have to. Later, after she had permanent custody of Emma, she could explore a relationship with Grayson.

*Don't kid yourself, Sid. If you're not spreading your legs for him, Grayson isn't going to stick around and wait. The minute you have permanent custody of Emma, he'll break the engagement and find someone his type. You heard him - he's doing this for GG.*

She swallowed and reached for the soap. If she concentrated on Emma and weren't going to take him into her bed, Grayson would lose interest in her quickly. He hadn't been in a serious relationship since high school, and her broke, skinny little ass was not the girl who would change that. She ignored the sick feeling in the pit of her stomach. It was for the best.

# CHAPTER 14

Grayson studied Sydney carefully. She was sitting on the small couch in the living room with a book on her lap, but in the last half hour, she hadn't turned a single page. He didn't know what was wrong. She had joined them in the kitchen after her shower, and although she had smiled, laughed, and played with Emma, there was a noticeable sadness about her.

Even worse was the way she reacted whenever he was close to her. He could see her body tensing and her eyes widening whenever he was in touching distance. She had skittered away from him when he accidentally brushed against her while helping her load the dishwasher.

He frowned and apologized before asking her if she was okay. She nodded nervously before gathering Emma up and taking her to the bedroom to help her wash and change her clothes.

He had suggested they go into town and shop for Emma's room, but she had shaken her head immediately. She made sure Emma was immersed in the toys she had brought with her before saying quietly that she didn't have the cash right now to decorate Emma's room.

He wanted to reach out and touch her, but instead, he shoved his hands into his pocket and said, "I'll pay for it, and you can pay me back later."

She bit at her bottom lip. "No, thank you, Grayson. I already owe you too much money."

"It doesn't matter, Sid. I want to do this."

"Please, Grayson." She'd finally looked at him, and he was surprised that her blue eyes were bright with unshed tears. "I'd prefer if you didn't."

He nodded, and then Emma pulled on his arm and asked him to take her to GG. They'd spent the day alternating between the farmhouse and the barn before joining GG for dinner again. He and Sydney had brought Emma to Jacob's promptly at seven. He had waited in the truck, his stomach burning with jealousy as he watched Sydney, Emma, and Jacob stand on the front porch together. Despite knowing how fractured the relationship was, they looked like the perfect little family, and he had to remind himself that Sydney had no interest in Jacob.

Now, he muted the television and crossed the room to sit beside her. She started to stand, and he gently touched her forearm, stopping her. He frowned at how she trembled beneath his touch and slid closer to her.

"Sydney, tell me what's wrong," he said softly. He reached to smooth her hair back from her face, and she twitched backwards.

"Have I done something to make you afraid of me?" His gut lurched at the thought. He had been rough with her in the bed this morning, ignoring her protests and touching her like she belonged to him. He would never forgive himself if he had frightened her.

"What? No, of course not," she said.

"Then tell me why you're upset," he coaxed. He moved a little closer until his thigh was against hers and bent his head, brushing his lips across hers before she could move away. She made a soft sound of pleasure in the back of her throat, and he deepened the kiss, slipping his tongue into her mouth. She returned his kiss for a moment before she wriggled out of his grip and nearly fell off the couch.

"Sydney? What's wrong?"

"This is wrong." She paced back and forth in the small room. "For the first time in years, I have a chance at custody of Emma, and this morning, I didn't even think about her."

Shame crossed her face. "I was so anxious to have you between my legs that I forgot about my child."

"She was fine, honey. She was watching cartoons."

"What if she had decided to cook breakfast herself? What if she had tried to go to the barn to see the kittens, and something happened to her?"

"Honey, that wouldn't have happened. I was listening for her," Grayson said.

"Great. So you're a better parent than I am. Jacob was right. I don't deserve to have Emma by myself." Large tears slipped down her cheeks, and she wiped them away angrily as he stood up.

"Sydney, you're a great mom." He reached for her, and she yanked herself out of his grip, nearly tripping over the small footstool behind her.

"Don't, Grayson. Please, don't," she said. "I'm sorry. I know I've been giving you mixed messages and – and leading you on, and that's a shitty thing of me to do. I can't tell you how much I appreciate everything you've done for me. I know you're the reason I even have Emma, and I will never be able to repay you for that. But please, I can't do this right now. Emma has to be my only priority. I have three months to prove I'm a good mother and should have partial custody of Emma. I can't do anything that would jeopardize that, and being with you makes me lose focus. Do you understand that?"

He nodded, and she gave him a weak smile of relief. "Maybe once I've gotten permanent partial custody of Emma, we could - I don't know – revisit what's happening between us?"

He hesitated, and she flushed bright red. "Sorry. I didn't mean to put you on the spot like that."

"Sydney, I -"

She held up her hand and then rubbed at her forehead. "Don't worry about it, Grayson. I promise I'll prove I'm a good mother, so we only have to keep this fake engagement going for three months. After that, we can go our separate ways. It's probably best if we're just friends anyway. I have a lot of baggage. Besides, I have to get serious, pay off my debt, and start saving for college in January. I'll be pretty busy between going back to school and Emma."

He stayed silent, and she gave him an anxious look. "Are you – do you understand?"

He nodded reluctantly. "Yeah, I understand."

"Thank you, Grayson. Truly." She rubbed her hands nervously on her jeans. "I think I'll go to bed. Could I borrow your truck tomorrow? I have some errands to run before my shift at the bookstore."

"Yes. Good night, Sydney."

"Good night, Grayson."

* * *

"SYDNEY DID WHAT?" GG PLACED A SANDWICH IN FRONT OF him before sitting down at the table.

"She's taken a third job. On Tuesday, she went into town before her shift at the bookstore and asked Ivan if he needed help. As luck would have it, one of his servers had just quit on him. He hired her to work at the diner on Thursday, Friday and Saturday. She started there this week."

With Sydney working at Ivan's and Dawson's now, he'd barely seen her. Despite her protests, he had picked her up at Ivan's on Thursday and Friday and then driven her to the bar. He had returned each night when the bar closed to drive her home. She had been quiet and withdrawn both nights, and he hadn't pressed her, afraid she would close herself off completely from him. She would shower and eat a quick dinner before excusing herself to her bedroom.

"I thought she worked at Dawson's on those days," GG said.

"She does. She's working during the day at Ivan's and then goes to the bar from there," Grayson said. He stared miserably at his sandwich as GG frowned.

"She'll work herself to death. Why on earth did she take a third job?"

"It's my fault. She feels like she needs to make extra money to return to school in January." He sighed and pushed away his sandwich. "I would never have told the judge she was returning to college if I thought she wouldn't let me pay for it. I assumed she would be fine with me loaning her the money."

GG smiled. "Oh, Grayson. Sydney has way too much pride for that."

"She's just being stubborn," he snorted. "But I can't convince her to let me loan her the money. Whenever I bring it up, she mumbles about how she already owes me the hospital bill and legal fees."

He slammed his fist on the table, making GG jump

slightly. "I was trying to help, and now I've made things worse for her."

"Why are you so anxious to help her, honey?" GG asked softly.

Caught off guard by her question, he stared at her momentarily. "Well, because she's had a terrible life, but she never complains, and she's always so damn cheerful. I really admire that. She deserves better."

He flushed at the look on GG's face.

"Plus, I know how much she means to you." He grasped onto that thought triumphantly. "I wanted to make you happy."

"Oh." GG gave him a thoughtful look. "You were trying to make me happy."

"Yes."

"Right, of course. You're so kind to try to make an old woman happy."

He scowled at her and stood as she gave him a teasing smile. "Where are you going, sweetie?"

He glanced at his watch before jamming his cowboy hat onto his head. "Her shift at Ivan's is almost done. I'm going to run into town and drive her to Dawson's. She says she can walk, but this is her third fourteen-hour workday. She's tired, I know she is."

He glanced out the window at the darkening sky. "Besides, it's cold out, and she still doesn't have a damn winter jacket. And it'll be dark by the time she gets to Dawson's, and I don't want her walking alone in that neighbourhood. She's too little to protect herself."

"Take your sandwich with you," GG urged.

"I'll take it for Sydney. She can eat it in the truck on the way to Dawson's."

She wrapped the sandwich quickly, and he kissed her

worn check gently. "Good night, GG. I'll see you tomorrow, okay?"

"You're not stopping by later?"

"No, I've got some errands to do, and then I'll just go to Dawson's until her shift ends." He paused. "Unless you need me to come home?"

She laughed. "No, I don't. Alex and the girls are coming by in an hour or so – we'll pretend to play bridge while we gossip."

* * *

"Where's your ring, Sid?" Belinda asked.

Sydney glanced at her bare left hand. Against her wishes, Grayson had taken the ring in to be sized. It was a pointless gesture. She would return it to him in three months but couldn't convince him not to do it.

"It's just getting sized." She smiled tiredly at Belinda before looking around nervously. "Listen, Belinda, I'm trying to keep a low profile with the whole engagement thing. I don't want- "

Belinda held up her hand. "Say no more, Sid. It's the same reason I don't wear my wedding rings here. It drives Bill crazy, but the extra money I make in tips doesn't bother him."

She rolled her eyes and then suddenly grinned at her. "Have I mentioned how cute it is that Grayson picks you up and drops you off for your shifts? Bill would do almost anything for me, but getting out of his nice warm bed at one in the morning to drive to the bar? Forget it."

She waved to Grayson, who nodded before taking another drink of beer. "He's got it so bad for you, Sydney. It's adorable."

Sydney blushed a little. Grayson was only doing it

because he was a nice guy and felt sorry for her broke ass, but she supposed it worked well for keeping up the image of a doting fiancé. "I feel bad that he's doing that. I've tried multiple times to convince him to let me drive my car, but he refuses. The one morning I tried to sneak out early, he busted me before I could even get to my car."

She sighed. "It's a huge inconvenience for him. The only reason he's hanging around is to drive me home, and I know he has better things to do."

She glanced at her watch. Grayson had walked into the bar about fifteen minutes ago. It was only ten o'clock, and she still had another three hours to go.

Belinda shrugged. "Or he could just want to spend some time with his fiancée. With you working at Ivan's, you can't have much alone time together."

She cocked her head at Sydney. "Why are you working three jobs again?"

"I already told you. I'm returning to college in January and need to save up for it," Sydney said.

"Yeah, but, honey – and don't take this the wrong way – your fiancé is filthy rich. Why are you killing yourself working three jobs to go to college when Grayson could easily pay for it?"

"He's not filthy rich." Sydney frowned.

"Uh yeah, Sid, he is. His father was worth millions when he died, and he left the bulk of it to Grayson. How could you not know that?"

"How do *you* know that?" Sydney asked.

Belinda gave her an embarrassed look. "Bill works at the firm that handled his father's accounting needs. I haven't said anything to anyone about it, but I don't think it's a big secret or anything. Most people know that the O'Reilly's have money, but I swear I don't gossip about Bill's clients, Sid. I just assumed that you would know."

"We haven't really talked about money. I mean, I knew he was well-off, but I didn't realize that he, uh..."

Sydney trailed off awkwardly. She could feel their fake engagement story already starting to fall apart, making her nervous as hell.

"You're kidding me." Belinda was staring at her with undisguised shock. "You mean Grayson hasn't asked you to sign a prenup agreement?"

"Um, not yet." Sydney fidgeted against the bar. "But I'm sure he will."

"Will you sign it?"

Before Sydney could reply, Belinda shook her head. "Stupid question. You're working three jobs when he could easily pay off your entire debt and send you to college, probably with just the money he has in his wallet right now. Of course you'll sign it."

She cupped Sydney's arm. "Honey, I know you love him, and you're not in this for the money, but just make sure that the prenup agreement protects you as well, okay?"

"Don't worry about me, Belinda. I can take care of myself and don't need any of Grayson's money to do it. Things are taking a turn for the better for me, you know? I have Emma back again. I'm going back to college to finish my degree, and," she swallowed guiltily, "I'm engaged to a wonderful guy. Things are good."

Belinda smiled at her. "And it couldn't have happened to a nicer person."

Sydney blushed, and Belinda laughed. "I mean it, Sydney. We haven't known each other for that long, but you're really important to me. I was so worried about you for a while there. You were getting so skinny, and I was sure your stupid car would, like, I don't know, blow up or something."

Sydney hugged her impulsively. "Thanks, Belinda. I'm glad we're friends."

They broke apart, and Belinda picked up the tray of drinks before winking saucily at Greg. The bartender was frowning at them, obviously wondering why they were still standing there talking, and Belinda winked again before sauntering toward her section.

Sydney gave Greg a small smile of apology before tugging down her jean skirt. Her hug with Belinda had caused it to ride up, and she could almost feel the hot gaze of the guy sitting at the bar behind her. She started a little when he stood and brushed past her, close enough for her to feel his crotch touching her ass.

"Excuse me, beautiful." He smiled and stroked her arm as he squeezed past her, and she gave him a polite smile as he looked her up and down, his gaze lingering on her cleavage and then her painted lips.

"No problem." She picked up her tray and glanced at Grayson. Her stomach dropped. He was watching the guy at the bar, and she recognized the look on his face. He had placed his cowboy hat on the table, and she watched as his hand squeezed and loosened on it compulsively. He was about thirty seconds away from stalking over and punching the guy in the face. She could see it in the set of his body and narrowed eyes, and she hurried over to him.

"Stop it," she said.

"Stop what?" He growled without taking his eyes off the guy at the bar.

"You know what." She stood in front of him, blocking his view of the man at the bar. He let his gaze drop to her small breasts, and the heat in his gaze made her nipples harden immediately. They were easily noticeable against her bra and thin tank top, and she would have smacked the smug smile off his face if the table hadn't been between them.

"And stop doing that," she said in a fierce mutter.

"Doing what?" he asked innocently.

"Looking at me like I'm your favourite flavour of ice cream."

He chuckled, a warm sound that made her lady bits tingle. "Comparing yourself to ice cream? Are you asking me to lick you, Sydney? Because I'd be more than happy to lick you wherever you want to be licked."

His gaze wandered down her body again. Now it wasn't just her nipples that were reacting to him, her pussy was too, and for one mad moment, she was tempted to pull Grayson outside to his truck and ride him until she came screaming around him.

She took a deep breath. "Grayson, we talked about this."

"I'm not touching you. I haven't touched you in four days," he said grouchily.

She bit at her bottom lip. "I'm sorry, Grayson. I know this is hard on you."

He laughed bitterly. "Hard? Yeah, that's a surprisingly accurate way to put it."

"Listen, why don't you head out? I know you're tired. You've been picking me up late every night."

He shook his head. "No."

"I'll take an Uber home." She smiled tentatively at him. "I'm sure you have better things to do."

"Will you let me pay for the Uber?"

She hesitated, and he rolled his eyes. "Either I pay for the Uber, or I stay here."

"Then yes," she said hurriedly, "you can pay for it."

SYDNEY'S QUICK ACCEPTANCE TO GET HIM TO LEAVE SENT HURT rippling through Grayson. He pulled his wallet out of the back pocket of his jeans and rudely tossed some bills down on the table. "Here, then."

She collected them quietly as he stood and shoved his cowboy hat on before shrugging into his jacket.

"Will that be enough?" he asked gruffly.

She smiled at him, a thin, wavering smile that did nothing to hide the deep shame in her eyes, and guilt rippled through his belly. He knew she hated taking money from him, knew how embarrassed she was by her lack of cash, and he had deliberately used that knowledge to hurt her. Even worse, she was still trying to be nice to him. He was an asshole.

"More than enough. Thank you. I'll see you tomorrow," she said.

She turned away, and he said, "Sid, wait I -"

"Hey, Sydney."

Sydney smiled at the tall, thin man suddenly standing beside her. "Hi, Chad."

Grayson scowled as the intern hesitated and then hugged her briefly. "How are you?"

She gave him another warm smile. "I'm good, thank you. How are you?"

He shrugged. "I can't complain. You're not getting into any more bar fights, are you?"

She laughed. "Nope. I've been good."

"Good, good." He scanned her up and down for a minute. "If you need me to look at the scar, just let me know."

Grayson cleared his throat, and Chad glanced at him.

"Evening, Chad." Grayson could hear the annoyance in his voice.

"Chad, you remember Grayson," Sydney said.

"I do." Chad held his hand out, and after a moment, Grayson shook it briefly. "How's it going?"

"Fine," Grayson said.

"Looks like you were just heading out," Chad said.

"He is. Bye, Grayson. I'll talk with you later." She turned

back to Chad, dismissing him completely, and thick jealousy rocketed through Grayson.

"Have a seat, Chad. What can I get you to drink?" Sydney asked.

"Just a beer, please." He scanned the bar. "Which section is yours?"

"This area is mine," Sydney said.

"Great." Chad smiled at Grayson and sat at the table. "I'll take Grayson's table since he's leaving."

Grayson gave him a tight smile that didn't reach his eyes. He turned to Sydney, but she had already disappeared towards the bar. He glared at Chad and stomped out of the bar.

He had only driven a few blocks when he had to pull the truck over. He shook with anger and jealousy and slammed his hands against the steering wheel. He had to get a hold of himself. He was acting ridiculous, and his inability to control himself around Sydney had him acting like a complete jackass to her.

He sighed and stared out the window, his breath puffing like smoke in the cold truck. He had only agreed to let her take an Uber home because watching her walk around in her tight tank top and skimpy skirt had driven him nearly mad with need.

Over the last four days, she had been careful to wear baggy clothes and little makeup whenever they were in the house together. He would have laughed if he hadn't been so frustrated. Although seeing her in her tight work clothes was driving him crazy, her attempt to look less attractive at home was pointless.

He didn't know how to tell her that it didn't matter what she was wearing – he had seen her naked. Christ, he had been *inside* of her. He knew how wet and tight she was, knew what it sounded like when she moaned his name with pleasure. It didn't matter what the hell she wore. He had half a hard-on - hell, a full-on erection if he was being completely honest - whenever he was around her.

And now she was at the bar by herself, men groping her every time she walked by them, and Chad, the Wonder Intern, sitting in her section. He muttered an expletive and turned the truck around.

# CHAPTER 15

S ydney glanced nervously at Grayson. Ten minutes after he had stormed out of the bar, he had returned. He sat in Belinda's section and ordered a whiskey. He had continued to order them over the last two hours.

"How many has he had?" she whispered to Belinda as she walked by.

"I've lost track," the brunette said. "Did you two fight?"

"Sort of," Sydney said.

She walked through the bar and toward the ladies' room. She was on bathroom duty this week and ducked into the ladies' room to check its state, breathing a sigh of relief when there was no vomit to clean up.

She was deeply tired, her feet and back hurt so much she could hardly walk, and she kept seeing the look on Grayson's face when he tossed the money at her. She had hurt him, but she didn't have a clue how. She thought he would be happy that she accepted his help for once.

She rubbed her aching lower back and headed out of the bathroom. Just twenty minutes and she could go home. She'd have to drive Grayson home. He was in no condition to drive. Lost in her thoughts, she didn't see Chad until he was directly in front of her.

She gave a small shriek of surprise as she ran face-first into his chest and stumbled back. She tripped over her feet and hit the floor ass first. Her ass screamed in protest, but her feet were positively singing with relief. She sat there for a moment, trying to decide if she should rub her butt or her feet before Chad reached down and helped her to her feet.

She winced as her feet throbbed again, and he patted her arms gingerly. "I'm so sorry, Sid. Are you okay?"

"Just fine. Nothing hurt but my pride."

She paused and reached behind her to rub her butt. "Well, maybe my ass."

She expected him to laugh, but he frowned. "You fell pretty hard, Sid, and this floor is solid. You could have cracked your tailbone. Here, let me feel."

He reached behind her, and she batted his hand away. "I'm fine, Chad."

He gave her a boyish grin. "You can trust me, Sid. I'm almost a doctor."

That made her laugh, and she let him turn her sideways. He pressed firmly on her lower back. "Does that hurt?"

She shook her head, and he moved his hand lower, pressing down on the top of her butt. She flinched a little, and he frowned again. "You should come to the hospital for an X-ray. It's probably just bruised, but better safe than -"

He was torn violently away from her, and she nearly fell to the floor again as Grayson shoved Chad against the wall. "Get away from her!"

Chad scowled at him and, with unexpected force, elbowed Grayson away. "Get your hands off me, asshole."

Sydney groaned. Chad was a couple of inches taller than Grayson, but Chad was thin, and Grayson was heavily muscled. He would flatten Chad in minutes.

Before she could step between them, Grayson growled. "Keep your hands off my fiancée's ass then."

Chad's mouth dropped open, and he stared at Sydney as she gripped Grayson's upper arm.

"You're engaged?"

"You didn't tell him?" Weaving back and forth, Grayson scowled at her.

Sydney gave him an impatient look. "No."

"Why not?" He took a step backward and nearly fell over.

Sydney pushed him back until he was leaning against the wall. "Because I'm *working*, Grayson, not socializing."

"You call letting him touch your ass working?" he said.

"Oh, for God's sake. I fell on my butt, and he thought I might have cracked my tailbone. He was being nice," Sydney said.

Grayson snorted and glared at Chad. "Bullshit."

Chad rolled his eyes. "Whatever, man. Sydney, I can drive you to the hospital for that X-ray."

"No thanks, Chad. I'm sure it'll be fine," Sydney said.

"If it still hurts after a couple of days, come by the hospital, okay?" Chad said.

"Okay."

He stepped forward, hesitating when Grayson stiffened and pushed away from the wall. He stepped in front of Sydney and stared at Chad. "You thinking of touching her again?"

"Stop it, Grayson. You're drunk and being a complete asshole," Sydney scolded. She moved around him and reached for Chad's hand, squeezing it firmly. "Thank you, Chad. I appreciate your help."

"Yeah, anytime. Do you need a ride home?"

"No. I'll drive Grayson home."

"That's right," Grayson drawled impudently. "We live

together now because we're *engaged*. She's sleeping in my bed tonight because we're *engaged*."

He wrapped his arm around her waist and kissed the side of her head with a loud smacking sound.

"She'll drive me home, and then we'll have sex because we're *engaged*," he said.

"Grayson!" Sydney elbowed him in the ribs, her cheeks heating up as Chad grinned.

"Yeah, well, just be careful. She could have a cracked tail-bone," Chad said.

"I'll be careful. She can be on top," Grayson said solemnly, and Sydney elbowed him again as Chad burst into laughter.

"Congratulations, Sydney. I hope you're very happy with him." He squeezed her hand and, still laughing, left the hallway.

The minute he disappeared, Sydney turned on Grayson. "What the hell were you -"

She squeaked in surprise when Grayson pushed her against the wall and pressed his body against hers. "You're mine, Sydney Wright. Do you hear me? Mine."

He gave her a searingly hot kiss. His tongue pushed between her lips, and he raked it through her mouth. He tasted heavily of whiskey, and she moaned despite her anger with him. It had been four days since she had been close to him, and her body melted into him as she returned his kisses frantically. He raised her arms above her head and pinned them against the wall.

"You won't let your fiancé touch you, but some random asshole can?" he growled into her ear.

"Chad's a friend, and he was checking that I hadn't hurt myself," she gasped as he nipped at her earlobe.

"That skinny jackass wants to be more than friends." He tasted her neck with his tongue.

"It doesn't matter. I'm not interested in Chad." She rubbed herself against the obvious bulge in Grayson's jeans.

He kissed her again, sucking her tongue into his mouth and pressing his erection against her. He was still holding her arms above her head, and as he trailed hot kisses down her throat, she glanced up. Desire flooded through her body at the way his hard hands looked wrapped around her wrists.

"Sid, the bar's closed. What are you -" Belinda's mouth dropped open when she entered the hallway. "Whoops! Sorry!"

Sydney pulled free of Grayson's grip and walked toward her.

"I see you've made up," Belinda laughed as Grayson staggered after Sydney. He took Sydney's hand, and she led him out into the bar and pushed him into a chair.

"Stay there while I cash out, and then I'll drive us home."

"Yes, honey," he said meekly before tipping his cowboy hat at Belinda. "Ma'am."

* * *

"Why didn't you tell him we're engaged?" Grayson asked.

"Why didn't you tell me you're a friggin' millionaire?" she countered.

He stared moodily out the truck's passenger window at the dark trees whipping by. "I didn't think it mattered to you. Does it?"

"No, it doesn't," she said.

"Now that you know, will you let me help you pay for college?" He gave her a hopeful look, and she sighed.

"No, Grayson. I told you, I already owe you too much."

He snorted in reply and rested his head against the window.

"You still haven't told me why you didn't tell Dr. Love back there that we're engaged."

"I thought it would be better to keep our engagement quiet since it's not real. The less people that know, the less awkward it will be when we end it." She gave him another glance, confused by the hurt on his face.

"Plus," she said, "I don't know anything about you. We're engaged, but I don't even know when your birthday is, what your favourite colour is, or anything that engaged people are supposed to know. I've already been tripped up a couple of times by Belinda. The more people who know we're engaged, the more questions I'll be asked that I can't answer."

"October fourth and blue," he replied. "When's your birthday?"

"February twenty-sixth."

He was quiet, his head nodding back and forth on the window, and she thought he might have passed out when he began to speak quietly.

"My mom died when I was six. A car accident. It was dark and raining, and a deer ran out in front of the car. When I was eight, GG moved from the guesthouse back to the farm-house with my dad and me. He had begun to drink heavily by then, and she never came right out and said it, but I know she was afraid for me."

She gave him a sympathetic look, but he was still looking out the passenger window. "I hated him by the time I was ten. GG tried to tell me he acted that way because he missed my mom, but she was wrong. He was mean and nasty before my mom died. I suppose it's hard for a mother to think badly of her child, and so GG used my mom's death as a reason for his behaviour. When I was fourteen, he started beating me whenever he got drunk, which was pretty much every weekend."

He glanced at her. "But you already knew that."

She nodded. "I remember the bruises from the locker room."

"Frank, our lead hand, was running the farm by that time. When my dad wasn't drunk, he was holed up in his room doing God knows what. I helped a lot before and after school, and Frank taught me how to run the cattle farm. He also kept Dad off my back as much as he could. He was a good man, and he's why GG and I are so well-off now. If it had been left to Dad, we would have lost everything."

"What happened to him?"

"He died when I was in my last year of high school. He had a heart attack in his sleep. I cried for weeks. He was more of a dad to me than my own father ever was."

"I'm so sorry, honey," she said.

"After Frank died, Dad really started cranking out the beatings. He was drunk nearly every day by that point."

"I can't believe you didn't run away."

"I was going to, but I was still working up my nerve to leave when I came home from school one day to see GG sitting in the kitchen with a bloody nose and black eye. Dad was sitting across from her, drinking a beer and acting like nothing was wrong."

He laughed bitterly. "GG tried to tell me she fell down the stairs. As if I would believe that with the drunken motherfucker sitting right there with her blood still on his knuckles."

"What happened then?" she asked.

He looked at her, and she shrank back from the fierce light in his eyes. "By then, I had started to fill out some, and he had gotten soft from years of drinking and sitting on his ass. I told him to get out, and he just – just sneered at me and told me I was a spoiled little pussy. He took a swing at me, and then I beat the bastard into a coma."

"Oh, honey." She turned into the farmhouse's driveway and shut the truck off before staring silently at him.

"GG pulled me off of him before I could kill him. She sent me to Alan's house for the night. He was my best friend in high school - still is - and then she called the police. She told them that he had gotten drunk and tried to kill her, and she had protected herself with a cast iron frying pan."

He stared down at his tightly closed fists. "When Dad woke up from the coma, he confirmed her story – why, I don't know - and because neither of them pressed charges, the whole thing was dropped."

She wanted to slide across the seat and put her arms around him, but she cleared her throat instead. "What happened then?"

"He never touched GG or me again, although he continued to drink steadily. I moved to the guesthouse and continued to work the farm. Three years later, he was dead from a combination of liver failure and a heart attack, and we were free."

"I'm very sorry, Grayson."

He stared out the windshield. "It was a long time ago. I wanted to be a professional basketball player when I grew up."

"I'm sorry?" The sudden change of topic had her blinking in surprise.

"When I was a kid, I thought I would play professional basketball. I used to practice constantly, and I wasn't bad."

"Is that why there's a basketball court behind the barn?" she asked.

He nodded. "Yeah. GG had it built for me as a surprise. Do you think Emma would like to learn to play basketball?"

She smiled. "You could ask her."

"I hate eggs. Hate them. Just the smell of them cooking makes me sick to my stomach. I want to get a tattoo, but I'm afraid of needles. I broke my right ankle when I was twelve because Alan dared me to jump out of the hayloft, and I was stupid enough to do it."

He smiled a little. "I screamed bloody murder, and Frank came running into the barn. His face went white, and his hands shook so badly he could hardly carry me to the house. He scolded me the entire time for being so dumb and then nearly passed out himself at the hospital when they set the bone."

He gave her a shy look. "I like to sing karaoke."

She giggled, and he blushed but continued on gamely. "My first crush was Becky Wellens in second grade. I tried to kiss her at recess, and she punched me in the stomach and then ratted me out to the teacher."

"My first real girlfriend was Donna Smith. I dated her for most of high school, and she was the first girl I slept with. I loved her more than she loved me. I asked her to marry me after high school, and she said no. She said she wanted to go to university and make something of herself. She couldn't stand the thought of being tied to a farm and living the rest of her life in our small town."

He shifted a bit in the seat. "After she dumped me, I dated a girl named Alison Moore. Nothing serious. She wanted more, but I didn't, and eventually, she started up with some guy in the rodeo. A couple of years later, I sold off all the cattle on the farm and told GG I wanted to travel. I travelled for a year and realized I missed GG and my home. So I came back. I'm thinking of getting into the cattle business again. I can't sit around forever doing nothing, and raising cattle is what I know. I'm good at it, and I enjoy it."

"Then you should do it." She smiled at him.

"Yeah." He yawned, and she glanced at her watch before opening the driver's door. She slid out of the truck, slamming the door shut and wincing at the pain shooting through her feet as she hurried around to the other side of the truck.

Grayson had already opened the door and was wobbling out of the truck. He stumbled and nearly fell, grabbing on to Sydney for support.

"C'mon, cowboy. You need to go to bed."

"Hey, there are two of you now. Nice," Grayson mumbled.

She tucked her arm around his waist and led him into the guesthouse and down the hall to Emma's bedroom. She helped him out of his jacket, swept his cowboy hat off his head and then pulled his t-shirt over his head, her mouth going dry at the sight of his lean torso. He sat heavily on the bed, and she bent over and picked up one foot. He grinned like a little boy and stared shamelessly down her tank-top at her breasts as she yanked at his boot. It finally came loose with a small grunt of effort, and she repeated her efforts with his left boot.

"C'mon, Grayson, stand up for a minute." She tugged on his arms, and he stood obediently. She reached for his belt buckle, unbuckling it quickly before unbuttoning his jeans and pulling down the zipper.

"Why, Ms. Wright, what kind of guy do you think I am?" He wiggled his eyebrows at her. "I don't know what you've heard, but I'm respectable."

"Uh-huh." She shoved his jeans down his hips, ignoring his growing erection as she pushed him gently onto the bed and pulled his jeans free. She tucked him under the covers, and he sighed and closed his eyes.

She ran a cool hand over his forehead. "Good night, Grayson."

His eyes popped open, and he grabbed at her hand. "You're so pretty, Sydney. I love your mouth and your hair and your eyes and your breasts."

She laughed. "Thanks, Romeo. Now, go to sleep."

He didn't let go of her hand. "It was my turn to talk too much tonight, wasn't it?"

"No. I liked it."

"I'm sorry I was such an asshole to you tonight, Sid. It hurt my feelings that you were so anxious for me to leave the bar."

She stroked his forehead again. "I didn't want you to leave. I felt bad that you had to wait for me all night."

He sighed and muttered something she didn't hear. "What was that?"

"I like waiting for you," he mumbled.

She dropped a soft kiss on his cheek. "Good night, Grayson. Sleep tight, don't let the bedbugs bite."

He turned on his side and began to snore softly, and she crept out of his room and down to her room. She turned on the shower and undressed quickly before stepping into the shower. She let the hot water run over her sore and weary body and did her best not to think about Grayson.

# CHAPTER 16

G rayson rubbed his aching head as he moved quietly down the hallway. It was still early on Sunday morning, but he had woken with a terrible taste in his mouth and a throbbing headache. He had brushed his teeth and taken a long hot shower until the pain in his head had started to recede, and he felt mostly human again.

He had only a vague recollection of what happened last night. He knew he had tried to beat up Chad for touching Sydney, and he was pretty sure he had told Sydney about his old man, but everything else was a confusing blur. Something about his first crush, Becky, and basketball and maybe karaoke.

He rubbed his head again and said a silent prayer that he hadn't told Sydney about his love for singing karaoke. He stopped in front of her room and listened carefully. It was quiet, and he wasn't surprised that she was still sleeping. The last three days had tired her out, and then she'd had to deal with his drunken ass. He was an idiot.

He started past her door, but a loud thud came from her

room, and her muffled curse stopped him in his tracks. "Sid? Are you okay?"

She didn't answer, and he knocked briefly before opening the door. "Sid?"

Sydney sat cross-legged on the floor. Her bedhead was so epic in size that it looked like she had been electrocuted, and she was rubbing her right foot, her mouth drawn down in a little moue of pain.

"Sydney? What's wrong?"

She looked up at him, and his brow furrowed at the dark circles under her eyes.

"Nothing's wrong."

"There's something wrong with your foot. Did you step on something?"

"No. They're just sore," she said.

He started towards her, and she scooted toward the bathroom on her butt. "It's fine, Grayson. They'll toughen up."

He scooped her up and carried her back to the bed. "This is ridiculous, Sydney. You can't even walk."

"I can walk," she protested. "I just wasn't expecting them to be that sore this morning."

He dropped her in the middle of the bed and opened the nightstand drawer.

"What are you doing?"

He didn't answer, rifling through it and grunting with satisfaction when he found a small tube of body lotion.

He sat on the bed and squeezed some lotion into his hand before pushing up the pant leg of her flannel pajamas and pulling her foot into his lap.

"Grayson, I don't need -"

Her protest turned into a long moan of pleasure as he rubbed the bottom of her foot with firm strokes.

"Oh my God," she groaned as he massaged and circled and rubbed the lotion into her foot. She fell back on to the

kay!" Emma crowed with delight before pushing her
o the side of her plate.

at those too, honey," Sydney urged her.

mma made a face. "I don't like peas. They're gross."

ist try a couple," Sydney coaxed. "You might like them

Jope, I won't," Emma said cheerfully.

nable to stop himself, Grayson ruffled Emma's hair.
t else did your dad say, Emma Lou?"

Grayson, it doesn't matter," Sydney said.

e ignored her and smiled at Emma, who was piling her
into a small mountain on her plate. "Emma?"

don't know." She shrugged disinterestedly. "He asked if
and Mama kiss in front of me. And he asked me if you
in the same bed."

he brightened. "I told him yes, and that Mama let me
in the bed with you after I had a bad dream, and that
wear shorts and not pajamas, and that Mama has really
hair when she wakes up."

he stared solemnly at Sydney. "You do, Mama."

ydney smiled at her. "I know I do."

Will the horse baby be in the barn tomorrow?" Emma
d Grayson.

He shook his head. "No, honey."

"Next time I visit?" she asked hopefully.

No, but I won't be home the next time you visit, so you'd
e to wait anyway."

Sydney gave Grayson a startled look as dark thunder-
ids rose on Emma's brow. "I thought you liked playing
h me."

"I do, Emma Lou." Grayson patted her arm gently. "But I
e to go out of town to look at some cattle, and I won't be
k until after your visit."

"When do you leave?" Sydney asked.

bed, her arms stretched above her head and her body
twitching with pleasure as he continued to massage her foot.

"Ohhh..." She gasped sharply, and he stopped.

"Did that hurt?" he asked.

"Oh God, do not stop, Grayson. Please," she begged. "It
hurts in a really good way."

He laughed and rubbed her small foot for a few more
minutes before reaching out and snagging her left foot. She
moved it eagerly into his lap, her whole body tensing as he
squeezed more lotion into his hands. At the first touch of his
fingers, she arched off the bed a little bit, another moan of
pleasure escaping her lips as her hands grabbed the side of
the bed above her and squeezed tightly.

Watching her move on the bed, listening to her small,
breathless groans of pleasure, he was not surprised to
discover that he had a raging hard-on. He took a deep breath
and kept her foot away from his crotch.

"God," she breathed. "You have no idea how good this
feels. Seriously, it's better than sex."

"Sweetheart, if this feels better than sex, he wasn't doing
it right," he said dryly.

She snickered and then gave another breathless moan
when he ran the ball of his thumb firmly down the middle of
her foot.

"Is it getting better?" he asked.

"Yes, thank you so much." She smiled sweetly at him, and
something in his chest tightened with pleasure. He wanted to
kiss her, hell, needed to kiss her, and his hands tightened
around her foot.

She swallowed at the look on his face. "Grayson -"

"Just one kiss, Sydney. That's all I want. One small kiss."
He pulled her toward him when her cell phone rang on the
nightstand.

She twisted out of his grip and sat up, smiling nervously

at him before answering the phone. A large grin crossed her face. "Hi, sweetie. Yes, today is the day you're coming over. I know - I'm excited, too."

She inched past him and put her feet down on the floor. She stood and stepped forward gingerly before turning, giving him a thumbs-up, and mouthing "thank you".

"Hmm? What was that, Emma? I'm not sure. I can ask him. Right now? Okay, just a minute." She turned to him. "Emma wants to know if you're coming with me to pick her up?"

He nodded. "Of course."

She smiled happily. "He says yes. Yup, you can see the kittens again." She wandered to the bathroom, and Grayson stood and slipped out of her room.

\* \* \*

"Mama, are you knocked up?" Emma asked.

Sydney coughed and choked on the water she was drinking. Grayson was getting up to thump her on the back when she finally controlled the coughing fit and stared wide-eyed at Emma.

"Honey, where did you learn that word?"

"I heard Daddy talking to Monica. He said that you were marrying Grayson because you were probably knocked up. He said you probably tricked Grayson like you tricked him because you need money and because you want custard."

Sydney could feel her face reddening, and she didn't dare look at Grayson as Emma speared a piece of pasta and popped it into her mouth.

"What do you mean by custard, Emma?" Grayson asked quietly.

"You know – custard." Emma waved her hand vaguely. "Daddy said Mama wants my custard."

Grayson pressed his lips together. "L of you?"

She shrugged. "I don't know."

Grayson gave Sydney a look of disgus "Don't let him get to you."

"What kind of trick did you play ( asked, chewing the pasta slowly.

Sydney forced herself to smile. "I did Daddy, honey. He was making a joke to Mo

"Oh." Emma speared another piece of p into her glass of milk before putting it in he

Sydney snuck another look at Grayson. her, his eyes dark and glittering with ange give him what she hoped was a calming smi

"Mama?"

"Yeah?"

"What does knocked-up mean?"

Sydney sighed and put down her fork. to say a baby is in your tummy. Most people knocked-up though – they say they're pregn

Emma looked at her and then at Grayson delightedly. "There's a baby in your tummy? I want a boy baby! How did it get in your tu it get out?"

"Honey, slow down." Despite her ang Sydney couldn't help but grin at Emma's entl isn't a baby in my tummy. Daddy was maki Monica, remember?"

Emma's face fell. "But I want a baby." She edge of her pink cast.

Grayson patted her arm. "One of the h barn has a baby in its tummy, Emma. Whe born, you can name it, and I'll teach you how it, okay?"

"Thursday morning. I won't be back until the following Tuesday." He gave Sydney an apologetic look. "Sorry, I should have told you sooner."

She tried to shrug nonchalantly. "That's fine. Emma, why don't you get your colouring books from your room? I'll colour with you as soon as I'm done tidying up the supper dishes."

"Okay, Mama." Emma slid out of her chair and skipped out of the kitchen as Sydney stood and silently put the leftovers in plastic containers.

Grayson started to load the dishwasher. After a moment, he said, "I should have mentioned the trip before now."

"Don't be ridiculous, Grayson. You're not obligated to tell me anything. It's all good."

Feeling weirdly upset, she said, "It does seem like a long time to be gone just to look at cattle, though."

He poured the rest of Emma's milk into the sink and placed the glass in the top rack of the dishwasher. "I'll be visiting with an old friend as well. It's a friend I haven't seen in a while, so I figured I would take a few extra days to visit."

"Oh, that's nice." She smiled brightly at him before putting the plastic containers in the fridge. She had to grit her teeth to stop asking him if the old friend was a woman. What if he said yes? What would she do then? Ask him if they were friends with benefits? It was none of her business, and she had no right to feel the surge of jealousy she was feeling now.

She had told him repeatedly that she couldn't sleep with him. She didn't get to be angry or upset if he found someone else who would. Her stomach twisted painfully, and she slammed the fridge door harder than necessary.

He shut the dishwasher door. "What's wrong?"

"Nothing." She scrubbed at a splash of pasta sauce on the counter before blurting out, "What's your friend's name?"

"Mitch." Relief washed over her in a hot rush.

He stepped a little closer. "Did you think it was a woman I would see?"

"I hadn't thought about it," she lied.

He grinned. "You're a terrible liar, Sydney."

She ignored him and scrubbed a little harder at the counter.

"Maybe you should kiss me goodbye. It seems like the type of thing that a jealous fiancée would do."

"I'm not jealous, and you don't leave until Thursday," she pointed out.

"True. This could be a practice one," he said, dipping his head toward her.

Disappointment flooded her body when Emma came barrelling back into the kitchen. "I'm ready, Mama.

Sydney sat next to Emma at the table, staring blankly at the colouring book in front of her and ignoring her urge to kiss Grayson.

* * *

"SID, WAKE UP." A SOFT VOICE AND HARD HAND SHOOK HER awake. She peeled back the covers and stared blearily at the alarm clock.

"Grayson? What's wrong?"

"Nothing. My Uber is here, and I wanted to say goodbye."

She sat up, pushing her hair out of her face and shivering in the cool morning air. "I told you I would drive you to the airport. Why didn't you wake me earlier?"

He reached out and tugged gently on one blonde curl. "You're working thirteen hours today. You need all the sleep you can get."

He shifted a little closer. "I don't want you driving your car. Use my truck, okay? I filled it with gas and left more money in the cupboard above the stove. And don't walk from the bar to the truck by yourself after your shift. Ask Mark or Frank to walk you to the truck. Promise me."

"I promise." She yawned.

"I've left Alan's number on the fridge. If anything goes wrong, or you need anything, call him."

"I don't even know him," she protested.

"That doesn't matter. He knows who you are and can be here in less than twenty minutes," he said.

"Grayson," she patted his arm, "I'll be perfectly fine. I've lived on my own for a long time. I can handle any problems."

"I know." He hesitated and then cupped her neck and gave her a soft and gentle kiss.

"Sorry," he said against her lips. "I know I'm not supposed to."

He stood and strode across the room.

"Grayson!"

He looked back at her. "Yeah?"

"Have – have a good trip. Be careful," she said.

He smiled. "I will. See you Tuesday."

# CHAPTER 17

Sydney stepped out of the bath and wrapped the towel around her body. Shivering a little, she went into her bedroom and sat on the side of the bed. Emma had left tonight to return to Jacob's, and Sydney already missed her.

She listened to the quietness of the house. Although she had lived here for nearly a year alone, after only a few weeks of having Emma and Grayson in the house, it already felt strange to be alone.

Normally, she enjoyed her own company but only felt lonely and blue tonight. Grayson wouldn't return until tomorrow, and as she stood and turned on some music, she told herself that she was not excited about him coming back.

*And I will not make a fool of myself by inviting him into my bed.*

She turned the music up until the sound blared in the room, and the walls practically vibrated, and she dropped her towel at the foot of her bed. Naked, she moved to her dresser and reached into the top drawer for some underwear.

She paused and then lifted a stack of her panties, staring at the red box that was hidden beneath them. She looked around guiltily and then tipped the lid off the box, pulled the collar out, and ran her fingers along the buckle. She took a deep breath, looking around again before lifting the box from the drawer. *It wouldn't hurt to try it on. Just to see what it looked like.*

Ten minutes later, she stared critically at herself in the mirror. The corset was maybe a bit too snug, she decided. Even just a few weeks of eating regularly helped her regain some of the lost weight.

She had chosen to try the corset without the shoulder straps, and she frowned and reached beneath it to tuck her boobs more firmly into the cups. The corset squeezed her slender waist and pushed her breasts up until they were high little mounds on her chest. Her nipples were nearly showing, and she readjusted her boobs again, wondering if they were supposed to be practically overflowing out of the cups.

Probably, she thought, thinking about her push-up bra and how much it had generated in tips for her. She rolled her eyes before twisting and looking behind her. The corset had come with a tiny red thong that barely covered her crotch, and she stared at her ass. The store clerk had been right, she decided. The extra weight had gone straight to her ass and boobs.

She swayed her hips in time with the music as she leaned forward and stared at her throat. A dark spear of pleasure pierced her lower belly, and her pelvis throbbed as she looked at the collar. It fit around her slender neck perfectly, and as she ran her fingers across the soft leather, her nipples tightened beneath the fabric of the corset.

She had pinned her hair on top of her head before her bath, and some strands had fallen free to curl around her face and neck. They brushed against the leather of the collar, and she ran her fingers over the silver buckle at the back.

*It looks good*, she thought hazily. Another surge of pleasure went through her, and she could feel the wetness between her legs. *No foreplay needed. If Grayson were here, he could just –*

She cut that thought off. Thinking about Grayson wasn't a good idea. Even if he was here, she had told him nothing could happen between them.

She ran her hands down the lace-covered bodice of the corset. For the first time, she wished she owned a vibrator. Her entire pelvis was throbbing and aching now, and she closed her eyes and permitted herself to relive the memory of Grayson's cock sliding deep inside of her.

*Jesus, girl, get control. Now, you're just deliberately torturing yourself.*

She opened her eyes and reached for the front fasteners on the corset when the red scarves in the box caught her attention. She picked up one, feeling the silky smoothness between her fingertips as she brought it to her face and rubbed it against her cheek.

She hesitated and then wrapped the scarf around one wrist before putting her hands behind her back. She took the other end of the scarf and awkwardly wrapped it around her other wrist, holding the ends with the fingers of one hand. She pulled tightly on it and looked in the mirror. Having her hands behind her had made her back arch a bit, and she arched it even more, pulling the scarves as tight as she could with one hand and admiring the way the position pushed both her chest and her ass out.

What would it feel like, she wondered, to have her hands tied firmly behind her back while Grayson touched her, kissed her, and slowly pulled the corset from her willing body?

The song ended, and she had enough time to hear the soft groan behind her before the next song blared into life. Her heart thumping wildly, she whirled around, staring straight into Grayson O'Reilly's shocked gaze.

* * *

GRAYSON STARED SILENTLY AT SYDNEY. EARLIER, AS HE HAD taken an Uber from the airport to the farm, he had hoped that Sydney would still be awake despite how late it was. He had even pictured her giving him a welcome home hug, maybe brushing her mouth across his cheek. He had pictured her doing this in her shapeless blue flannel pajamas, rolling his eyes a little at the realization that flannel pajamas were now considered a turn-on for him.

He hadn't expected to enter the house and hear the loud beat of the music blaring from Sydney's room. The pictures on the wall vibrated, and he shook his head with a small grin as he dropped his suitcase in the hallway. She was awake, and he had kicked off his boots and shrugged off his jacket. It wouldn't hurt to say a quick hello. Her bedroom door was open, and he ducked into her bedroom, the greeting dying on his lips.

Her back was to him, and she stared at herself in the mirror. Instead of the flannel pajamas, she wore the red corset. It clung to her slender body, and his eyes dropped to her ass. She had gained some weight in the last couple of weeks, and her ass was even curvier than he remembered. She had her hands behind her back, a red scarf wrapped around her wrists, and he watched as she pulled tightly on the scarves and arched her back.

He groaned, and she whirled around to stare at him with wide, startled eyes.

His breath stopped in his throat at the sight of the collar around her neck. His cock, already starting to stiffen, turned into a pounding, throbbing, hard-as-a-rock erection immediately. He could feel it pushing against the worn fabric of his jeans as he stepped toward her.

She took a step backward. "What are you doing home?"

He didn't answer, couldn't answer. He couldn't stop staring at the collar around Sydney's neck, at the scarf holding her slender arms behind her back. He had never been so turned on in his life, and all he could think about was how badly he wanted, *needed*, to fuck her. He strode towards her, praying like hell that she wouldn't push him away.

She opened her mouth to say something, but he slanted his mouth hungrily over hers and thrust his tongue deep into her mouth. He explored the wet, hot, slickness of her mouth as she moaned and rubbed her tongue eagerly against his.

He reached behind her, tugging the end of the scarf from her fingers and then wrapping it around her wrist. He released her mouth and stared at her, the question obvious in his eyes. She nodded, and he felt another surge of pleasure go straight to his cock as he pulled the scarf tight, making her back arch, and tied it firmly around her wrists.

He bent his head and trailed kisses down her throat before tugging lightly on the collar she wore with his teeth.

"Do you know how often I've lain in my bed and pictured you wearing this?" he whispered into her ear.

"Grayson," she moaned.

"Of course, it's the only thing you wear in my fantasies." He grinned wickedly at her before bending and kissing the tops of her breasts.

"You don't like the corset?" she asked.

He ran his hands over the fabric. "I like it. I just prefer to have you naked when I'm fucking you."

She bit her bottom lip, and he shook his head. "No, let me."

He sucked her lip into his mouth, pulling on it gently, then not-so-gently as she moaned. He reached around her, his hands grazing over her restrained ones before he cupped her ass and pushed her against him. She could feel his erection against her belly, and she whimpered as he squeezed her ass firmly.

He stroked the tops of her breasts, watching as she pulled helplessly at the scarf before he reached for the small silver fasteners at the front of her corset. He undid them quickly and pulled the fabric from her body, dropping it indifferently to the floor. He stepped back and looked down at her, his eyes darkening with desire. He had never wanted anyone so much in his entire life, and he stripped quickly before reaching for the impossibly small thong she wore. He pulled it down her legs and off her feet, tossing it to the floor as well.

She moaned at the feel of his chest against her breasts. Her nipples were hard and poking into his chest, and he cupped one breast in his large hand, her nipple a hard pebble against his palm.

"Grayson, please," she begged as he bent his head and licked first one nipple, then the other. He licked and teased them with just the tip of his tongue as she squirmed and pulled uselessly at her restraint.

"Please, what?" he asked hoarsely.

"I need – I want you to..." She trailed off, her face flushing, and he grinned at her.

"This?" He took her nipple into his mouth and sucked hard on it. She cried out with pleasure, her body arching against him.

"Yes!" she cried, her head dropping back as he teased and tormented both her nipples.

Christ, if he didn't fuck her now, he would come all over her. With a muttered curse, he picked her up, groaning when she wrapped her legs around his waist, and he felt her wet heat rub against his dick.

He backed up and sat on the bed, arranging her on his lap

so that her knees were on either side of his hips. She was spread wide open, and he reached between them, grabbing his cock and rubbing it against her as she whimpered above him. He positioned his cock at her opening and pushed just the head in. They both moaned, and she leaned forward, trying to take more of him into her. He grabbed her bound arms and pulled her back. She groaned in frustration and tried to wiggle free of his grip, but he was much stronger than her. He pushed a little further into her, watching her face as he filled her.

"Look at me," he demanded.

Sydney opened her eyes obediently, and he groaned as her muscles clamped down on him. "Jesus, Sid, you're killing me. Stop doing that."

"I can't help it," she moaned. She wiggled on top of him, pulling at the scarf around her wrists and trying to push forward and take more of him into her.

"Grayson, stop teasing me! I need -"

She cried out as he thrust upward, pushing her down at the same time until the entire length of his thick shaft was sheathed in her.

"Oh, oh, oh..." she gasped repeatedly as she stretched around his thick, hard length. He waited a few minutes, gritting his teeth and staring grimly at a spot on the floor until he was sure he wouldn't come.

He reclined on the bed and stared up at Sydney. She was straddling him with her arms still bound behind her. He had pulled the scarf tightly enough around her arms that it forced a continuous arch to her back. Her nipples were hard and swollen from his mouth and teeth, and he watched her breasts sway gently as she squirmed on top of him. His eyes lingered on the collar for a long moment before he reached up and tugged lightly on it.

"I like seeing this on you," he confessed.

She swallowed hard, the collar shifting gently with the motion.

"Do you like wearing it?"

She closed her eyes, her cheeks turning pink, and refused to answer.

He pinched her nipples lightly with the tips of his fingers. She cried out with pleasure, and her back arched further, her pelvis grinding down onto his.

He sat up again, steadying her when she nearly tipped over, and cupped her throat, running his thumb over the soft leather.

"Do you like wearing it, Sydney?" he breathed into her ear before following the curve with his tongue. She moaned and pushed her breasts against his chest, rubbing her nipples against his chest hair before bouncing up and down on his lap.

He let her move for a few seconds, fiercely controlling his need to come as she bounced and wiggled and rubbed against him. When he sensed she was close to coming, he forced her to stop, easily holding her steady on his lap with one large arm around her waist.

"Grayson, please," she moaned softly.

"Tell me if you like wearing the collar," he said. "Tell me if you like being tied up with this soft red scarf, if you like having my cock inside of you, and then I'll fuck you."

"Yes!" she cried immediately. "Yes, I like it. I like all of it."

He thrust into her, and she made a cry of pleasure, her body tightening around his again. He groaned and reached behind her, quickly untying the scarf from her wrists. The moment she was free, she wrapped her arms around his neck and, using his shoulders for leverage, rode him hard.

He tugged lightly on the collar around her neck, forcing her mouth down on his as he slid his hands into her hair. He held her firmly as she parted her lips, and he thrust his tongue in and out of her mouth, mimicking the movement of his cock.

She rode him harder and faster, searching for her release until, with a short, loud cry, she stiffened against him and came. He could feel the surge of wetness, feel the agonizing pleasure of her inner muscles clenching around his cock, and he echoed her cry, his hips thrusting upward as his orgasm tore through him.

# CHAPTER 18

S he woke the moment he glided his tongue over her. It was dark in the room, but she didn't need light to know that it was Grayson's dark head between her legs, Grayson's fingers parting the lips of her pussy, Grayson's tongue flicking against her suddenly throbbing clit.

"Grayson!" she cried out.

"Yeah, Sid?" His voice was muffled, and her breath exploded from her mouth in a loud moan when he sucked on her clit.

"That – that feels so good," she gasped.

"Good." He kissed the inside of her thigh before moving her legs up over his shoulders. He cupped her ass with his big, hard hands and lifted her to his mouth again.

"Oh my God," she moaned, her hips arching and her heels digging into his back. She had never had a man go down on her before. Jacob had never shown any interest in it and hadn't even seemed that enthusiastic about her going down on him. He had been very much a standard missionary-style type of man, or what Belinda referred to as a "vanilla lover", and now the brand new sensations Grayson created with his lips and tongue were nearly driving her mad with excitement and need.

As his tongue flicked and teased and danced across her wet and swollen clit, she clenched the sheets in her hands until, with a loud cry and her thighs tightening around his head, she came fiercely. She fell back on the bed, the pleasure pulsing through her and filling her with a lovely type of warmth, and was only vaguely aware of Grayson flipping her onto her stomach.

Grayson covered her small body with his large one. He had pushed her thighs apart, and his cock was sliding into her before she had even recovered from her orgasm.

"Ohhh!" She moaned with pleasure as he thrust hard into her. She was trapped under him, his hard chest rubbing against her sleek back and his hot, hurried breath blowing into her hair, and she loved it.

He pushed harder as she moaned his name repeatedly. Each downward thrust made her voice cut out a little as he plunged in and out, bouncing her on the mattress.

To her surprise, she could feel another orgasm starting, the tingling starting in her toes and moving up her thighs. Before she could come, Grayson stopped and pulled out of her, kneeling behind her. She cried out with frustration and need.

"Get on your hands and knees, Sid," he growled.

She hesitated briefly. Being fucked on her hands and knees had always played a prominent role in her fantasies, but she had never actually tried the position. The one time she asked Jacob if he wanted to try it, he looked at her like she had sprouted a second head.

"Now, Sid." Grayson's hard hands were on her hips, pulling them up, and she was left with no choice but to move into the position. He caressed her ass for a moment and then pushed her legs further apart. He nestled in behind her, his cock sliding across her slit and then straight into her tight opening.

They both moaned, and Sydney tightened involuntarily around him as he shoved himself in to the hilt, his pelvis slapping against her ass. He groaned a curse and reached around her, cupping one small breast and teasing the nipple with his thumb.

"Relax."

He trailed wet kisses down her spine, smiling a little at the tattoo on her lower back as she panted harshly.

"Relax, honey," he coaxed.

"I'm trying," she gritted out. She had no idea why this was happening. She mentally told herself to relax, but her pussy continued to grip Grayson's cock tightly. Her entire body was tingling and throbbing. She had been so close to coming, and it felt like every nerve ending in her body screamed with the need for relief.

Grayson's hand slipped between her legs, his fingers pushing past her wet pussy lips to find her equally wet clit. He rubbed with firm pressure, and her ability to form coherent thoughts was lost. She climaxed almost immediately, screaming his name and arching her back as the pleasure consumed her small body. Her muscles first tightened and then eased around him, and he moved in and out of her, making a low groan of delight every time her soft ass slapped against his pelvis.

Shaking from her orgasm, she locked her arms and held herself upright on her hands and knees, pushing her hips back to meet each of Grayson's strokes. He swept her mass of hair to the side. She still wore the collar, and he moaned at the sight of it and thrust harder. He pressed roughly on her upper back, and she buried her upper body into the mattress obediently, lifting her ass high into the air and widening her legs.

Holy fuck, she was going to come again. She couldn't understand her body's reaction, but there was no denying the climax building inside her.

"You feel so good, Sid," Grayson whispered as he slid in and out of her.

His hands clamped down on her hips, and she reached back and wrapped her small hand around his wrist, holding his hand against her as she panted and thrust back against him. With a thin bird-like cry of pleasure, she stiffened and came. Her body shook as she held his wrist with fierce determination. He thrust into her a few more times and cried out hoarsely as he climaxed in her.

* * *

"Grayson?" Sydney's voice drifted out of the darkness.

"Yeah?" His hand continued to trace lazy circles on her bare back.

"I'm sorry."

"For what?"

She leaned over him and turned on the bedside light. The dim light illuminated the room, and he smiled at her.

She gave him a tentative smile in return, but when she tried to sit up, he pulled her closer. She rested her arms on his chest and stared at him.

"Why are you sorry?" he asked.

She shrugged uncomfortably. "For leading you on and being a tease."

"Why would you think you're a tease, Sid?"

She sighed. "Because I told you repeatedly that we couldn't have sex, and yet…"

"Here we are having sex?" Grayson trailed her hand down her smooth back to her ass and squeezed it gently.

"Yeah." She hesitated. "It's just – I've wanted you for a while now. I've had a crush on you since you rescued me in the locker room."

He squeezed her ass again. "I've wanted you too. And you're not a tease."

She sighed and rested her head on his chest, listening to his heart thump steadily beneath her ear. "I thought you weren't back until tomorrow."

"I decided to come back a day early."

She kissed his chest gently and said, "Did you have a good visit with your friend?"

"I did. And I purchased some cattle."

"You did? That's great! You must be excited."

"I am," he said with a cute grin. He traced the collar that was still around her neck. "And I'm very glad I came home a day early. I would have missed my chance to see you in this."

She blushed bright red and buried her face in his shoulder. Now that some of her lust for Grayson had been satiated, she was embarrassed by her behaviour. Fantasizing about being tied up and fucked was one thing, but she never thought she would go through with it. She shivered a little. The look in Grayson's eyes when he had caught her in the collar had made her lose any inhibitions she might have had.

"Sid? What's wrong?" Grayson's voice rumbled in her ear.

She took a deep breath and made herself look at him. "Nice girls don't do stuff like this."

"I think you'd be surprised what nice girls do, Sid," he said dryly.

She stared at him doubtfully. She was starting to suspect that she was much more naive about sex than she thought. In one night, Grayson had already done things to her in the bedroom that Jacob had never done in nearly three years of dating.

"Why did Belinda give you this stuff as a gift?" Grayson asked.

"We were at that new store, 'Dirty Little Secrets'. Belinda wanted to buy something for Bill." She stared down at his chest. "I was wandering around looking at stuff, and the clerk caught me looking at the collar and scarves and assumed that I was, um, into the bondage thing. Then Belinda showed up, and I was holding the collar and the scarves, and she laughed and told me I was kinky. Then I dragged her butt out of there."

She hesitated. "Do you think I'm kinky, Grayson?"

She waited for him to laugh or tease her about her naivety, but he shook his head without a hint of amusement. "No, Sid. I think you're a normal, healthy woman with a normal and healthy appetite for sex."

She stared solemnly at him. "I used to think that I was pretty knowledgeable about sex, but now I'm not so sure."

"What do you mean?"

She blushed but carried on gamely. "Well, uh, we've already done stuff that I've never done before, and I'm..."

He gently tipped her chin up. "And you're what, Sid?"

"I'm worried that maybe you were disappointed, and I have much more to learn than I thought."

He flipped her onto her back and stared down at her. "Trust me, Sid – I was not disappointed. What happened between us was the best sex of my life. And," he leaned down and kissed the tip of her nose, "it would be my absolute pleasure to teach you anything you want to know."

She should have told him then that what had happened tonight was a one-time thing, but he was staring down at her, his eyes growing dark with desire, and she could feel his erect cock against her hip. Her need for him was a raging fire inside her, and she put her arms around his neck and pulled him closer.

"Should we start lesson one right now?" she asked.

His hands tightened convulsively on her hips, and he nodded. "Yes, I think we should."

# CHAPTER 19

"**D**addy!" Emma skipped up the sidewalk to where Jacob waited on the front porch. He smiled as she hugged his thigh.

"Did you miss me?" she asked.

"I sure did, sweetheart. Did you have fun with your mom?"

"Yep."

He nodded at Sydney, who was walking slowly up the sidewalk. "Why are you limping?"

"Sore feet," Sydney replied briefly. Grayson rubbed and massaged her feet nearly every night, but they were still painful. She sighed. After a month of working fourteen-hour days, she had thought they would have toughened up by now. Grayson pestered her nearly daily to quit her job at Dawson's, but she couldn't do it. In just over a month, she would meet with the judge to review Emma's custody arrangement. Everything had gone so well that she was confident that she would have no problem getting permanent custody of Emma.

The thought filled her with both an indescribable joy and

an incredible sadness. Winning at least partial custody of Emma had been her only dream for the last three years, but at some point in the last three weeks, her dream widened to include having Grayson in her life.

It was a good, small, sweet dream that she found herself returning to time and time again. When she was shelving books at the bookstore, when she was carrying heavy trays of food at Ivan's diner, and when she was avoiding the hands of her customers at Dawson's.

It was an easy enough dream to fall into. Living with Grayson *made* it easy. They had spent plenty of time together in her old four-poster bed, Grayson showing her all sorts of pleasure she had never even dreamed of, and they had shared stories and learned each other's likes and dislikes. They had fallen into a sweet and easy pattern in the last month. She was tired - working three jobs made it impossible not to be - and Grayson had been spending much of his time preparing the farm for the cattle arriving next week, but it had still been the best month of her life. It was so easy to pretend their engagement was real. Except they had never spoken about the future, and in less than a month, if all went well at Emma's custody hearing, they would be calling off their fake engagement.

She knew that Grayson cared about her. At least she was pretty sure – she had, after all, thought that Jacob had loved her and look how that had turned out – but his caring didn't mean he would be willing to carry on with their fake engagement once she had permanent custody of Emma.

Because of that, because of her uncertainty about the future, she wasn't willing to give up any of her jobs. As it was, she already knew there was no way she could return to college in January. Once they broke off their fake engagement and Grayson moved out, she would be paying rent to GG, plus paying back the lawyer fees, and her hospital bill to Grayson. She would need all three jobs to stay afloat.

"Guess what, Daddy?" Shrill with excitement, Emma's voice brought her back to the present.

"What's that, sweetheart?"

"Grayson let me ride a horse! He said I was really good at it and the horse liked me. And I got to pet the baby horse again. I named it Cinnamon, and Grayson said it was a good name. It sniffed me, and it tickled! Plus, there's another knocked-up horse, and Grayson said I could name that baby horse too!"

"Emma," Sydney chided gently, "we don't say knocked-up, we say pregnant. Remember?"

Emma nodded. "Okay, Mama."

She looked pointedly at Jacob, who flushed a little. "Kids pick up the craziest words, huh, Sid?"

"Yeah," Sydney said.

"Okay, Emma, kiss your mom goodbye. It's time for your bath."

"Wait, I gotta give Grayson a kiss goodbye too." Emma flew back down the sidewalk, her cast glowing brightly in the growing gloom, toward Grayson, leaning against his truck.

Jacob peered around Sydney and frowned when Grayson scooped Emma up and tossed her gently into the air. She screeched with delight and hooked her arm around his neck, kissing his cheek.

"I don't think it's safe for her to be on a horse right now, Sid. She has a broken arm, remember?" He scowled at her.

"Grayson was on the horse with her the entire time, Jacob. She had a helmet on and safety pads, and Grayson held onto her. She was safe," Sydney said.

"Yeah." Jacob stared again at Emma and Grayson. "C'mon, Emma."

Emma frowned. "Can I stay another night with Grayson and Mama?"

Jacob shook his head. "No, sweetheart. Say goodbye and come into the house."

Emma started to pout, but Grayson whispered something in her ear that made her giggle. She kissed him loudly on the cheek. "Bye, Grayson. I love you."

Sydney heard Jacob's sharp inhale and turned back to see him staring at Emma and Grayson with a hurt look. Before she could say anything, Emma skipped back up the sidewalk and latched on to her leg.

"Bye, Mama!"

Sydney crouched and hugged her. "Bye, Emma. You be good for Monica and your daddy, and I'll see you in a few days, okay?"

"Okay, Mama. I love you."

"I love you too, Emma."

* * *

SYDNEY STARED AT THE RED SCARVES IN THE TOP DRAWER OF her dresser. She reached out with trembling fingers and ran them along the smooth fabric. Grayson had taught her more things in the last month about her own body and sex than she could ever have imagined. They hadn't, however, used the scarves or the collar since that night he had come home to find her wearing them.

She was tempted to bring them out, to leave them on the bed and see what he said, but she was too shy. It was ridiculous, considering all the things they had done together. He had seen every part of her naked body up close and personal and had taken her in every position imaginable. She didn't understand why she was so shy about expressing her desire to be tied to the bed. He had already assured her that he was open to everything she suggested. She stroked the leather collar and wished again that she could tell him she wanted to be tied down and have him tease and torment her. She could feel her pulse quickening at the thought. What would it feel like to be helpless, to have no control over what Grayson did to her oh-so-willing body?

"Sid? You okay?"

She jumped and tried to shove the drawer shut, cursing under her breath when it jammed.

"Sid?"

She whirled around. Grayson was leaning against the open doorway and smiling at her. "Whatcha doin' over there?"

"Uh – nothing." She flushed brightly and tried to casually shut the drawer by leaning on it. It refused to budge, and she could feel the sweat on her forehead when Grayson stripped off his shirt and approached her.

"How was your bath?" He looked her up and down. His eyes lingered on her nipples, poking against the sheer fabric of her nightie and then at the area between her thighs.

"It was nice." She pushed again at the drawer as Grayson drew closer.

"I like your new nightgown, Sydney."

Sydney smiled and glanced at her body. Thursday, after her shift at Ivan's and before her shift at Dawson's, she met Belinda at 'Dirty Little Secrets.' She had found the sheer blue, baby-doll nightgown on the sale rack and couldn't resist buying it. Belinda had teased her gently, but Sydney had been undeterred. Her flannel pajamas were seriously unsexy.

"Thank you. It's not as warm as the flannel pajamas." She grinned at him.

"You don't need the flannels to keep you warm. I'll keep you warm," he growled playfully.

He was standing in front of her now, and she moaned

when he reached out and traced the outline of her nipple with one long finger. He stepped closer and kissed her lightly on the mouth. "I've missed you."

She smiled a little. "It was one night, Grayson."

She still wasn't comfortable having sex with Grayson while Emma was in the house. All Grayson had to do was touch her, and she forgot about everything else but how good it felt to be in his arms. Although she knew it was ludicrous, she couldn't shake her fear that something would happen to Emma while Grayson distracted her. She had been more grateful than she could say when Grayson had not pushed the subject and kept things strictly platonic on the night Emma stayed overnight.

"True," Grayson acknowledged as he pressed his lean body against hers. "But you have no idea how difficult it is to lie next to you and not touch you."

"I'm sorry. Thank you for -"

He shook his head. "You have nothing to be sorry about, Sydney. Emma comes first. Besides, it's not your fault I'm a horny son of a bitch."

She burst into loud giggles as he nuzzled her neck. "Actually, it might be a little bit your fault. You do tend to rub yourself against me while you sleep."

"I do not!" She blushed furiously.

He laughed. "Yes, you do. And I find it delightful."

He reached behind her and pulled the collar out of the open drawer. "Will you wear this tonight, Sydney?"

"Yes." She lifted her hair so he could buckle it around her neck. It felt good around her throat, and she liked how Grayson's eyes darkened with need when she wore it.

He kissed her skin just above the collar as she put her arms around his waist and leaned into him. A flash of red caught her eye, and she realized he had pulled the red scarves out of the drawer. He rubbed them against her bare shoulder, their silky smoothness sending tingles down her spine. He put his arms around her and kissed her, his tongue flicking against hers with sensual sweetness.

"Grayson," she sighed into his mouth and glanced at the scarves. Her gaze flickered to the bed posts, and she quickly dropped her eyes to Grayson's broad chest.

He kissed her forehead. "Tell me what you want, Sid."

"Grayson, I – "

"Tell me," he whispered when she hesitated.

She took a deep breath. "I want you to tie me to the bedposts."

She could feel the blush rising up her chest, and she closed her eyes for a moment before forcing herself to look at Grayson's face. She gasped a little. The look on his face was one of raw hunger and need, and her body throbbed in response.

"Would you – would you like that, Grayson?" She asked, already knowing the answer but needing to hear him say it.

"Yes." His voice was hoarse, and he cleared his throat roughly. "Yes, Sid. I would like that very much."

He took her hand and led her to the bed. She helped him out of his clothes, stopping to stroke his hard cock with one small hand until he was thrusting his hips against her. He tugged her hand away and raised her arms. He trailed his hands down the sensitive undersides of her arms before grasping the bottom of her nightgown, easing it over her head and tossing it on the dresser.

"Lie down, Sid."

Her stomach churned with nerves and desire, and she did as he asked. He took her right hand and kissed the palm of it gently before stretching her arm toward the bedpost. He wrapped the scarf around her wrist and tied it firmly to the bedpost.

"Okay?"

She nodded, and he picked up her left hand, transferred another gentle kiss to the palm of it and tied it to the other bedpost.

He gazed down at her outstretched and naked body. "You're so beautiful, Sid."

He stood and walked to the dresser. He rummaged in the top drawer, and her breath caught in her throat when he turned around, and she saw the feather in his hand.

He sat on the bed and leaned over her, kissing her lightly on the mouth. "Anytime you want me to stop, just say so, okay?"

She nodded her eyes on the large black feather in his hand. "Yes."

Her body jerked when he ran the feather down her bound right arm. It tickled, and she squirmed and giggled when he ran it over her underarm.

He stopped and grinned down at her, and she flushed a little. "Sorry."

"Don't be. I like it when you laugh." He ran the feather over her ribs, and she giggled again. She thought the feather would be more erotic, but so far, the feeling was nothing more than a tickling sensation.

He drifted it across her flat belly, and she squirmed when he circled her navel with it. It was still creating nothing more than a light ticklish feeling, and she was starting to wonder if maybe the feather just wasn't for her when he brushed it across her left nipple. A moan exploded from her throat as desire flamed in her belly. He repeated the motion, trailing the feather across her nipple until it was hard and throbbing.

"Grayson," she moaned quietly when he made lazy figure eights between her breasts before circling her right nipple with the tip of the feather.

"Yes, Sid?"

"That feels so good," she panted.

He circled and traced her nipples for what felt like hours. Each brush of the feather against her sensitive nipples sent a jolt of pleasure straight from her nipples to her pelvis. Her arms strained at the scarves, and she arched her back, light moans and gasps pouring from her mouth in a steady stream.

"Grayson, please! Your mouth – I need your mouth!" she finally cried.

He leaned down and sucked her nipple into his mouth, tracing it with his tongue like he had with the feather, and she cried out. He used the feather to tease her left nipple as his mouth and tongue teased her right.

Sydney could barely breathe. She wondered if it was possible to come from having her nipples touched alone. Her pelvis was throbbing and aching with a white-hot fire, and she didn't even realize she was pumping her hips back and forth.

She cried out when Grayson stopped touching her, but he was only moving between her spread legs. He lifted her leg and kissed her calf and then her knee before leisurely moving the feather in small circles over her shin and calf.

He moved it up to her thigh, running it lightly across her inner thigh up to her warm, wet pussy. She waited breathlessly for the light touch of the feather, but he didn't touch her with it. Instead, he brushed it across her lower abdomen and down to her other thigh.

"Oh my God! Grayson, please!" She pulled frantically at the scarves that held her captive as he smiled at her.

"Please, what, Sydney?" He circled the feather down her left leg.

"Please touch me," she begged.

"I am touching you." He ran the feather across the soft curls between her legs.

"Grayson!" She stared at him. "Touch me."

"Tell me where you want to be touched, honey." He leaned

over her and licked her flat abdomen, circling her navel and then blowing lightly on her wet skin.

"You know where," she groaned.

"Here?" He nibbled on her hip.

"No!" she gasped out.

"Here?" He eased up her body and nibbled the undersides of her breasts.

She rubbed herself against his chest. "Please, Grayson. I can't stand it."

He sat up and traced each of her ribs with the feather. "I want to hear you say it, Sid."

"Oh my God." She panted and bit her lower lip hard. "I – I can't."

"Yes, you can," he whispered as she bit at her lip again. He leaned over her and licked her mouth. "Don't do that, my love. You'll make yourself bleed."

He sucked gently on her lower lip, and she licked eagerly at his mouth. She had never been so turned on in her life. Everything Grayson said and did was only heightening her pleasure, and she panted and moaned and twisted against him.

"Tell me what you want, and I'll do it, honey," he said.

She pulled furiously at the scarves, exquisite pleasure radiating through her body when she realized she truly was helpless.

"Touch my pussy, Grayson," she moaned quietly.

"Whatever you want, Sydney." He ran his hand down her body and between her legs. He touched her clit with two delicate strokes, and she arched her back, her arms straining against her restraints, and swallowed back her scream of pleasure as she climaxed wildly.

She fell back against the bed, gasping for air as Grayson knelt between her legs. He grabbed her thighs roughly and entered her with one hard thrust. She cried out at the feel of his cock and squeezed her legs around his waist.

"Sydney, oh Sid, oh Sid," he panted.

He pounded into her small body, pushing her deep into the mattress as she arched her hips to meet his. After only a few minutes, he cried out and shuddered above her as warm wetness filled her core. He collapsed against her, and she gently kissed the top of his head.

He rolled off of her and quickly untied the scarves, freeing her from the bedposts so she could lie on her side beside him. He put his hand on her hip and pulled her closer as she rested her hand on his chest and felt the rapid beat of his heart beneath her palm. They stared at each other silently for a moment, both breathing heavily.

"Jesus, Sid," he finally said. "I'm sorry."

"For what?" she asked.

"I've never lost control like that. Did I hurt you?"

She shook her head immediately. "No. It was amazing, Grayson."

"Fucking amazing," he muttered, and she grinned at him.

"Have you ever done that with anyone else?" She had to know.

He shook his head immediately. "No - only you. Are you sure I didn't hurt you?"

She kissed him lightly. "I'm positive. I'd like to try it again."

He grinned at her soft blush and brushed some wayward curls from her face. "Give me ten minutes."

# CHAPTER 20

"God, that ring is so gorgeous, Sid." Belinda grabbed her hand and stared at the engagement ring.

Sydney smiled. "Thanks. Did I tell you it belonged to GG's grandmother?"

"You did," Belinda said. She glanced at her ring-less left hand. "Grayson didn't like you not wearing it at work, huh?"

"No." Sydney shrugged. "He didn't say anything about it. I just like wearing it, even if it makes my tips go down."

She ran her finger over the pearls that surrounded the diamond. She did like wearing it. It helped support her sweet little fantasy that what was happening between her and Grayson was real. She knew it wasn't, just like she knew that she would soon have to return the ring. Despite that, or perhaps because of it, she always wore it - even when working at the bar.

"Do you have Grayson's truck tonight?" Belinda lifted her tray of drinks, nodding her thanks to Greg.

"No. He's going to pick me up." Sydney heaved her tray of drinks from the bar and followed Belinda, ignoring her aching feet.

"He's so sweet," Belinda called over her shoulder before disappearing into the crowd gathering around the dance floor.

He *was* sweet - unbelievably so. He was kind and patient with Emma, helped GG with whatever she needed, rubbed her feet after every shift at the bar, and helped out around the house despite his busy schedule with the farm. He wasn't perfect – he tended to drop his clothes wherever and had an unhealthy obsession with college basketball – but he was a good man.

*Once he's done being a Good Samaritan with you, he'll make some lucky woman very happy,* her inner voice whispered snidely. She flinched and shoved the voice out of her head. It was late, she was tired, and she had a table full of rowdy out-of-towners who had no idea how to keep their hands to themselves. Sighing, she shifted the heavy tray and glanced at her watch. Half an hour to go – Grayson would be here anytime now.

"Sydney?"

She turned and stared thoughtfully at Jacob. "Hello, Jacob. What are you doing here?"

He shrugged and glanced around the bar with distaste. "I wanted to talk to you."

"So you came by my work? I could speak with you on Sunday when I pick up Emma." She frowned at him.

"I didn't want to talk to you with Emma overhearing. Do you have a minute?"

"I don't, actually. But if you want to wait half an hour, the bar will be closed, and I can speak to you then."

He nodded. "Yeah, that's fine."

"Do you want a drink?"

"No. Come find me when you're done."

She gave him one final, puzzled look before continuing to the table of out-of-towners. What on earth could Jacob want to talk to her about that he was willing to come to Dawson's?

"There's our little sweetpea. We were starting to think you'd forgotten about us, darlin'." The man was tall and lanky with a pot belly and a receding hairline.

She forced herself to smile. "Not at all. Just busy in here tonight."

She handed out the drinks as the man looked her up and down. "You sure you can't hang out with me after work, little sweetpea?"

She shook her head. "Nope. I already told you – I'm engaged."

"True," the man drawled. "But I ain't got a problem with dippin' my wick in another man's pot."

She gave him a thin smile. "Yeah, well, I do, and so does my fiancé. He's the jealous type."

"He ain't gotta know," the man crooned softly, putting his arm around her waist. "C'mon, sweetpea, why don't we head somewhere quieter? You can use those big lips of yours for something else other than talking."

"Watch your mouth, cowboy," Sydney said coldly, "or I'll get your ass kicked out of here. And get your hand off of me."

"Speaking of asses…" The man let his hand drift down to her bottom and gave it a firm squeeze.

Sydney sighed and looked around for Mark. He was at the far end of the bar and not looking her way. "Last chance. Move your hand, or I'll move it for you."

"A little bitty thing like you? I doubt it." The man laughed and stood up before pulling her hard against him. "Give us a kiss, sweetheart." He leaned his face down as Sydney struggled to free herself.

"C'mon, honeypot, just one little -"

"Take your fucking hands off her."

Sydney had never been so happy to hear Grayson's low

growl as she was at that moment. She twisted her head to look at him, and her heart rattled to a stop when she saw the anger on his face. "Grayson -"

"Get your hands off of her," he repeated.

The man sneered at him. "And if I don't?"

"I'll break them." Grayson removed his cowboy hat and set it on the empty table beside him. He stood silently, his face calm and his body relaxed, as he waited for the man to decide.

The man looked around at his friends before turning back to Grayson. "I'd like to see you try."

"Fine with me." Grayson stepped forward and pulled Sydney free of the man's grip.

"Grayson, honey, he's drunk. Please don't do this. Just walk away, okay?" Sydney pleaded.

He ignored her completely, and when she tried to use her small body to block him, he lifted her out of the way and set her aside.

"Grayson, please." Sydney turned and signaled frantically for Mark as the man stepped away from the table and toward Grayson.

The two men stared at each other, and the man turned to look behind him at his friends again. "Aww hell, this is going to be a piece of -"

He balled his hand into a fist and suddenly turned, swinging at Grayson in an attempt to catch him off-guard. It didn't work. Grayson was ready for him and he ducked under the man's swinging arm and charged him. He rammed his shoulder into the man's belly, knocking him backward onto the table. Glasses exploded and beer rained to the floor as the man's friends scrambled back from the table.

"Mark!" Sydney screamed as Grayson held the man down and punched him repeatedly in the face. Blood flew from the man's mouth, and he screamed pitifully as Grayson continued to ram his fist into his face.

"Grayson! Enough man! Enough!" Mark, his biceps bulging, grabbed the back of Grayson's shirt and struggled to pull him off the thinner man.

"I said enough, man!" Mark shouted and put his arm around Grayson's neck. He dragged him away as the man groaned softly and touched his battered face.

"Sid?" Belinda was suddenly standing beside her. "Are you okay?"

"Yeah," Sydney said shakily. "The guy wouldn't take no for an answer, and then he wouldn't let go of me, and then Grayson showed up."

The entire bar stared at them as Wayne charged out of his office.

"What the fuck is going on?" He shouted. He stared at the man still lying on his back on the table, blood pouring from his nose and mouth, and then at Mark with his arm wrapped loosely around Grayson's neck.

"Let him go, Mark," Wayne said as the man's friends helped him sit up.

"He attacked me!" The man gasped, pointing one shaking finger at Grayson. "For no reason."

"Liar!" Sydney shouted. She turned to Wayne. "Wayne, this asshole had his hands all over me and ignored me when I asked him to stop. Grayson told him to let me go, and he refused."

She ran to Grayson and wrapped her arms around his waist. "Are you okay? Are you hurt?" She stared up at him anxiously.

"No. I'm fine." He ran his fingers through his hair before jamming his cowboy hat back onto his head. He put his arm around her shoulders and tucked her against him as the man he had beaten up leaned over and spit blood and at least one tooth onto the bar floor.

"I'm suing," he said weakly. "I want this man arrested for assault."

"*Jesus wept!*" Wayne shouted and then clapped his hands together. "Get out, everyone. The bar's closing early tonight. Pay your tab and go home."

As the rest of the bar patrons gathered their things and left, Wayne turned back to Grayson and the out-of-towner. "Both of you come to my office. We'll have a drink and discuss this calmly. I'm sure we can all leave friends."

He turned and walked towards his office without looking at either of them. After hesitating, the man and Grayson, Sydney still clinging to him, followed him.

* * *

"You okay, Sid?" Grayson glanced worriedly at her as he drove them home.

"I'm fine. Are *you* okay?" she asked

"Yeah."

"Grayson, I love that you're so protective of me, but you really shouldn't have done that," she said softly.

He grimaced. "Do we have to talk about this, Sid? It ended fine. I'm not in jail, and the guy isn't suing."

"Only because Wayne told him I would charge him with sexual assault if he didn't," she said. "And the guy was just drunk and stupid enough to believe it."

Grayson winced at her anger. "The guy deserved it."

"I'm not saying he didn't, but there are better ways to solve these problems than with your fists."

"You're right. You're quitting the bar," Grayson said.

She glared at him. "Don't start that again, Grayson. I'm not quitting the bar."

"Sydney, this is ridiculous! You can't continue to work three jobs, and the bar is no place for a girl like you."

She snorted. "A girl like me? Trust me – I fit in just fine at the bar." Bitterness tinged her words. She didn't want to work at the bar, and she didn't want to become a career waitress, but she didn't have much of a choice. Going back to college to become a teacher was nothing more than a sweet dream.

"No, you don't. It doesn't matter – you'll have to quit in two months anyway. You'll be starting college in January."

She didn't say anything, and he glanced over at her. "Have you applied for your courses yet, Sid?"

"Not yet," she muttered.

He scowled. "You need to get on that, Sydney. There will probably be placement tests you have to take and meetings with a counsellor. You can't wait much longer."

"I know." She cleared her throat. "I'll look into it this week while you're out of town looking at cattle."

"Promise?"

"Yeah." She could look into it without actually applying for anything.

They drove in silence until they reached the farmhouse. Grayson shut the truck off with a sigh and stared at her.

"I'm sorry, Sid."

She sighed. "I know. And it isn't that I don't appreciate you defending my honour, Grayson. It's just that I don't want to be fired from this job."

He started to protest, and she put up her hand. "I know, I know – I'll be leaving in two months anyway. But for now, I need this job, okay?"

Grayson nodded. "Okay."

He stared out the window for a moment. "I don't want to fight tonight. I'm leaving tomorrow and will be gone the entire week. I don't want to leave with you angry at me."

"I don't want to fight either," Sydney admitted. She slid across the seat and leaned her head against his solid arm. "Grayson, I'm not angry with you. I -"

She grabbed his hand. "You're hurt!"

He glanced down at his scraped and swollen knuckles. "It'll be fine."

"Come on. There's a first aid kit in the guesthouse."

He stopped her before she could slide away from him. "I hate leaving you for this long, Sid. I'm going to miss you."

She kissed him softly on the mouth. "I'll miss you too. Let's clean up your hand, and then you can show me exactly how much you'll miss me."

He grinned. "You have yourself a deal."

## CHAPTER 21

"I could have dropped Emma off, Jacob." Sydney watched as Jacob picked up Emma and kissed her on the cheek.

"I know." He smiled down at Emma. "Honey, Monica is in the car waiting for you. Why don't you sit with her while I talk to your mom? Then we'll go for ice cream, okay?"

"Okay! Bye, Mama!" Emma blew her a kiss and ran out the door.

"Do you have a minute, Sid?"

"Yeah. Sorry, I know you wanted to speak to me on Saturday night. Things got a little crazy at the end of my shift," Sid said.

"I noticed." He sat in the kitchen chair and shifted uncomfortably as Sydney sat across from him.

"What's going on, Jacob?"

"I don't think Grayson is good for Emma," Jacob said bluntly.

"What?" Sydney stared at him in astonishment. "Grayson is excellent with Emma, and she loves him. He's all she's talked about this weekend."

"Emma is fond of everyone, Sydney. Grayson isn't that special to her," Jacob said sullenly.

She frowned. "That's not true, and you know it."

"Listen, Sid," Jacob said, "I don't want Grayson near Emma. He's dangerous, and his temper is too short. Who's to say he won't lose his temper with Emma like he lost it with that guy last night?"

Sydney would have laughed if she hadn't been so flabbergasted. "Are you crazy? Grayson would never lose his temper with Emma. He's always patient and sweet with her."

"I don't want him going near her anymore!" Jacob snapped.

Understanding hit Sydney in a hard rush. "You're jealous."

"I'm not jealous," Jacob said.

"You are. Emma loves Grayson, and it's the first time you've had to compete for her affection."

When Jacob didn't reply, she pressed on. "Jacob, you have nothing to worry about. Emma is very fond of Grayson, but you're her dad. She loves you to death, and nothing will ever change that."

Jacob flushed. "I told you, I'm not jealous of Grayson!"

"I get it, I do. Do you know how difficult it was for me when you started dating Monica? During every visit, all Emma did was talk about Monica. How much she loved her, how fun Monica was. It ripped my heart out, but eventually, I realized that Monica loved Emma, and I was happy she was in Emma's life. Emma has enough love for all of us."

"Monica is a hell of a lot better for our daughter than Grayson will ever be," Jacob snarled. "Emma loves her like a mother, and thank God for that because God knows her own mother is useless."

Sydney recoiled. "That's not fair. I made one mistake, and it was a long time ago. You can't punish me forever for that. I was young and scared and -"

"Listen, Sid, I don't care about that, okay? But I'm telling you that Grayson is not to have anything to do with Emma anymore. Keep her away from him. Do you understand?"

"I do understand." Sydney nodded. "But lucky for me, you don't get to tell me what to do."

"That's where you're wrong, Sydney," Jacob said softly. "You forget that what you have with Emma is only temporary. Either you break it off with Grayson and keep him away from Emma, or I'll ruin your chance of getting permanent custody of her."

"You can't do that," she said, the blood draining from her face.

"I can and I will," Jacob said. "Listen, I don't want to do this, but I will if I have to. The next court date is in less than three weeks. If you don't break off your engagement with Grayson, I'll tell the judge about Grayson's inability to keep his temper and that he's dangerous, and I'm worried for Emma's safety."

"One bar fight doesn't make him dangerous, Jacob. The judge will dismiss it entirely once we explain why he got into that fight." Sydney clenched her shaking hands together under the table.

"Maybe, maybe not." Jacob shrugged. "Do you want to take that risk? You already have so much working against you. You're broke, you're deeply in debt, your mother has a history of mental illness, and you've tried to kidnap my daughter before. Do you really want to add a fiancé with anger issues to the mix?"

Sydney could feel the tears starting, and she blinked them back fiercely. "Don't do this, Jacob. Please. Do you hate me that much? This will only hurt Emma."

Jacob stood up and brushed at some lint on his pants. "I don't hate you at all, Sydney. Why would you think that? I'm doing what's best for Emma, and what's best is that she has nothing to do with your fiancé."

He hesitated. "Listen, if you do this, I'll tell the judge I think you deserve permanent partial custody of Emma. I'll split it evenly with you, not just a couple of days a week."

"You bastard," Sydney said.

He gave her a hurt look. "I thought that would have made you happy, Sid. Isn't that what you want? To have Emma permanently?"

"Get out." She gave him a look of such smoking hatred that he blanched.

"Will you do what I'm asking?"

"Yes!" she shouted. "I'll do what you want, you goddamn son of a bitch! Just get the fuck out of my house!"

"There's no need to shout," Jacob said primly, leaving the kitchen. When she heard the front door close, Sydney buried her head in her hands and burst into tears.

* * *

GRAYSON OPENED THE FRONT DOOR TO THE GUESTHOUSE. "Sid? I'm home."

He dropped his suitcase in the front hallway and headed to the kitchen. He was dying to see her. Besides a few odd texts, he hadn't spoken to her all week. He had tried a couple of times to call, but it had gone to voicemail. He knew she was busy, but he was still a little hurt that she hadn't returned any of his calls.

He stepped into the warm light of the kitchen, a grin lighting up his face when he saw Sydney sitting at the table.

"Hi there." He leaned down to kiss her, stopping when she flinched back.

"Sid? What's wrong?"

"Sit down, Grayson. We need to talk."

He sat in the chair across from her and reached for her hand. She moved it away, and he realized with something like terror in his heart that she wasn't wearing his engagement ring.

"Sydney? Tell me what's wrong."

She blew her breath out in a shuddering sigh. "I'm leaving, Grayson."

He stared at her, dumbfounded. "You're what? Why?"

"I'm sorry. I wish I could explain, but I can't. Just trust me that this is the right thing to do, okay?"

"The right thing to do? Sid, I don't understand. What's going on? Everything was fine between us when I left, and now you're just done?"

"I'm sorry, Grayson, but I can't stay here with you any longer. Thank you for everything you've done for me. I promise you I'll start sending you money for the hospital bill and for the lawyer fees and -"

"I don't care about the money!" Grayson said. "Sydney, you can't just leave it like this. At least not without telling me why. You owe me that much, dammit!"

Sydney stared at her trembling hands. "The night of the – the fight in the bar, Jacob was there. He's threatening to tell the judge about it, threatening to tell him that you're dangerous and could hurt Emma."

His mouth dropped open. "I would never hurt Emma."

"I know," she whispered miserably. "This isn't about the bar fight. Jacob is jealous that Emma loves you and is using this to keep you away. But if the judge takes his side, I'll lose custody of Emma again. I can't – I'll go crazy if that happens."

"Honey, that won't happen. We'll explain what happened that night at the bar. The judge is a reasonable guy. He'll understand."

"And if he doesn't? I already have so many strikes against me. What if he looks at this as the final one?"

He didn't have an answer, and she smiled grimly. "Jacob said if I broke off my engagement with you, he would tell the judge that he would share custody of Emma with me. Permanent custody and not just two days a week – we would split it evenly."

"Do you believe him?" Grayson swallowed thickly.

She shrugged, looking so tired and sad that his heart ached for her. "I don't know. But I have to do what's best for Emma. And I believe - *I know* - that she needs me in her life. And I need her."

She squared her shoulders. "It's only a few weeks before we planned to end the engagement anyway, right?"

"Right," Grayson said quietly. "You have to do what's best for Emma. I get it. I'll move my things out tomorrow."

"I've already moved my stuff out."

He stared at her. "What? No! Sydney, you can stay in the guesthouse. You don't have to leave." He could feel the panic bubbling up in his throat. It would be bad enough not to be living in the guesthouse with Sydney, but not even to catch the occasional glimpse of her would be more than he could stand.

"Grayson, I can't stay here. You know that," she said softly.

"Where will you go?"

"I'll stay with Belinda and Bill until the next court date. They have a couple of extra rooms and don't mind that Emma will be there a couple of days a week. After I have more permanent custody of her, I'll find a place in town. It'll probably be better to be in town anyway. I have a feeling my car won't last much longer," she said.

"It's closer to the college as well."

"Yeah, it is." She wouldn't look him in the eye.

She stood and walked around the table. Gray kept his eyes on the worn wood. His hands clenched into tight fists in his lap as she paused beside him. She placed a cool hand on the back of his neck and squeezed lightly.

"Thank you again for everything. I'll always be grateful. Goodbye, Grayson."

There was a small clink as she placed the engagement ring on the table before him. He stared at the ring as she walked out the front door and out of his life forever.

# CHAPTER 22

"Grayson, wake up! Grayson! Get your butt out of bed right now."

Grayson groaned as a hard hand shook him out of his stupor. He squinted at the alarm clock beside the bed. It was two in the afternoon, and he had the mother of all headaches.

"Grayson!"

He blinked up at his grandmother. "What, GG? What's wrong?" He rasped out.

"Meet me in the kitchen. We need to talk."

She left the bedroom, and he sat up and rubbed his hand across his face. It scraped across his three-day beard, and he swung his legs over the side of the bed and waited to see if he was going to vomit. It wouldn't be the first time.

Sydney had walked out three weeks ago, and he had spent most of it self-medicating with copious amounts of alcohol. He was managing, just barely, to run the cattle farm that used to be so important to him but a shamefully large part of it was being taken care of by GG and Derek.

He groaned and staggered to his feet, gripping his head as

a bolt of pain skated through his skull. He wasn't even entirely sure what day it was. He thought it might be Saturday. He was almost certain that when the cab had dropped him in front of the guesthouse last night, the driver had said it was Friday, but the days were blurring together.

Once he was sure he wasn't going to vomit, he dragged himself to the kitchen. GG opened the curtains and held his hand up to block the light. "Could you close the curtains, GG?"

"Nope. This house needs some sun and some airing out. Sit down, Grayson," GG said firmly.

Grayson sat. He had learned at a young age that when GG used that tone of voice, there was no point in arguing with her.

"Boy, you look terrible. And you smell terrible, too," GG said disgustedly.

"Did you wake me up just to tell me I smelled, or is there something else you want to talk about?" he asked grouchily.

"Don't give me lip, Grayson."

"Sorry, ma'am," he muttered.

She stood and poured them both cups of coffee. She set the cup of dark, rich brew before him, and he took a cautious sip.

"Do you know how many times I sat across the table from your father and gave him coffee in a vain attempt to sober him up?" she asked.

He stared at her. "GG, I'm not -"

"You've always taken after your mama, Grayson. Did you know that? Not in looks – you take after your daddy in looks - but your personality was your mama's through and through. She was such a sweet woman. I know you don't remember her well, but everyone loved her. She was always willing to help out, always ready to give someone the shirt off her back if she thought they could use it."

She took a sip of coffee. "I was happy when you got that same sweetness. I was so proud of you and just damn thrilled that you weren't like your daddy. He was such a mean, miserable bastard. I know that's an awful thing to say about my own son, but he was an awful man, and there ain't no point in trying to pretend he wasn't."

She gave him a grave look. "And now I'm sitting here staring at you, and all I can see is your daddy. And not just in looks anymore, Grayson."

Grayson stared at her, wounded to the core. "How could you say that, GG?"

"Because it's the truth, Grayson, and you need to hear it. I spent enough of my life telling lies and covering up for your father that when he finally died, I swore I'd never lie again."

She reached out and took his hand. "I love you, sweet boy. You are the dearest thing in my life, and I will not watch you turn into the man your daddy was. I know you miss Sydney, but drinking yourself to death like your daddy did isn't going to get her back."

"It's too late, GG," Grayson said miserably. "I screwed up, and being with me could cost Sydney custody of Emma. Jacob said he would tell the judge that -"

GG held up her hand. "I know the story, Grayson. Your Sydney told me everything before she left."

"Then you know we can't be together," he said.

She snorted. "Listen, Ricky might be a fancy judge now, but I've known that man for years. As a teenager, he got into more than his fair share of bar fights. He's not the kind of man who will look at one bar fight where you were protecting her mama as a reason to keep Emma away from Sydney."

"It's not just that, GG." Grayson rubbed at his throbbing head. "This whole engagement was fake, remember? Sydney has no reason to get back together with me. Jacob told her he'd give her permanent custody of Emma if she called off the engagement."

"You and I both know that snake in the grass won't keep his word." GG slammed her hand down on the table, and Grayson winced as the sound reverberated through his aching head.

"GG -"

"Here's what I know, Grayson O'Reilly. I know that you love Sydney and that she loves you too. If you don't go and fight for her, don't tell her exactly how you feel and ask her to marry you for real this time, you'll regret it for the rest of your life. Even if she says no, which she won't, you'll have had the chance to tell her how you feel about her."

"I do love her, GG. So much." Just saying the words lifted a huge weight from his chest that he hadn't realized was there.

"I know, sweet boy. I know. Now, go and tell her." GG smiled at him and squeezed his hand as he stood up. "But first – take a shower and shave. You smell like a dead skunk that got dragged through the mud."

* * *

"Hello, Belinda."

"Hey, Grayson." Belinda looked at him warily as he sat down at the bar.

"Why are you behind the bar tonight?"

She shrugged. "Greg's on a break. What can I get you to drink?"

"Just a soda." He looked casually around the bar. For a Saturday night, it was surprisingly quiet. Only a few tables were taken, and no one was dancing on the dance floor. Of course, it was still early. He didn't see Sydney and wondered if she was on a break.

"She's not here, Grayson." Belinda put the soda down in front of him.

"What do you mean? Did she quit?"

Belinda shook her head. "No. She's sick tonight."

"Sick? Is she okay? What happened? Did she -"

Belinda laughed and held up her hand. "Relax, big guy. She has a bad cold. She came into work, and after about two hours, Wayne sent her home. She put up a fuss about it, but Wayne wouldn't take no for an answer."

She leaned against the bar. "Why are you here, Grayson?"

He opened his mouth, and the truth came spilling out. "I love Sydney, and I want her to know."

Belinda smacked him hard on the shoulder. "Finally! Christ, Grayson, you're damn lucky you're good looking because you've been a right idiot for the last three weeks."

He blinked at her in shock, and she grinned again before lowering her voice. "Sydney told me everything. She got drunk one night and just spilled her guts. From what she told me, it was obvious that you two are in love with each other. I've been waiting two weeks for you to get your ass in here and confess your love for her. It figures it would happen the night the poor girl went home sick."

She swiped a rag across the top of the bar before brightening. "Did you bring the ring with you?"

"Yes." He blushed a little, and Belinda smiled before pulling a pad of paper from her apron pocket. She scribbled something on it and handed it to him.

"What's this?"

"My home address. Bill's not home. He's at a conference this weekend, so you've got her all to yourself. Go tell her you love her."

\* \* \*

SYDNEY SNEEZED AND BLEW HER NOSE BEFORE SINKING DEEPER into the couch. She had fallen asleep for a few hours and thought she might feel marginally better. She sighed. She shouldn't be surprised that she had finally gotten sick. She had been running herself ragged for the last few months, and her body could only take so much.

She flipped channels aimlessly. She would have Emma tomorrow, and she hoped she was feeling better. She would only have her for the day because Monday was the day she would be back in court. Her stomach churned nervously. She'd tried again to fire Martin, but he refused. He had insisted that there was still plenty of money left on the retainer that Grayson had given him, and after only a few minutes, Sydney had given in.

She had left Grayson, destroying her heart and her only chance of happiness, and she couldn't stand the thought of losing Emma, too. She needed Martin, so she swallowed her pride and let him continue to represent her. She already owed Grayson a bunch of money. What was a few thousand more?

Grayson. She did her best not to think about him, not to worry about him, or wonder how he was. It was impossible. During the day, he was always there, lurking in the back of her head, and she dreamed of him at night. She blew her nose again and shut off the TV. Would she ever stop missing him?

The doorbell rang, and she sank deeper into the couch, pulling the blanket over her head. Who the hell would be dropping by at nine at night? No one for her, that's for sure.

The doorbell rang again, and she grumbled to herself. She threw back the blanket and climbed off the couch. She pulled self-consciously at her flannel pajamas and turned on the hallway light as she limped toward the front door. She looked through the peephole in the door, stretching onto her tiptoes to reach it, and her breath stopped in her throat.

Grayson was standing in the doorway, looking handsome as ever in his cowboy hat and tight jeans. She looked around frantically and thought about creeping back to the living room.

"Sid? I know you're in there. Let me in," Grayson called through the door.

Dammit! She caught a glimpse of herself in the hallway mirror. She looked terrible. Her nose was swollen and red, there were dark circles under her eyes and her hair – oh God, her hair. She tried to flatten it down, but her blonde curls refused to be tamed.

"Sydney, let me in," Grayson said.

Sighing, she opened the door. "Hello, Grayson." Her voice was raspy from her cold.

He smiled at her, the smile that she had grown to love, and she felt her knees weakening and her pulse speeding up.

"Hi, Sydney. Can I come in?"

He didn't wait for her to reply, just shouldered past her and closed the door gently. He looked her up and down, and she blushed.

"Back to the flannels?" he said with a small smile.

"I have a cold," she said stupidly.

"I know. Belinda told me." He hesitated. "You look beautiful, Sid."

She laughed. "Yeah, thanks. Um, come into the living room. Can I get you something to drink?"

Frowning at how she limped, he shook his head and followed her down the hallway and into the small living room. She stared nervously at him, clasping her hands behind her back, and waited for him to say something. The silence ticked on, and she grew more and more nervous. Her hands were sweating, and she could feel sweat breaking out on her forehead.

Unable to stand it any longer, she cleared her throat. "What are you doing here, Grayson?"

"I love you, Sydney," he said in a low, clear voice.

Her mouth dropped open, and she stared at him in bewilderment.

"Sydney? Say something, honey. Please," he said.

She closed her mouth and opened it again, and he gave her an encouraging look.

"I – I..." She suddenly grabbed a tissue and sneezed explosively into it. The force of it nearly knocked her small body over, and he rushed over and grabbed her arms.

"Sydney, will you please say something?"

"Say it again," she said.

"I love you," he said.

She burst into tears and pulled out of his arms, stumbling away and nearly falling onto the couch. He followed her, his heart dropping to his stomach, and sat beside her. Her hands were over her face, and each sob that tore out of her throat was like a knife to his heart.

"I'm sorry, Sid. I should have told you earlier. I know this doesn't change anything. I know we can't be together, but I need you to know I love you. Please don't cry, honey. Please. I never meant to hurt you, and I should never have forced you into this fake engagement thing. I only did it because I wanted to be close to you, and I thought -"

"Grayson, be quiet." She brushed the tears from her face and wiped her nose. "I love you too."

He cupped her face. "Say it again."

"I love you, Grayson." She hiccupped and then started to cry again.

He pulled her into his embrace, planting kisses all over

her red, puffy face, and whispered repeatedly, "I love you, I love you, I love you."

She pushed him back onto the couch and curled up against him. "I've missed you so much."

"I missed you too, honey."

They sat silently for a while, Sydney sniffing and wiping her nose occasionally until she lifted her head and smiled at him. "What made you confess your love?"

He kissed the tip of her nose. "GG. She told me to straighten up and tell you I loved you, and I always do what GG tells me."

"Thank God," she sighed.

He shifted down the couch and pulled her feet into his lap. He rubbed the bottom of them with his strong hands, and she moaned with a combination of pain and pleasure. "Oh God, I've really missed that."

He pulled lightly on her foot. "I'll pretend you aren't just using me for the foot rubs."

"Sure, whatever you say, honey," she groaned.

He rubbed her feet, listening to her soft sighs of pleasure, before he squeezed them lightly. "Sid, we need to talk about Emma."

She shook her head. "We'll make it work, Grayson. It was wrong of me to let Jacob use Emma to dictate how I live my life. I love Emma, she's the most important person in my life, but I love you, too, and you are just as important to me. We'll fight for custody of her together. On Monday, we'll convince the judge that I deserve both of you in my life."

"We could keep it hidden until after the court date." He was trying to be casual, but she could see the anxiety on his face.

"No. I won't hide how I feel about you for a minute longer. Besides, even if we did hide it, Jacob would find some other reason to keep me from getting custody of Emma. I won't allow him to control us any longer. Emma will be thrilled to see you tomorrow."

He smiled. "I don't want to hide anymore either, Sid, but I should probably use tomorrow to get things back in order at the farm. I went a little nuts without you for the last three weeks. And if things don't go well with the judge, tomorrow might be your last unsupervised day with Emma. You should spend it alone with her."

She smiled at him. "Tomorrow won't be my last day with Emma, but I understand needing to finish the farm stuff. But you should know that Emma has missed you terribly, and she'll be thrilled to see you next weekend."

"I've missed her too. I love that crazy kid." Grayson smiled.

"I love that you love her, and I love you, Grayson O'Reilly," Sydney said.

Her eyes widened when he slipped off the couch and onto one knee beside her. "I love you too, Sydney."

He reached into his pocket and pulled out the engagement ring. "Will you marry me? For real this time?"

Happiness flooded through her, and she held out her hand. "Yes, Grayson. I'll marry you."

He slipped the ring onto her finger and then kissed the palm of her hand. She tugged her hand free. "You need to stop kissing me, cowboy. In case you haven't noticed, I have a terrible cold.

He kissed her forehead. "I did notice."

"Yeah, the red and swollen nose makes it hard to hide."

"I love your nose." He kissed the tip of it before sitting on the couch beside her.

"Honey, there's something else we need to talk about."

She gave him a curious look. "What?"

"Your debt."

She flushed and looked down at her hands. "Grayson, I promise I'll work hard and pay it down. I -"

"Stop, Sid. I meant I want you to let me pay off your debt so you can attend college in January."

"I can't let you do that. It's my debt, not yours."

He kissed her knuckles. "I want to do this, Sydney. Not to sound arrogant, but your debt won't even dent my bank account. Plus, I want you to be happy. Finishing college and becoming a teacher will make you happy, won't it?"

She nodded as hot tears dripped down her cheeks.

"Don't cry, honey." He wiped at her tears.

"Thank you, Grayson."

"Does that mean you'll let me pay it off?"

She nodded and then squealed when he stood and lifted her off the couch, spinning her around.

"Which way to your bedroom, honey?"

She kissed his neck. "Down the hall, last door on the right, but we can't do this. You'll catch my cold."

"It's worth it." He winked at her and then paused. "Unless you're not feeling well enough? Shit – I'm an idiot. You need sleep, not sex."

He carried her to her bedroom and placed her carefully on the bed. He started to tuck her in, and with surprising strength, she pulled him down onto the bed beside her. She kissed his neck, her hands unbuttoning his shirt, smiling at his low groan.

"Sid, you need rest."

"I need you," she said. "I've missed you."

"Oh God, Sid," he moaned as she slipped her hand inside the front of his jeans and gripped his rapidly hardening cock.

"Are you sure?"

"I'm positive." She straddled his hips and smiled down at him. "Just no kissing on the mouth. I'm not giving you my cold."

He ran his hands over her flannel pajamas. "Well, you are making it difficult to resist. You know how sexy I find your flannels."

She giggled as his hands went to the buttons on her shirt. "I aim to please, cowboy. I aim to please."

# CHAPTER 23

"So, we're here to discuss the custody matter of Emma Louise Young." Judge Hawkins looked over his glasses at Sydney and Martin. "I assume everything has gone well in the last three months?"

"Yes, Your Honour," Martin said.

The judge turned his attention to Jacob and his lawyer as the courtroom door opened, and Grayson slipped inside. He sat down in the front row behind Sydney, and she turned to give him a quick, confident smile.

"Does your client agree, Tobias? There's no issue with giving Ms. Wright permanent, partial custody of the child?"

"Actually, Your Honour." Jacob's lawyer cleared his throat. "Ms. Wright has recently called off her engagement with her fiancé Grayson O'Reilly and moved out of the guesthouse she shared with him. She's now living in a rented room in the house of one of the servers from the bar. Because she's once again alone and without family to help, not to mention her previous track record of kidnapping Emma, my client feels it would be best if Ms. Wright went back to supervised visits.

At least until Ms. Wright proves she can provide her child a stable home life."

The judge frowned. "Is this true, Martin? Is your client no longer engaged to Mr. O'Reilly?"

Martin stood. "No, Your Honour. It's not true. Ms. Wright is still engaged to Mr. O'Reilly."

"She's lying!" Jacob stood and stared furiously at Sydney. "This is ridiculous! She's not with Grayson O'Reilly!"

The judge banged his gavel. "Mr. Young, sit down!"

Jacob's lawyer pulled him back to his chair as Judge Hawkins peered at Grayson. "Mr. O'Reilly, are you engaged to Ms. Wright?"

Grayson stood. "Yes, sir, I am."

The judge frowned at Martin. "Then why is Mr. Young insisting that your client is not engaged?"

Martin shrugged. "I have no idea, Your Honour."

"Bullshit!" Jacob jumped to his feet again. "She's not even living with him!"

"Mr. Young, I will not tell you again to sit down. I don't appreciate the language or the outbursts."

Tobias stood and pushed Jacob violently into his chair. He smoothed his suit jacket and straightened his tie. "Your Honour, Ms. Wright has been living with a co-worker from the bar for the last three weeks. She has not been -"

"She's been staying with a friend who's going through a rough time," Martin interrupted smoothly. "She's no longer engaged because she's helping out a friend? That's ridiculous."

"That's a lie, and you know it, Martin," Tobias said heatedly. "Numerous people will attest that Ms. Wright and Mr. O'Reilly called off their engagement. Do I need to call each one of them in to testify to that?"

"I think you need to start questioning your client's stories, Tobias." Martin smiled at him. "Considering that he tried to blackmail Ms. Wright into ending her engagement to Mr. O'Reilly by telling her she would never see Emma again if she didn't, I'm not entirely sure your client is trustworthy."

"I did not blackmail her! That idiot Grayson is dangerous for Emma. He got into a bar fight and nearly killed a man!" Jacob remained seated, but his face was bright red, and his lawyer kept a restraining hand on his shoulder.

Martin rolled his eyes. "That's ridiculous. He didn't -"

"Sydney told me she was breaking off her engagement to Grayson!" Jacob snarled. "She agreed that he was dangerous."

"Dangerous? Grayson O'Reilly has been a model citizen of this town for his entire life. His grandmother is -"

"We're not discussing Grayson O'Reilly's grandmother," Tobias said. "Could we try to -"

"Enough!" Judge Hawkins banged his gavel so hard that Sydney thought the end of it would fly off. "Martin, Tobias - bring your clients to my chambers now. You as well, Mr. O'Reilly."

* * *

JUDGE HAWKINS LEANED BACK IN HIS LEATHER CHAIR AND pulled irritably at his robe. "Well, this has certainly turned into a shit show, hasn't it?"

Sydney stared at the judge. She was so nervous she thought she would wet her pants, and she took Grayson's hand and squeezed it tightly. He squeezed it back and gave her his own anxious look.

He stared at Martin. "Explain to me what's going on, Martin."

Martin cleared his throat. "Your Honour, a few weeks ago, Sydney was attacked by a man in the bar. Mr. O'Reilly was there, and he stepped in and defended Sydney. He punched the guy a few times, and that was it. No charges were laid, and the man admitted he had gone too far. Two days later, Mr. Young told my client that he believed Grayson was a threat to Emma and demanded that she break off her engagement. My client, recognizing that Jacob was jealous of Grayson's relationship with Emma, naturally refused."

"Mr. Young continued to insist that she break off the engagement, and when Sydney refused, he threatened to take Emma away from her. When that still didn't work, he then promised to put in a good word for her with you and offered her permanent custody, split evenly between them if she would break off her engagement. This is simply because Mr. Young is jealous of Emma's affection for Grayson."

Judge Hawkins stared at Jacob. "Is this true, Mr. Young?"

"Your Honour, Emma is young and impressionable. Mr. O'Reilly is a bad influence, and I don't want -"

The judge held up his hand and sighed irritably. "Where is Emma right now?"

Jacob hesitated. "She's with my fiancée, Your Honour."

"Then I suggest you get your fiancée on the phone and have her bring Emma to my chambers, Mr. Young. I want to speak with her."

* * *

SYDNEY'S BREATH CAUGHT IN HER THROAT WHEN THERE WAS A soft knock on the door. They had been waiting nearly fifteen minutes for Monica to bring Emma, and she thought for one moment that she might throw up when the knock came.

"Come in," Judge Hawkins called, and Monica, looking nervous and uncertain, entered the room, leading Emma by the hand.

"Hello, Emma." Judge Hawkins leaned forward and smiled in a friendly manner at the young girl. "My name is -"

Emma shrieked in delight and dropped Monica's hand. "Hi, Grayson!"

She ran forward and leaped at Grayson. He gave a soft grunt of surprise and caught her, lifting her onto his lap as she wrapped her tiny arms around his neck and hugged him.

"Hi, Emma."

"I've missed you! Have you missed me?" the little girl asked excitedly.

"I have," he said.

"Mama says you've been busy working and that you're starting up the cow farm again. She said you would show me how to milk a cow when you weren't so busy!" Emma patted his face with her hand as Sydney said a brief prayer of thankfulness that she had been too chicken to tell Emma the truth about her and Grayson.

"I can do that." Grayson grinned at her.

"Did the other knocked-up horse have her baby yet? I'm going to name it Muffin. Daddy said that Muffin is a good name for a horse. Do you think it's a good name for a horse?" she asked.

"Muffin is a great name and nope, the horse hasn't had her baby yet."

Emma scanned the room. "Is GG here?"

"No, my love. GG is at the farmhouse," Sydney said.

"Hi, Mama. Grayson is here!"

"I know, honey." Sydney squeezed the little girl's chubby leg as she settled against Grayson.

Emma waved at Jacob. "Hi, Daddy."

"Hi, Emma." Jacob gave her a weak smile.

Emma stared at Judge Hawkins. She looked him up and down before staring up at Grayson. "Why is that man wearing a dress?"

Grayson snorted back soft laughter and kissed the top of Emma's head. "Um…"

Judge Hawkins grinned before staring at Sydney and Jacob. "I guess I don't need to speak with Emma to find out if she likes Mr. O'Reilly or living at the farm. It seems clear to me."

He folded his hands on his desk. "I've made my decision. Ms. Wright's temporary custody of Emma is now permanent. And," he eyed Jacob shrewdly, "since Mr. Young seems so eager to share custody of Emma with Ms. Wright, I'm upping her custody rights to three and a half days a week. You'll split the week evenly with Ms. Wright. Do I make myself clear, Mr. Young?"

"Yes, Your Honour," Jacob said stiffly.

Sydney could feel tears sliding down her cheeks, and she squeezed Grayson's hand so tightly that her knuckles went white.

"Congratulations, Ms. Wright," the judge said briskly. "Case dismissed."

# EPILOGUE

"Are you scared, Mama?" Emma peered at her from the circle of Grayson's arms.

"A little, honey." Sydney smiled at her daughter as Grayson handed her a small bag. "What's this?"

"Your lunch." Grayson kissed her lightly on the forehead. "I've put an apple in there. Don't trade it for junk food with the other kids in the cafeteria."

She laughed and wrapped her arm around his waist, leaning against him as he tucked Emma's scarf more firmly around her neck.

"Good luck on your first day of school, honey." He kissed her and stepped back as she climbed into the truck and shut the door. She rolled down the window and stuck out her head.

"Give your mama a kiss, Emma."

The little girl leaned forward and kissed her loudly on the lips. "Have fun, Mama!"

"Thank you, honey."

The little girl turned to Grayson. "Can we go and see Muffin now?"

"Yup." Grayson kissed her cheek, which was red from the cold, and then leaned into the truck and kissed Sydney.

"I'll see you tonight, Sid," he said. "We'll do something special to celebrate your first day at college."

She shivered at the sweet promise in his voice and smiled happily at him. "I'm looking forward to it, cowboy."

Keep reading for an excerpt of The Rancher's Daughter

# THE RANCHER'S DAUGHTER
## EXCERPT

He didn't recognize her at first. He had checked her out, of course, just like every other man in the bar had. She was hard to miss in that tight, short skirt. The combination of her heels and skirt made her legs look impossibly long.

She obviously was not used to heels. Even he could see the way she wobbled a little on them as she shifted from foot to foot and tossed her long blonde hair nervously. It made her cute in an awkward, newborn colt kind of way, and if there hadn't been a cluster of men already standing around her, he would have considered buying her a drink.

He sat back in the booth and took a drink of beer, studying the way the skirt clung to her ass. She was curvy in all the right places. He smiled a little. He liked curvy. Always had and always would. There was something about a full ass, large breasts, and a nice round tummy that made his blood hot.

He took another sip of beer. He knew exactly where the attraction came from. His childhood babysitter, and his first crush, was a girl named Betty. She carried an extra forty pounds on her small frame, and she was soft and sweet with large breasts and wide hips. He'd loved her fiercely, and his ten-year-old heart was broken when her family moved away.

He finished his beer, briefly considered muscling his way in beside the other three men standing in front of her, and then stood and jammed his cowboy hat on his head. He would be better off to head home. Tomorrow was going to be a long day, and besides, a man pushing forty was too old to be picking up women at the bar.

He crossed the crowded bar and took one final look at the blonde's ass before heading toward the door. One of the men standing next to her said something, and she laughed - a low and husky sound that he immediately recognized. The hair on the back of his neck stood up, and he twisted around to stare at the woman. It couldn't be - there was no way it was her. She didn't go to bars, and even if she did, she certainly wouldn't dress like that.

She laughed again, and his feet propelled him forward before his brain fully comprehended what he was doing. He grabbed the woman's arm, not failing to notice the firmness of her arm under her shirt, and spun her around.

"Hey! What the hell -"

She squeaked to a stop and stared up at him in shock. "What are you doing here, Thomas?"

He couldn't speak - hell, he couldn't breathe. She wore a loose shirt, but it was unbuttoned nearly to her navel. Under it, she wore a white bustier. The white material contrasted sharply with her tanned skin. He couldn't stop staring at the way the bustier hugged her large breasts like a lover's touch. Her breasts strained at the material, the tops of them barely covered by the bustier, and he wondered how long it would take before they simply busted free of the overstressed fabric.

"Thomas!" The woman said sharply. He dragged his eyes away from her exquisite breasts and up to her face.

"What am I doing here? What are you doing here, Evelyn? Does your father know you're here?"

"I'm twenty-eight years old, Thomas. I don't need my father's permission to go to a bar." She tugged at his hand. "Let go of me, please."

"No. I'm taking you home."

"Like hell you are," she said with a light whack on his broad chest.

He scowled at her. "This place is nothing but a meat market. I'm taking you home."

She snatched her arm free and teetered on her high heels. She would have fallen if he hadn't reached out and snagged her arm again.

"I'm not a child, Thomas. Stop treating me like one."

His eyes shifted to her breasts again. They rose and fell rapidly with her anger, and his dick stirred in his pants. Jesus, she definitely wasn't a child.

"Evelyn, you -"

"What gives you the right to tell me what to do?" she said before glancing over her shoulder at the men behind them.

"I'm your stepbrother," he said grimly.

"Ex-stepbrother. My dad divorced your mom three wives ago."

One of the men stepped forward and placed a meaty hand on Evelyn's shoulder. "Is there a problem?"

"No, not at all." Evelyn smiled sweetly at him. "Just give me a minute."

"Take your hand off her," Thomas growled at the man.

The man frowned but didn't move his hand. "The lady and I were just about to dance. I suggest you remove *your* hand, friend."

Thomas stared steadily at the man. He was tall like

Thomas. Although at 6'3", Thomas still had the height advantage, and he could tell the man was soft. He could see it in the man's manicured hand, in the expensive shirt he wore, and in the way his belly protruded over his belt.

"You would be wise, *friend*," Thomas said with a cool glance at the man, "to walk away."

The man hesitated and then removed his hand from Evelyn's shoulder before slowly walking away.

"Thank you so much, Thomas." Evelyn scowled at him. "God, you're such an ass."

Ignoring her insult, he said, "Let's go, Evelyn," and then grunted with frustration when she yanked her arm free of his grip again.

"No. I came here to dance, and I'm going to dance." She turned, wobbling like crazy on her heels, and yelped in surprise when he took her upper arm and steered her towards the dance floor. "What are you doing?"

"You want to dance? Fine, we'll dance one dance and then I'm taking you home. No arguments, Evelyn."

Thomas nearly pushed her onto the smooth dance floor as the band finished playing, and the people on the dance floor whooped and clapped. They stood in awkward silence until the band started up the next song.

"This next one is for all the lovers out there." The lead singer grinned into the microphone as they played a slow song.

Thomas hesitated before putting his arm around Evelyn's waist and pulling her against him. He took her right hand in his left and moved her around the small dance floor.

"Thomas, this is ridiculous. I don't want to dance with you." She pounded him on his back with her left hand.

He winced a little. It wasn't surprising how strong she was. Hell, he'd seen her lift sixty-five-pound bales of hay easily. She was a ranch kid. She might be curvy, but she also had muscles from years of outdoor work.

"Too bad," he said. He dragged Evelyn closer until her body pressed tightly against his and clamped his hand firmly around her hip. "One dance, and then I'm taking you home. I don't care if I have to throw you over my shoulder and carry you out of here kicking and screaming. Do you get it, Evelyn?"

She snorted in defeat. "Yeah, I get it."

"Good. Maybe you should tell me just what the hell you're doing here. This is no place for a -"

"Maybe *you* could shut it for a minute, Thomas. What do you say? If this is going to be my only dance of the night, then I'd like to close my eyes and pretend you're someone else. Your yapping is ruining the effect," she said.

"Fine," he huffed.

He held her a little tighter and steered her around the dance floor. He took a deep breath. She smelled like violets. He'd never noticed her scent before. Did she always smell like violets? He'd worked beside her for years, baling hay, milking cows, and riding horses, and he had never once noticed her scent. Maybe it was because he had never allowed himself to be this close to her before.

He couldn't say that he'd never noticed her body. He was a guy, after all. But she wore jeans and loose t-shirts when working the ranch. He had checked her ass out a time or two, and her breasts weren't completely hidden under the loose t-shirts, but he'd always felt guilty about it.

In the last few years, though, he'd found it increasingly difficult not to wonder if her skin was as soft as it looked, not to imagine what it would sound like to have her low voice moaning his name, and not to picture how good she would look naked in his bed. He used to have some control over his thoughts, and now he was a goddamn pervert.

Forgetting that she was ten years younger than him, she was his stepsister. It may have only been for a year, and maybe it'd been twenty years ago, but it didn't change the fact that for a brief time, their parents were married. He used to find it easy to keep his eyes to himself when it came to her.

Well, most of the time anyway. There had been that one time when Evelyn was eighteen and had come to the guesthouse. She would never know just how difficult it was to send her back to her own house. Thank God she left the ranch for college soon after that. When she returned four years later, he had almost forgotten the way she looked that night.

Of course, he thought grimly, the white bustier did a fine job of reminding him. Sweat broke out on his forehead, and he grimaced and moved his pelvis away from hers. Jesus, he was not about to get an erection while dancing with Evelyn. He stared down at the floor. It was a mistake. He could see the luscious curve of her ass in her indecently tight skirt, not to mention her long legs clad in black nylon. He wondered if she was wearing stockings and if her panties were a thong. The must be. There was no sign of a panty line.

*Maybe she's not wearing any panties at all.*

His hand tightened on her hip, and he pressed her against him as he fought to keep from moving his hand to her ass and finding out for himself the state of her underwear.

He realized two things an instant too late. One – his efforts to not have an erection had failed miserably, and two – Evelyn's soft gasp clearly indicated that she was well aware of what the hardness was pushing against her hip.

# ABOUT THE AUTHOR

Elizabeth Kelly was born and raised in Ontario, Canada. She moved west as a teenager and now lives in Alberta with her husband and a menagerie of pets. She firmly believes that a person can survive solely on sushi and coffee, and only her husband's mad cooking skills prevents her from proving that theory.

For more information about Elizabeth, check out her website at

www.elizabethkelly.ca

facebook.com/EKellyBooks

x.com/ElizabethKBooks

instagram.com/elizabethkelly_author

amazon.com/Elizabeth-Kelly/e/B00EOHZ0MS

bookbub.com/authors/elizabeth-kelly

# ALSO BY ELIZABETH KELLY

Place Your Trust in Me (Book Three)

## Individual Books

The Necessary Engagement

Amelia's Touch

The Rancher's Daughter

Healing Gabriel

The Contract

A Home for Lily

Saving Charlotte

Shameless

The Fairy Tales Collection

Broken

An Unlikely Seduction

## Holiday Romance

The Christmas Wife

The Christmas Rescue

The Christmas Nanny

The Christmas Boss

Sordid Games